"EASY THERE," HE MURMURED, HIS VOICE LOW AND HIS BREATH WARMING HER EAR.

Embarrassed, Bethany tried not to look up. She started to take a step backward, but he still held her. Curious, she tilted her head enough so that she could raise her eyes and meet his gaze.

"You okay?"

She gave a single nod.

"Sorry about that," John said and relaxed his hands. "Didn't mean to sneak up behind you."

She took a deep breath. There had been something comforting about being so close to him, her cheek practically resting against his shoulder. "I should've looked where I was going."

Still, he didn't release her and remained standing there, silent staring intently into her face. His eyes narrowed as he studied her.

"What's wrong?"

Slowly, John leaned over, lifting up one hand and running the backs of his fingers across her cheek. "You splashed water on your face."

Instinctively, she reached up and touched her cheek where he had. "Did I?"

"It's gon[illegible] nd took a step away fro[illegible] rprised to see you still h[illegible]

Also by Sarah Price

Belle: An Amish Retelling of Beauty and the Beast

Ella: An Amish Retelling of Cinderella

Sadie: An Amish Retelling of Snow White

The Amish Cookie Club

Published by Kensington Publishing Corporation

An Amish Cookie Club Christmas

SARAH PRICE

www.kensingtonbooks.com

ZEBRA BOOKS are published by

Kensington Publishing Corp.
119 West 40th Street
New York, NY 10018

All Kensington titles, imprints, and distributed lines are available at special quantity discounts for bulk purchases for sales promotion, premiums, fund-raising, educational, or institutional use.

Special book excerpts or customized printings can also be created to fit specific needs. For details, write or phone the office of the Kensington Sales Manager: Attn.: Sales Department. Kensington Publishing Corp., 119 West 40th Street, New York, NY 10018. Phone: 1-800-221-2647.

First Printing: October 2019
ISBN-13: 978-1-4201-4918-0
ISBN-10: 1-4201-4918-0

ISBN-13: 978-1-4201-4921-0 (eBook)
ISBN-10: 1-4201-4921-0 (eBook)

10 9 8 7 6 5 4 3 2 1

Printed in the United States of America

Chapter One

Edna sat at the kitchen table, her calendar book opened to the month of November. In the past, the calendar pages might have had a scribble or two here and there. But not this year. The rest of November and all of the December pages were anything but empty.

Removing her reading glasses, she rubbed the bridge of her nose and sighed. Not only was every Friday and Saturday leading up to Christmas scheduled for serving the noon meal to tourists, but starting next week, so was every Wednesday and Thursday. Even Thanksgiving week was full, with Tuesday scheduled as a makeup for the holiday.

She felt as if she might just succumb to tears. How on earth had she let this happen?

"Maem?"

She looked up as her eldest son, John, walked into the kitchen.

Forcing a smile—no sense in letting him see her fret—Edna set down her glasses and turned around in order to better see him. With his dark pants and white shirt, he wore the traditional clothing of an Amish man. But it was his piercing blue eyes that made him stand out in a crowd. Regardless of how handsome he was, John would always hold a special place in her heart, not just because he was her eldest child but because he was the most caring of her three boys.

"You're home early from the auction *haus*." Her eyes shifted to the clock on the wall. Was it already four thirty? She hadn't even started supper yet! "Oh help!"

John leaned against the counter and smiled at her, his eyes sparkling with amusement. "Let me guess." He reached up and tipped back his straw hat. "Lost track of time again, *ja*?"

Edna took a deep breath, willing away the sense of anxiety that grew inside her chest. "Seems to be happening a lot these days."

"You work too hard."

She couldn't argue that point, so instead, she changed the subject. "Speaking of work, how was *your* day?"

Something changed in his expression. A dullness, she thought, replaced the twinkle in his eyes as he shrugged. "Usual. Busy like most Thursdays. Lots of horses coming in tonight for tomorrow's auction. Had to get the stalls ready for them."

The lack of joy on his face said it all. At twenty-six, John was old enough to run his own farm. The only problem was that the family farm wasn't large—or profitable—enough to sustain the entire family. Dairy farming had taken a hit in recent years due to the decrease in milk prices. And that meant the family needed supplemental income in order to survive.

A few years back, Edna had started serving the midday meal to tourists during the late spring and summer months. This year, however, she'd agreed to continue hosting the *Englischers* throughout the autumn season, too. And not just one or two days a week, but four days. The family needed the money, after all.

Shortly afterward, John had been the next one to seek other work in order to help the family pay the bills. His love of livestock made him a natural hire for the local auction house. He worked Tuesdays through Fridays, helping to prepare for and oversee the livestock auctions on Wednesdays and horse auctions on Fridays. Unfortunately, Edna knew that while he was happy to contribute to the family, John should've been the one to stay home, while his two younger brothers, Jonas and Jeremiah, should've been the ones to leave the farm and find employment elsewhere.

But sometimes what *should've* been wasn't what *actually* happened.

John glanced over her shoulder at her calendar. His eyes widened and he whistled under his breath.

"Overbooked again, eh?"

Shutting the calendar, Edna pursed her lips, a feigned expression of irritation on her face. Truth be told, she could *never* be irritated with John. Of her three sons, John had always been her rock. Unlike Jonas and Jeremiah, John was sensible and responsible, a levelheaded man with a righteous reputation and a strong faith in God. And, of course, he was a man devoted to his family.

The only problem was that his family consisted of his parents and brothers. Most of his friends had already settled down with children of their own now. It was high time for John to do the same, but he showed no inclination to court any of the Amish women in their church district.

"Oh! You know me far too well, John Esh!"

The last thing she wanted to do was complain to John about her having taken on far too much work during the holiday season. Because she'd had no choice. No sense in complaining about something she couldn't change.

Standing up, she made her way toward the kitchen counter.

"And it seems I'm far behind on making supper for you men."

It was Tuesday and she had promised the boys—for she

always referred to Jonas and Jeremiah as "the boys"—steak and mashed potatoes for supper. They'd spent the day spreading manure in the fields, preparing the soil for next year's crops. With the weather turning crisp and cold, a hearty supper was definitely in order.

"Need help?"

Edna gave him a soft smile. "*Nee*, John. You relax a spell. Seems you've been working extra hard of late."

She watched as he took a seat at the table and stretched out, his long legs crossing at the ankles. "*Ja*, the auction *haus* has been busier than usual. Reckon that's good. Lots of horses and livestock, even though it's nearly winter."

"What about buyers?"

He sighed and rubbed his eyes. "*Ja*, plenty of those, too."

It broke Edna's heart to see him so tired. All he wanted was to work on the farm. But he'd never complained about having to find outside employment. *If only Jonas and Jeremiah were inclined to do the same,* she thought. Maybe then John could work on the farm year-round.

"Reckon that's *gut*, eh?" She hurried about the kitchen, trying to refocus her mind on supper and not on how overbooked she was for the next six weeks leading up to Christmas.

"They really need the help," John continued, but there was a forlorn undertone to his voice. He paused long enough for Edna to look at him. "Mayhaps that's what you need, Maem. Help."

She smiled to herself. "I already told you, I'm fine. Supper won't take but half an hour."

"I meant *real* help. With your business."

Not that again, she thought. She'd been struggling with so much for so long, and both John and her husband, Elmer, had been after her to hire someone to assist her with the meal preparations and serving the guests when they came. But she'd fought it.

"And I already said I'd think about it," she said.

The truth was that she *had* thought about it. Hiring help would cut into her profits, and they really needed every dollar.

"You can't keep doing all these things by yourself," John retorted. "You work too hard, Maem. Now you're taking on more. And just before the holidays."

The holidays.

Edna loved Thanksgiving and Christmas, that was for sure and certain. There'd be family suppers with Elmer's siblings, as well as with her own. Not just one or two supper invitations, but a dozen or more. Edna knew that they'd try to attend as many as they could. After all, it wasn't often that they could get together and see everyone: nieces, nephews, cousins, new babies.

And, of course, they'd attend the school pageant, as they did every year. Despite not having children attending the school anymore, Edna always enjoyed seeing the young children as they sang hymns, recited Scripture, and reenacted the Nativity scene.

Yes, the holidays were a busy time for everyone.

Despite her love of the holiday season, inwardly, Edna groaned. This year would be different, for John was right: she was working too hard and, most likely, wouldn't come up for air until just a few days before Christmas which left little time to actually enjoy the season. Between meeting every week to bake cookies with Verna, Mary, and Wilma for Yoders' Store in Shipshewana and running her own catering business, Edna wondered if she'd taken on more than she could chew. Or "swallow," in this case.

At least tomorrow was Wednesday. Her friends would be coming over to bake the cookies for Yoders' Store.

She'd have to tell them that it would be her last Wednesday helping. Hopefully she could keep meeting with her friends to bake cookies every other Friday morning, for they always made goodies to share at fellowship after their respective worship services. No matter how busy she was, she certainly enjoyed meeting with her friends, but she knew she'd have to forfeit Wednesdays for a while.

The Cookie Club. That's what people called it. And while Edna didn't particularly care for that nickname, she'd grown used to hearing it over the years.

"You really do need some help," John repeated.

"I'll think about it," she agreed for the dozenth time, trying not to glance at him over her shoulder.

Leveling his gaze at her, his expression doubtful, John raised an eyebrow. "You say that all the time, but thinking and doing are two different things."

Edna couldn't help but laugh. That had been her most often repeated expression to the boys growing up, especially Jonas and Jeremiah, who tended to think more than do, unless doing was something *they* wanted done.

Turning around to face him, she gave him a warm smile. "*Danke* for your concern, John. And since you are so insistent, mayhaps I *will* let you help me by peeling these potatoes." She walked over to the table and plopped down a large bowl of unpeeled potatoes. "Now, what do you think about that?"

He laughed at her as he picked up the peeler. "Think I put my foot in my mouth this time."

"That you did, John," she said in a lighthearted tone. "That you did."

Chapter Two

On Wednesday, Mary sat at Edna's kitchen table, one hand wrapped around a mug of hot coffee while she plucked at a cinnamon bun that Edna must've made earlier that morning. Inhaling the sweet smell of cookies baking in the oven, Mary couldn't help but smile. She loved coming to Edna's house with Verna and Wilma, especially every other Friday. It was such a nice tradition that they'd made, baking cookies for their congregations.

A few years back, they'd begun meeting on a regular basis. Edna had suggested it as a way to support their friend Wilma who'd been going through a rough patch when her youngest daughters, twins named Rachel and Ella Mae, began their *rumschpringe*. Though she was usually overly opinionated and vociferous, Wilma had encountered a blue spell, clearly missing her youngest daughters always being around the house. Getting together had been a way for the friends to provide support for Wilma during that time, but they'd kept the gatherings going afterward. As it turned out, they *all* needed support over the years.

"Guess who I saw on Sunday after worship?" Verna gushed.

Mary didn't need to guess. Ever since her daughter, Myrna, had married the widower Ezekiel Riehl, Verna rarely spoke of anything else. To be truthful, Mary had grown more than just a little weary of hearing about Myrna. Four months had passed since the wedding, but Verna acted as if Myrna was the first Amish woman to ever get married. Myrna, Myrna, Myrna. That's all she ever talked about.

Of course, Mary would never say such a thing to her cousin out loud, but she certainly thought it.

"And I just can't believe there are no babies yet!" Verna gushed. "I just can't wait for a grandbaby!"

Wilma made a guttural noise, deep in her throat. "Appears you have to, don't it?"

Mary glanced at her friend, too aware that Wilma sounded as exasperated as she felt regarding Verna's constant chatter about Myrna. However, feeling the sting of Wilma's words on behalf of their friend, Mary forced a pleasant smile and reached over to pat Verna's hand. "All things in God's time, not ours."

Edna cleared her throat. "Reckon I might as well tell you all now."

The room fell silent as three pairs of eyes, including Mary's, turned to her.

From the expression on Edna's face, it was clear that she was not about to share good news. Mary braced herself for the worst.

Edna sighed and shut her eyes as she spoke. "Well, it appears I won't be able to host our weekly cookie sessions for Yoders' Store for the next few weeks."

A stunned silence overcame the room.

For the past year, ever since MayFest, they'd begun baking cookies on Wednesday to sell in town at Yoders' Store. The bishop's wife had asked them to do so in order to raise money for the Amish Aid, the community fund that helped Amish families in need and was often used to cover medical bills since the Amish didn't subscribe to health insurance. While baking more cookies for Yoders' Store had created more work for all of them, it had also meant another excuse for them to get together.

Despite being disappointed, Mary was relieved that nothing was wrong with Edna or her family. It wouldn't be the same if Edna wasn't able to join the group, though.

And then it dawned on Mary that Edna hadn't explained why. Perhaps something *was* wrong with one of Edna's family members.

"Such unexpected news. Has . . . has something happened?" Mary asked, the first to speak. She knew better than to inquire further. Some Amish people were private about illnesses or problems. Even though Edna was one of her best friends, she wasn't going to pry if her friend didn't want to share more information.

Opening her eyes, Edna shook her head and exhaled. "Well, I needn't tell you about the problems with dairy prices." Her eyes scanned the table.

"It's hurting a lot of the farmers for certain," Verna said. "Why, even Ezekiel's looking to raise beef cattle in the spring to supplement the loss of dairy income."

Edna nodded. "Exactly. Remember my cousin Norma? Her husband gave up his dairy herd completely."

Mary clucked her tongue and shook her head. It was such a terrible thing, so many farmers having to leave the farm in order to provide for their families. Some days, she was thankful that her own husband, Abram Ropp, had never farmed at all. At least their small family didn't have to change their lifestyle so late in life to avoid struggling.

"And you all know that John's been working at the auction *haus* and I've been catering noon meals to the *Englische* a few days a week," Edna continued. "But it's just not enough, so I've extended my business throughout the holidays and added more days."

Verna gasped and Wilma made a noise of disapproval.

Mary, too, felt surprised. She knew how hard Edna worked during the spring and summer months. Normally she shut down her business after September so that she could enjoy the autumn season, so full of canning and quilting bees as well as weddings, before the holiday season.

"And I'm booked," Edna admitted with a sigh. "Overbooked, to be exact. I have people coming every Wednesday, Thursday, Friday, and Saturday until right before Christmas. And some of the parties are thirty or more people."

Wilma made a face, her cheeks squishing upward so that her eyes became narrow slits. "My word, Edna! Times might be tough, but I can't believe they're *that* tough. Might as well open a restaurant with such a busy schedule!"

Verna shot Wilma a look of reproach before she turned her attention toward Edna. "You can't do that on your own, Edna. You're going to need some help."

It wasn't the first time that the small group had recommended it was time for Edna to hire help. But Edna had been fighting doing so for a long time. "I agree," Mary said. "You'll be plumb worn out if you don't hire someone."

"That's what John said." Edna rested her elbow on the table and her chin against her hand. "Between setup, cooking, serving, and cleaning, it's such a commitment. Whomever could I possibly ask at such late notice?"

For a moment, no one spoke.

Mary held her breath and suspected that Verna was doing the same. Undoubtedly, she, too, knew what was coming.

"Well now," Wilma began slowly, her lips pursed and her cheeks becoming flush with excitement. She appeared to speak in a hesitant manner, as if mulling over an idea, but Mary knew that Wilma's brain had kicked into high gear. "I suppose I *could* spare Rachel and Ella Mae for the next few weeks."

Mary stared at the table, deliberately avoiding any eye contact with Verna or Edna. Why on earth had Edna opened herself up to Wilma in such a manner? Surely, she hadn't been thinking.

"Oh." Edna caught her breath. "I . . . well, that's a kind offer, Wilma, but I couldn't—"

Immediately, Wilma became animated. She leaned forward and reached out to cover Edna's hand with her own. "It would do my girls a world of good to help you," she said, her voice quivering with excitement. "They'd learn so much. And, of course, my Rachel is quite the cook."

Inwardly, Mary groaned. She knew that Rachel was anything but a good cook. In fact, Wilma's daughters might learn a lot from Edna, but at whose expense? Edna's, or her customers'? As for Wilma's comment about the girls helping Edna, Mary knew that they'd be more trouble than help. After all, Rachel and Ella Mae were renowned for being quarrelsome and difficult when together.

Sighing, Mary knew that there was only one way to rescue her friend from being forced to accept Wilma's offer.

"Oh, Wilma, that's so kind of you," Mary started. "But I think Edna might need someone more experienced in the kitchen."

"Experienced?" Wilma bristled at the remark as if Mary had personally insulted her daughters. "Like who?"

Looking at Edna, Mary smiled. "Like me."

Silence filled the room and every pair of eyes stared at her. Mary tried to act nonchalant, but she caught the look of gratitude in Edna's expression.

"Do you mean that, Mary?" she asked.

With only Bethany to care for, Mary wasn't as busy as she once had been. And while she wasn't necessarily looking for work, she knew that it wouldn't hurt her to help her friend. Besides, Bethany was almost twenty years old now. She could certainly take care of the house chores.

"I do, Edna." She looked down at her crocheting, noticing that she'd skipped a back loop. Quickly, she unfurled it and began crocheting at that spot again. "Why, it might be fun to meet some new people and listen to their stories. I've never spent much time around *Englischers*—"

Wilma gave a short laugh.

"—and we'd have a good time working together anyway."

For what felt like a long moment, Edna remained contemplative. She stared at the wall and her brows knit together. Mary wondered what she was thinking. Perhaps she didn't *want* her help. Had she assumed too much in offering to lend a hand?

"Well, Mary," Edna said at last, "if you really think you'd like to get me through the holidays, I sure would appreciate it, especially if you could start next week. That's when it's going to begin getting busy."

Mary breathed a sigh of relief.

"But talk it over with Abram first and let me know," Edna said, her shoulders relaxing a little as her attention returned to her own crocheting. "My feelings won't be hurt if he thinks it would be too much." She looked up and peered at Mary. "With all of your own chores and all."

Out of the corner of her eye, Mary noticed that Wilma frowned and focused on her knitting, her needles moving fast and furious. Surely, she was upset that *her* offer had been refused, but who could blame Edna? Those two daughters of Wilma's did nothing more than argue and bicker, constantly trying to outdo each other.

"Oh, I'm sure he'll be fine with it," Mary replied. "Bethany can surely cover everything that needs to be done at home anyway." She glanced up. "But I'll ask him just the same and let you know. Why, I can even ask Bethany to help by baking bread for you."

Wilma clucked her tongue in annoyance.

But Edna ignored Wilma's reaction and beamed in Mary's direction. Clearly *that* idea pleased Edna tremendously. "Oh, Mary, that would be such a big time-saver for me. And she always has been a great baker, hasn't she?"

The compliment made Mary beam. Not only would she enjoy spending time with Edna, it would do a world of good for Bethany to take on more responsibility at home.

Chapter Three

Bethany opened the oven and leaned down so that she could inhale the scent of freshly baked apple pies. She had baked eight of them for church service and—oh!—how that smell warmed her insides. If her mother was known for baking cookies, Bethany was known for baking pies. And bread. Baking just came naturally to her, and it was something she enjoyed doing, even if she rarely stuck around for the fellowship hour after worship.

"My word!" Her mother bustled through the door, a large box in her arms. She set it down on the kitchen table before she reached up to unpin her shawl. "Smells like autumn in here, for sure and certain."

Bethany shut the oven door. "Nothing says autumn like apple pie, don't you agree, Maem?"

Her mother smiled at her. "Indeed, Dochder. But it's almost winter now."

"Not for another five weeks," Bethany said. "December twenty-first, *ja*?"

Mary laughed. "Right you are. But it sure is starting to feel like winter. Why, Thanksgiving is less than two weeks away."

Glancing at the box, Bethany frowned. "What's all that?"

She stepped forward and peered at the items crammed inside it. "Flour? Sugar? Yeast?" A frown creased her forehead. "We've plenty of these dry goods in our pantry, Maem. Why'd you buy more?"

Mary sighed. "I'll be helping Edna Esh until the holidays are over."

Now *that* was curious news, but it didn't explain the extra goods. "Oh?" She started unpacking the box. "Helping her with what?"

"Cooking for her *Englische* visitors." Her mother sighed and sat down at the table. "She's overbooked and now has people coming four days a week! In a row, too. She can't do that alone, so . . ."

Bethany cocked her head at her mother. "You offered to help."

Her mother nodded. "I offered to help."

"You don't look happy about it."

"Oh, I don't mind helping her," her mother admitted. "I *always* enjoy Edna's company."

"But?"

Mary frowned. "But what?"

"Something is still bothering you," Bethany said. Her mother might not complain out loud too often, but she had never been one to hide her true emotions. "I can tell."

Her mother gave a small smile. "You know me too well, Bethany." She reached out and touched the bag of flour that Bethany had laid on the tabletop. "I just wish I didn't have to help so often. That's an awful lot of time away from home, and I do have my own chores."

Bethany swallowed. Surely her mother wasn't going to suggest that *she* help Edna, too. Just the thought of it made Bethany's chest feel tight and her heart race. She held her breath, waiting for her mother's next words.

"But I made the offer and now I must follow through,"

Mary continued. "Otherwise, Wilma will be sending Rachel and Ella Mae to help her." She glanced at Bethany. "And we both know how *that* would turn out."

Bethany's breath came out in a soft whoosh, an unsuppressed indication of her relief that her mother hadn't suggested *she* help one or two of the days each week. "While you're helping her, I'll do your house chores, Maem."

Her mother gave her a pleased look. "*Danke*, Bethany. I never doubted that for a moment, but it sure is nice to hear you offer." With a quick gesture toward the box, Mary continued. "She told me to start next Wednesday and, if you don't mind, mayhaps you could help by baking six extra loaves of bread next Tuesday for me to take to her. I know how much you love baking . . ."

The sentence remained unfinished, but Bethany could complete her mother's thought: . . . *and hate to leave the house.*

Bethany couldn't remember when her reluctance to socialize or leave home had begun. When she was younger, school and church were the only two places she went. Voluntarily, anyway. As she grew older, she avoided youth gatherings, and the two times her mother sent her to the market, Bethany had full-blown panic attacks. Her chest would feel constricted and her breath would come in short, shallow gulps.

It wasn't that she didn't *want* to have friends or socialize; it was just that she was afraid of people. Strangers, in particular.

Shyness plagued her to the point of physical illness.

"Oh, Maem!" Bethany felt as if a weight fell from her shoulders. Her mother understood her so well! "Baking bread would make me feel so helpful to Edna!"

Her mother gave her a reassuring smile. Bethany should've had more faith in her mother not to overcommit her. As usual, her mother had found a way for Bethany to help without forcing her to do something she dreaded: interact with strangers.

"I thought you'd agree," Mary said. "Poor Edna. She has over twenty-four women coming for a meal this Wednesday and another twenty on Thursday."

Bethany frowned. "That's an awful lot of people. Just to enjoy the noon meal?"

Her mother held up a finger. "*Nee*, Bethany. To enjoy the noon meal in an *Amish* home."

"Are our homes so different from theirs?" Bethany asked. She knew very little about *Englischers*. Despite her family living close to town, Bethany didn't have much cause to interact with non-Amish people.

Her mother surprised her, however, by responding, "Mayhaps our homes *are* different."

Bethany couldn't imagine what, exactly, would make *Englische* homes different. Whenever they rode to church or visiting other family members, they drove past many *Englische* homes. From the outside looking in, they certainly appeared the same. In fact, the house that *they* lived in used to be an *Englische* home. Her parents had moved into it shortly after they married, removing the electricity and converting everything to propane like other Amish houses.

"They are?" Bethany asked. "How so?"

Mary gave a soft smile, but there was a look of sorrow in her eyes. "I can't explain it, Bethany. I don't know that many *Englischers*, but I suspect there is something lacking in their world that draws so many of them to ours."

A sigh escaped Bethany's lips. She'd never understood why so many non-Amish held a fascination and curiosity about the Amish. Tourists came from all over the country to Shipshewana, to visit Amish Acres and attend the Round

Theater, to patronize the shops in town, and, increasingly, to enjoy a meal in an Amish home.

It hadn't been the first time that Bethany had wondered if *Englischers* thought it would be any different from dining in their own homes. Suddenly it dawned on her that maybe her mother was right. Even worse, maybe *Englischers didn't* dine in their own homes.

Often after the fellowship hour following worship, the older Amish women sat around the tables, nursing cups of coffee. They loved to gossip, a pastime that neither Mary nor Bethany participated in. However, Bethany sometimes sat beside her mother and listened to the stories. How could she help but be naturally curious? Sometimes the women shared news about their *Englische* neighbors, and on more than one occasion, someone would comment about the busy life of *Englischers*, how many of them put work before family.

Perhaps that was what was so different about the *Englische* and the Amish: Amish people always put God first and family second. After that, they focused on work, friends, and community—not always in that order.

Bethany simply could not imagine living any other way. She prayed silently, thanking God for all of the gifts He had given her—including being born into an Amish family—as she unpacked the box of goods that she'd need in order to bake bread for Edna on Tuesday.

Chapter Four

The following Wednesday, a large group of women filled Edna's kitchen, with both their physical presence and their noise. They talked among one another, laughing loudly from time to time. And they couldn't seem to get enough of her food. The desserts in particular.

"Do we have enough?" Mary whispered to Edna in Pennsylvania Dutch so that no one could understand her.

"I don't know," Edna whispered back. She hadn't realized how she'd grown immune to being around the *Englische* tourists until she'd seen Mary's reaction to them. Now, as she watched the women through the eyes of her friend, Edna realized just how different the Amish were from the *Englische*.

Mary frowned. "Why, I've never seen so many pies just disappear like that!"

Edna glanced at the two long tables that John and Elmer had set up in the kitchen the previous evening. Each table sat twelve ladies, and both were filled.

The women had arrived at twelve and were scheduled to leave at two o'clock. Two hours. The longest one hundred and twenty minutes of Edna's life, it seemed. This was the first group to visit Edna's since she had started working with Destination Amish, that new tour company out of

Sugar Creek, Ohio. It was also the largest group that Edna had ever served in her house, but, according to her schedule, even larger groups were coming in the weeks to come.

Now more than ever, Edna was beyond thankful for Mary's offer to help. She'd never have been able to handle such a large group on her own. Besides, just as Mary had predicted, it *was* more enjoyable to work alongside someone else.

"I sure hope you're charging them enough to cover your expenses," Mary teased.

Edna laughed. "If they keep eating so many pies, I'll have to rethink my prices, that's for sure and certain!"

Hurrying back to the section of the room where the guests sat, Edna scanned the tables. She'd baked six apple pies the day before, and only four pieces were left.

"Anyone for more pie?" she asked, hoping the answer was "no." Otherwise, she'd have nothing left to serve her husband and sons after *their* evening meal.

"My word!" one woman declared as she leaned back. "I don't think I could eat another bite."

Several other women nodded their heads in agreement.

Edna smiled and reached down to take the remaining pie plates away. As she set them on the counter, placing the empty plates in the sink and three that still had pieces of pie onto the counter, she glanced out the window.

The large tour bus looked so strange to her. She hated seeing it there, blocking her view of the barn and side paddock. *Less than five weeks left*, she reminded herself. Then there would be no more serving meals to strangers until the springtime. Her life would be hers again and she could enjoy the rest of the Christmas holiday in peace.

As the guests sat around the table, some drinking coffee while others preferred tea, they talked about their children and grandchildren. Edna caught snippets of the conversation as she cleared one table while Mary did the same for the other.

"Richard's planning a vacation in California next April so we can visit our son . . ."

"My grandchildren called the other day . . ."

"Bill can't stand the cold and he's insisting we buy a winter home in Florida . . ."

She tried to shut her eyes, tuning out the words that brought joy to the speakers but anguish to Edna. She couldn't imagine her sons living so far away that she couldn't see them every few days or visit with her future grandchildren regularly. And, while she knew several elderly couples who wintered down in Pinecraft, Florida, Edna would never want to leave her family or community for such a long period of time—and she couldn't stand cold weather, either!

Mary stood at the sink, already washing the dishes. Edna set some more dirty plates on the counter.

"*Danke*, Mary," she whispered in Pennsylvania Dutch. "I'd never have been able to handle this group without you."

She glanced over her shoulder, taking in the women seated around the two long tables. Some of them were talking while others listened. It was hard to follow their conversations, as several of them spoke over one another.

"You're welcome, Edna," Mary said as she returned her attention to her friend. "I'm glad that you asked me. You've taken on so much. I can't imagine how you would've done this alone."

Edna gave a little chuckle. "I reckon we manage. But I'm sure glad I didn't have to manage *this* one alone."

The door opened and Edna glanced over her shoulder. To her surprise, her middle son, Jonas, walked into the kitchen and, for the briefest of moments, appeared taken aback by the women seated around the two long tables. But then, true to his normal jovial nature, he gave the *Englischers* a charming grin.

"What ho!" He pushed back the brim of his hat, a few brown curls poking out and covering his forehead as he wiped his feet on the rug inside the door. "Where was *my* invitation?"

Several of the women tittered, delighted with the appearance of Jonas. Edna took a deep breath and exhaled slowly, leaning against the counter. He was always cordial and friendly to strangers, especially *Englischers*—apparently thriving on the attention. And the women clearly did not mind.

"You must be Edna's son?" one of the women said.

"That I am." He puffed out his chest. "Jonas. And I'd ask your all names but—why!—I don't think I could remember half of them! So many of you." He gave a small laugh as his eyes scanned the empty table. "Now I sure hope my *maem* fed you enough. Hope she didn't skimp on the apple pie." He leaned forward as if to share a secret. "Her apple pie is some of the best around, you know."

Edna clucked her tongue. "Such nonsense. My apple pie is no more special than anyone else's, Jonas!"

But several of the women disagreed and said just that, the compliments causing Edna to blush. If John was Edna's support, Jonas was her biggest cheerleader.

Jonas gave an exaggerated sigh. "What's a fellow to do?" he said in an overly dramatic way. "And here I was hoping my sweet talk might land me a piece of that pie!"

"Oh, there was some left," one of the women said. "Mayhaps your *maem* took it back to the kitchen already."

Jonas grinned and scurried toward the counter to retrieve it.

Edna made a stern face at him. Leave it to Jonas. Now Edna wouldn't have enough for *all* of the boys later. Ideally, she'd make another dessert to appease everyone's sweet tooth, but she was tired. She'd been baking all morning, having made the pies for today's group of women as well as tomorrow's. Besides, she knew that she didn't have enough supplies to make more; John was supposed to stop at the store tomorrow on his way home from the auction house.

I'll fix Jonas's little red wagon, Edna thought as she watched him shoveling a forkful of apple pie into his mouth. After the evening meal, when Elmer, John, and Jeremiah had pie, Jonas would have none. Maybe then he'd think twice about stealing the leftovers she'd earmarked for the entire family.

Chapter Five

On Thursday, when Mary arrived home after helping Edna, the kitchen smelled like fresh bread and she found Bethany standing at the sink, washing dishes.

"What a long day!" She sidled up to the sink and peered over Bethany's shoulder. Bread pans. "You made more bread loaves for Edna?"

"*Ja*. I figured she'd need them." Bethany gestured toward the bread on the cooling rack. "And I've rolls baking now for Friday."

Mary gave her a grateful smile. "That was thoughtful of you. She'll be quite appreciative, I'm sure."

Bethany gave a modest shrug. "I didn't mind. I'd already finished the laundry and cleaned the *haus*. Besides, I enjoy baking. No sense sitting around."

For a moment, Mary observed her daughter, a feeling of pride filling her chest. Without doubt, Bethany was a beautiful young woman, inside and out. She was hardworking and quiet, and there was something about her that set her apart from other Amish women. Her dark hair and even darker eyes offset her high cheekbones and porcelain skin, giving her an angelic aura. And when she smiled, her face lit up and her almond-shaped eyes sparkled. The only problem was that she didn't smile often enough.

"I reckon it doesn't hurt to sit around a little bit," Mary said lightly. "In fact, I've been on my feet all day, so I might just do that right now!" She walked to the back of the kitchen and sank down into her reclining chair. When they had first moved into the house, there had been a wall that separated the kitchen from the living room. But Abram had removed it so that the two rooms became one, making a sitting area within the kitchen such as most older Amish homes had. That way the family could always be together and not separated.

"Those *Englische* women!" Mary said. "Why, I've never seen so many pies disappear so quickly."

"You said that yesterday, too," Bethany observed.

"They like their sweets, that's for certain." Kicking off her black shoes, Mary reached down and rubbed her feet. She'd been standing all day and they ached. "I'd so like to make some of your apple pies for Edna. She works so hard, the poor dear. And I could surprise her with them in the morning so she doesn't have to make more."

Bethany wiped her hands on the kitchen towel. Her eyes glanced up at the clock on the wall. "It's early enough. I reckon we could still make them."

Mary hadn't thought that she'd hear anything different from Bethany. The only problem was that Mary had been helping Edna for the past two days and hadn't gone to the grocery store. From the looks of the freshly made bread sitting on the counter, she doubted there was enough flour to bake so many pies.

"Do we have enough flour for crusts and apples for the filling?"

She watched as her daughter turned toward the pantry. She opened the door and peered inside. Sure enough, when Bethany turned around, her face didn't appear optimistic.

Mary didn't need to hear the answer.

"Oh bother!" She leaned back in the chair and shut her eyes. "I so wanted to help Edna. She's so busy in the mornings, baking chicken and making side dishes. And then she bakes the pies, too. All before lunch."

The idea of having to bicycle into town made Mary cringe. She was exhausted, especially after having just biked all the way home from Edna's house. It was a long ride, almost three miles, and, after working all day, she just wanted to take a few moments and put her feet up.

Now she'd have to go to the store if she wanted Bethany's help making apple pies and wouldn't be able to make them until after supper.

Unless . . .

Mary opened her eyes and looked at her daughter. "Do you think . . . ?"

She didn't even have to finish the sentence. Immediately, she saw her daughter flinch. Clearly, Bethany knew what Mary was going to ask and the idea of it did not make her happy.

"Maem, please," Bethany pleaded, her eyes suddenly wide and the color disappearing from her cheeks.

Exasperated, Mary sighed. "It's just to town, Bethany."

"But you know how I dislike going there. And bicycling on the roads! All those cars—"

Mary held up her hand and interrupted her daughter. "Bethany, it's still early. Traffic will be light." She was used to her daughter's arguments about why she shouldn't have to go into town or run errands. *If only Abram hadn't instilled such fear into the girl when she was younger,* Mary thought. While she knew that her husband had just been trying to protect their only child, the long-term ramifications had certainly done all of them a disservice.

Bethany made a face.

"Now, now." Mary attempted to placate her. "You can get there and back before the roads get congested by rush hour traffic." She paused before adding a carefully calculated final comment. "And it would be a big help to me, Bethany, and to Edna."

She watched as her daughter swallowed. If there was one thing that could make Bethany crumble, it was the idea of being helpful to anyone. Just saying the word was enough to get her to do anything, even something as dreadful as bicycling into town on a Thursday afternoon.

Oh, Mary didn't *like* to play that card with her daughter; it felt too much like manipulation. But sometimes she had to succumb to exploiting that one weakness. Otherwise, she'd *never* get Bethany out of the house.

Unfortunately, this was one of those occasions.

"All right, Maem," Bethany mumbled at last. The hesitation in her voice was mirrored in the expression on her face, which told the true story of how she felt about going into town. Mary could read Bethany as if she were a book. Yes, her daughter would help her, but she did so only with the greatest of reluctance.

"That's a *gut* girl, Bethany." Mary gave her a soft, appreciative smile, hoping that her daughter wasn't too upset. She shut her eyes and leaned her head back against the recliner again. Now, with Bethany leaving for town, she'd finally get those thirty minutes of peace and quiet, interruption-free, to take a quick nap.

Chapter Six

Standing in the dry goods section of Yoders' Store, Bethany scanned the shelves looking for brewer's yeast. She always used some of that in her baking, not just because it added extra nutrition to her bread and pie crusts, but because it also made everything taste extra delicious.

The clear plastic bags of pre-weighed baking supplies made for a pretty display. All of the flours, sugars, salt, and yeasts were lined up, the colors blending together in soft whites, beiges, and even pink.

She reached out and plucked a bag of Himalayan salt from the shelf. Sometimes she splurged and bought a small bag, always using it sparingly because it was more dear than regular salt.

Perhaps she'd buy some today, she thought, and placed it in her basket.

Slowly she made her way down the empty aisle, grateful it was still early enough that the store wasn't crowded. She simply hated shopping, especially when the store was overflowing with tourists.

If only they didn't live so close to town, Bethany thought. But her father wasn't a farmer, and when he'd married her mother, they'd bought the small ranch house outside of Shipshewana. He worked with an Amish man who owned a woodcraft store that catered to tourists and locals alike. While it wasn't his own business, the store had served the Ropp family well over the years.

The only problem was that they lived in a converted *Englische* house and were surrounded by Amish and non-Amish alike.

Oh, how Bethany longed to live far away from the hustle and bustle of Shipshewana. She wished that she could live on a farm where the house was surrounded by large pastures and fields that grew crops in the spring and summer. She'd have loved a large garden to grow her own vegetables that she could sell throughout the summer and enjoy canning fruits and beets and tomatoes in late August and September.

But she didn't live on a farm and she wasn't far from town. In fact, she was standing in Yoders' Store right in the middle of town, surrounded by strangers.

She glanced around. Despite the feeling that a vise had tightened around her chest, she could still breathe. On the weekends, Yoders' Store was patronized mostly by tourists, but on a Thursday afternoon, there were mainly other Amish people and not so many *Englischers*.

Walking down the aisle, she spotted something on a shelf across the way.

Cookies.

Smiling to herself, Bethany walked over and looked. She recognized the label on the cookies, for she had written it herself: "AMISH COOKIE CLUB." It felt strange to see her mother's cookies for sale at the store. Surely Verna or Wilma had dropped them off earlier that day or, perhaps, the previous day. Bethany knew that they usually met on Wednesdays to bake them but, now that Edna was so busy and Mary helping her, it would be up to the other two women to not only bake them but wrap them in the clear baggies, affix the label to the packages, and drop them off at Yoders' Store.

Suddenly, Bethany's thoughts were interrupted by the feeling that someone was staring at her. She stiffened and felt that familiar sense of dread wash over her.

She didn't want to look around, to see who was watching her. Surely a tourist must have entered the store. It was always the tourists who stared, their eyes wide and their mouths pursed in curiosity. It was as if seeing an Amish person in a store was a rarity, like seeing a deer along the road.

Just the thought made Bethany's chest tighten even more, and she had to force herself to take deep breaths.

For a moment, she considered dropping her basket and making a polite dash for the door. But she had promised her mother that she'd bake those pies for Edna. If she deserted her groceries now, she'd have to break that promise, and that was one thing her mother had taught her never to do.

Without looking up, Bethany quickly made her way to the next aisle and started walking toward the cash register at the front of the store. Her eyes stayed glued to the floor; she was too afraid to look up.

She began to count: *One, two, three*. It was the one way she knew to calm her palpitating heart. *When I get to twenty*, she thought to herself, *I'll be at the register. I'll pay and leave by the time I count to fifty, and then I'll be on my bicycle and heading home.*

But she never made it to ten.

Her eyes saw the dark brown work boots poking out from the bottom of plain black pants before she hit eight. She'd just started thinking *nine* when she bumped into the person belonging to those boots.

"Oof." The wind escaped from her gut and she felt a hand on her arm, holding her as if to keep her from falling.

She didn't fall. Instead, the basket fell from her other arm and the contents spilled onto the floor.

"Are you all right?"

Bethany didn't look up, too afraid to see whom she had walked into. Quickly, she knelt down to begin gathering the items, but the man had already started doing the same. Her knees knocked into him and she fell backward, onto her rump.

"Oh!"

Once again, she felt his hand on her arm. This time, he gently guided her to her feet.

"What a time you're having," he said.

His voice. So soft and caring, not harsh or critical. Bethany couldn't help but glance upward, and when she saw the bright blue eyes staring at her, she felt a momentary shock course through her veins.

Immediately she averted her gaze, but not before noticing how undeniably handsome he was. The straw hat, tipped back on his head just a bit, revealed his thick, brown curls and cast a hint of a shadow over his face, which, like those of most Amish men, was tan and a bit weather-beaten. He was older than she—Bethany could tell that from his broad shoulders and towering height. But he wore no beard along his jawline or chin.

"I . . . I'm so sorry," she whispered. "I wasn't looking where I was going."

He paused. "*Ja*, I noticed that. Was wondering if you were going to notice me," he said, a teasing tone to his voice, "or merely try to walk through me."

She blinked and managed to sneak another peek at him. If he'd noticed that she wasn't looking where she was going, why hadn't *he* gotten out of her way? But while she might think that question, she would never have spoken it aloud.

"Must've been awful deep in thought," he continued. "Mayhaps thinking about something—or someone?—special?"

Startled by his question, she felt her mouth fall open. "That's a very familiar question," she managed to say as she averted her eyes. There was something about his face that seemed so familiar. Did she know him? His eyes never left her face.

He laughed. "*Ja*, I reckon it is. My apologies if it offended you." He tilted his head when she stole one last look at him. "Wasn't my intention, that's for sure."

No, Bethany didn't think she knew him. He wasn't from her church district, and while certainly unmarried, he probably didn't attend many youth gatherings—not that Bethany often attended them anyway. He was probably courting someone, or mayhaps even getting ready to marry. November and December *were* wedding season.

Bethany shifted her gaze back to the floor. "I . . . I'm sorry for bumping into you . . ."

"No need to apologize. I should've gotten out of your way." Another long pause. "I suppose I just thought you'd notice me—" He stopped talking midsentence, interrupting himself with abrupt silence.

She took a step backward and shifted the basket on her arm so that it created a barrier between them.

"Well, anyway." He must've taken the hint that she did not want to converse with him. She saw him shuffle his feet, taking his own step away from her. "You have a good rest of the day, then." Another step increased the distance between them.

She nodded and moved to the side as if to pass him, but he, too, had made a similar move.

She heard him chuckle, a soft and pleasant sound.

"Permit me," he said and gestured with his hand as he moved to the right, giving her enough room to walk past him.

"*Danke.*" It came out soft, almost a whisper, and she wondered if he'd heard her. She hoped so, for she would hate for him to think her rude. Of course, it didn't really matter, she told herself as she hurried away from him and toward the cash register. She'd never see the stranger again. And yet, long after she paid for her goods and left the store, she couldn't help but wonder about the man with the bright blue eyes. Who was he, she thought, and why did she have the distinct feeling that she *had*, indeed, met him before?

Chapter Seven

By the following week, Edna wondered how she'd ever catered so many meals and for so many people without having hired help.

Mary was truly a godsend, especially on Wednesday. For some reason, even though it was the day before Thanksgiving, over twenty women had come for the noon meal.

That Destination Amish tour company certainly attracts a lot of people, Edna thought. She'd have to write to the owner, Michelle, and thank her for sending so much new business to her house. It was a blessing to have the extra income and, frankly, Edna enjoyed meeting so many nice women, even if they were the hungriest *Englischers* she'd ever served.

Only once had she encountered a group with a woman—the organizer of the gathering, no less!—who was unkind. In fact, she'd been downright condescending. But Edna knew well enough that there was always one bad apple in a bunch. Fortunately, it had only been that one time.

Otherwise, Edna found her work rather fulfilling. She especially enjoyed receiving kind letters from some of her guests. They seemed to like writing letters, and, especially during the winter months, Edna was more than happy to reply to their correspondence.

Yes, God had blessed her with being able to help her family during difficult times. She was thankful for work that didn't take her away from the farm.

And yet, as she looked around and assessed the disaster left behind—supper plates, dessert plates, utensils, water glasses, coffee mugs, and serving platters—she couldn't help but sigh.

Well, she thought, *that's what I'm paid to do. Cook and clean up.*

"Best get started, I reckon," she muttered, more to herself than to Mary.

"You're so busy anymore," Mary said as she began clearing the table. "It was never like this before, was it now?"

For a moment, Edna didn't respond. Truth was that she'd noticed a difference after she'd teamed up with Destination Amish. Even though Michelle was based out of Sugar Creek, Ohio, she had begun promoting Edna's dinners to her clients. That was when Edna's business had boomed. In fact, she'd been booked months in advance. And then Michelle had asked her to consider adding additional days to her schedule to accommodate the holiday demand.

Only because of the continuing issue with declining dairy prices had Edna agreed.

While Edna knew that the company had something to do with the increase, she also knew that tourism in Shipshewana was increasing overall. That new play at the Amish Acres' Round Theater, *Belle*, had something to do with it, or so several of her guests had informed her. A retelling of a fairy tale that was popular among the *Englische*—but told in an Amish setting and with *Englische* actors and actresses—it had attracted a lot of new tourists. And, of course, people appeared to really enjoy the quaint town, with so many small shops and good restaurants.

"*Nee,*" she responded to Mary at last. "Not like this. And

with the holidays nearly upon us . . ." She left the sentence unfinished, for they both already knew that the busy schedule wouldn't change until just before Christmas. Turning to face Mary, Edna gave her a grateful smile. "I sure am thankful for your help," she repeated once again.

Silently, she said a prayer of gratitude, not just for the increase in business but for John having insisted that she find someone to work alongside her.

But now it was time to clean up.

"Well, I see that we've enough leftover cookies and rolls," Edna said as she surveyed the remaining platters. As before, there were scarcely enough leftovers to feed her family that night. "I can take the rolls to Ida's *haus* for Thanksgiving supper tomorrow, but it looks like I'll still have to make that corn casserole."

"Having the holiday meal with the Beachys again?"

Edna nodded. Elmer's sister, Ida, always hosted the main Thanksgiving gathering for the family, not just because the floor plan of their old farmhouse accommodated the large family, but also because Elmer's parents resided with their daughter and her family.

"Well, let's package these up, then. Where are your containers?" Mary finished carrying the last of the serving dishes to the sink. "I'll fetch one."

"Containers?" Edna dropped the hand holding a dish towel to her hip and pointed toward the small door at the back of the kitchen near the staircase. "I should have one or two in the pantry. But let me do that. Surely you must have things to do at home, being that tomorrow's Thanksgiving."

Mary, however, waved her off. "Don't be silly. We're only going to Verna's, and Bethany made two sides for us to bring. I'd never leave you with an unclean kitchen after you've worked hard all day."

Mary headed in the direction of the small room that Edna used to store her canned goods, dry food, and larger pots. Edna followed.

The shelves were lined with all of the jars of food that Edna had canned for the winter. While everything looked full, Edna suspected that it wouldn't last until spring. She'd worried about that during the canning season and now knew that she should've prepared even more. Most of her guests liked to have canned beets and chow chow with their meals.

Sighing, Edna scanned the shelves for her less-used containers. "Up there," she said and pointed. "Best wait for one of the boys to come in so they can reach it. John should be around here somewhere. He's not working this week, you know." She headed back toward the sink. "I didn't think to have one of them bring the containers down since we weren't baking for worship this week."

"Oh, I can reach it."

But Edna shook her head. The stepladder had broken the previous week and Elmer had yet to fix it. "We've enough to do until the boys come in."

Back at the sink, Edna turned on the faucet, waiting for the water to warm up. The water heater ran off propane, so it took a while. "I sure do enjoy listening to those women talk, don't you?" She ran her fingers under the water. "Come on, now," she grumbled. "It always takes so long to get hot."

There was no response.

"Mary?"

A voice called from the pantry. "What did you say?"

Edna leaned back and peered toward the doorway. "What're you doing?"

"Fetching those—"

Before Mary could finish her sentence, Edna heard the

sound of wood scraping against the floor, and her friend cried out.

When Edna heard the crash, she knew that something bad had happened.

“Mary!”

Quick as she could, Edna ran over to the pantry, only to find Mary on the floor, her foot stuck in between the lower rungs of the ladder.

“Oh, Mary! What happened?”

She didn’t have to ask, for it was obvious enough. Clearly Mary hadn’t listened to her and had seen the stepladder. She must not have noticed the broken hinge and had fallen to the ground when she tried to climb it.

“Don’t move.” Edna knelt beside her friend and grabbed her hand. “Did you hit your head?”

“*Nee.*” Wincing as she tried to sit up, Mary reached down and grabbed her leg just above her ankle. “But I think I hurt my leg.”

Edna stood and ran to the kitchen door. Throwing it open, she reached for the bell that hung there, pulling on the cord as she called out for her husband.

Within seconds, she saw him peer around the side of the dairy barn.

“*Kum!* Mary’s fallen!” She gestured toward the house. “She’s hurt.”

Immediately, Elmer broke into a run, racing across the yard that separated the barn from the house. As he approached the porch, Edna hurried back inside, praying that her friend hadn’t broken her leg.

Why, oh why, hadn’t Mary listened to her?

Chapter Eight

Mary rubbed her ankle, too aware that Edna and her husband, Elmer, hovered over her. She felt foolish. Why on earth had she climbed that stepladder?

"Oh, Mary!" Edna knelt beside her. "Does it hurt much?"

She felt the color flood her cheeks. She didn't want to admit that it did, but she felt the sting of tears in the corners of her eyes. "Mayhaps it's just my ankle. Just a little twist, I suspect."

She'd seen the stepladder against the back wall and thought only to help out by fetching those containers. It was too hard to clean a kitchen when food still needed to be put away. So, she'd fetched the stepladder, opened it, and then climbed it. But just as she'd been reaching for the containers, she felt the stepladder give underneath her feet.

When she had fallen, the room spun and she hit the floor. Hard. But it was the way her foot and leg had gotten caught in between the two steps that seemed to have caused her injury.

"Let's get you up." Edna's hand wrapped around her elbow and she nodded to her husband. "Gentle now, Elmer."

Carefully, they hoisted Mary to her feet, but the moment she tried to put pressure on her right foot, she winced in pain, fighting the urge to cry out. Shooting pain ran up her leg and she stumbled to the side, grabbing Elmer's arm.

"Oh help," she muttered.

The sound of footsteps on the stairs was immediately followed by John's voice. "What's happened here?" He didn't wait for a response as he hurried over and wrapped his arm around Mary's waist, lifting her up so that she leaned against him. "I gotcha."

This time, she couldn't hold back. Tears sprang to her eyes. Blinking rapidly, she willed them away. The last thing she wanted was to cry, but the pain radiating up her right leg toward her knee made it difficult. She'd never been one to tolerate pain very well.

Clearly concerned, Edna turned her eyes from Mary to John. "You best help her to the sofa, and mayhaps, Elmer, you should call for help."

Mary wanted to tell her friend not to bother, but she couldn't speak. The pain was greater than she could bear. So, instead, she let John practically carry her to the sofa. Only when she was seated could she catch her breath.

"I . . . I think I'm fine, Edna," she managed to say. "The fall just winded me some."

"Hmph." One look at Edna's face and Mary knew she didn't believe her. "You need a doctor to look at your leg." She turned toward her husband. "Mayhaps even the hospital."

Shaking her head, Mary refused. She didn't want a doctor, and she certainly didn't want to go to the hospital. It was bad enough that she felt foolish for having fallen, but she also felt terrible that she couldn't finish her job. She was supposed to be helping Edna, *not* burdening her. And with the next day being Thanksgiving, Mary certainly didn't want to be stuck in the emergency room with all of those big, fancy machines and fast-talking doctors.

"Too much fuss, I'm sure. It's probably just sprained."

"Or broken!" Edna shot back. "You don't set that right and you'll have problems for the rest of your life, Mary."

"I best go call Abram," Elmer said. "He's probably still at work, *ja*? See what he thinks to do."

As Elmer left, John knelt down and gestured toward her leg. "May I take a look?" he asked.

Embarrassed, Mary could only nod.

Gently, his fingers touched her ankle, applying pressure along the sides. "It's not warm to the touch," he said in a soft voice. "And you can wiggle your toes?"

She did as he asked.

"And if I touch your ankle here, does it hurt?" He pressed his fingers along the soft part of her ankle.

She winced. "*Ja*, it hurts."

He frowned, his forehead suddenly creased with deep wrinkles. "How about here?" Gently, he moved his fingers to the bone above her ankle.

She winced. "A little."

With a deep sigh, John stood up. "You really should go to the hospital, Mary, but it's up to you."

Mary clenched her teeth, willing herself to try ignoring the pain. "I reckon it won't hurt to wait until later . . . see how bad it still is." She just wanted to get home, take some aspirin, and rest with her leg elevated. Surely if it was broken, it would hurt much more, she told herself.

"Well then, I'll harness the horse and drive you home." John glanced at his mother. They exchanged a look, a secretive and silent communication between them.

"*Gut* idea," Edna said. "Abram will know what to do and whether or not to take you to the hospital. But either way, you best rest up. I don't expect you'll be coming back here on Friday or Saturday."

Mary averted her eyes. She didn't want to see the look of disappointment that surely covered Edna's face. It was, most likely, the same expression that she herself wore.

Not only was Edna hosting large groups on Friday and Saturday, but the weeks leading up to Christmas were just as chaotic, with large groups scheduled back-to-back. Mary had actually been looking forward to getting into the holiday spirit by assisting her friend. During the few days that she'd already worked for Edna, Mary had found she didn't mind interfacing with the *Englische* women and the occasional man who paid to enjoy a dinner meal at noon in an Amish house.

Her own house had never been filled with lots of people. Despite having wanted a large family, Mary only had Bethany. And when the holidays rolled around, their house was never as busy as it appeared to be for other, larger Amish families.

So Mary had found herself enjoying working at Edna's. It was nice to be surrounded by the conversations, laughter, and joviality of the guests who came to Edna's house. The people were kind and curious about the Amish way of life and seemed to genuinely enjoy conversing with her and Edna. Yes, she had definitely liked working there.

Plus, truth be told, Mary had found herself enjoying the one-on-one company with her friend. She couldn't remember the last time the two of them had spent so much time together without Verna and Wilma being with them.

But, even without seeing a doctor, she knew that Edna was right. With an injured ankle and leg, Mary *couldn't* help Edna. Never mind what a doctor might say; Abram would certainly tell her no, too. He'd be far too concerned about her further injuring herself if she didn't take the time to heal properly.

Mary took a deep breath and, shutting her eyes, rested her head against the back of the sofa. Why hadn't she listened to Edna? Instead of helping her friend out of a bind, Mary had now created a bigger problem, for who would assist Edna now?

Chapter Nine

When she heard the buggy pull up to the house, Bethany glanced at the clock. Who would be visiting at this time? No one was expected. Her mother was still at the Eshes', and her father wouldn't be home from work until four thirty.

Walking over to the front window, Bethany lifted the green shade and peered outside. To her surprise, she saw that it was Edna's buggy.

Frowning, Bethany wondered why her mother was home so early. And why on earth was Edna driving her? As she had the three previous days, her mother had bicycled to the Eshes' farm. The weather was fair, so that couldn't be the reason that Edna had driven her mother back to the house.

Besides, it was still early. Bethany hadn't expected her mother home until closer to four o'clock—she and Edna usually visited afterward—but it was barely three.

To Bethany's surprise, she watched as a man, not Edna, got out of the buggy and tied the horse to the wooden hitching post at the end of the driveway. Was that Elmer? She couldn't tell because his back was turned toward her. But when the man returned to the left side of the buggy, she didn't see Elmer's familiar white beard. Who on earth was driving the buggy?

Wiping her hands on a dry dish towel, Bethany hurried

over to the kitchen door in time to see the Amish man helping her mother from the buggy. His hat was tipped down and Bethany couldn't make out who it was.

With her arm draped around the man's shoulders and his around her waist, Mary hobbled on one leg along the path toward the house. The way she moved, her leg jerking quickly as she tried to walk and her arm over the man's shoulders, only created more questions. Surely something was wrong, indeed!

For a moment, Bethany felt a wave of panic—not over the strange man but over seeing her mother injured.

"Maem!" She flung open the door, not caring that it banged against the side of the house, and hurried outside to wrap her arm around her mother's waist. Her hand brushed against the man's, but she avoided looking at him. "What happened?"

"Oh, something silly." Mary tried to laugh it off, but Bethany saw through that fast enough. The paleness of her mother's face and the tears that welled in her eyes told Bethany that it wasn't something silly at all.

"Maem?"

"Well, I might have sprained my ankle," she admitted, then glanced at the man who was assisting her into the house. "John was kind enough to bring me home."

John? She hadn't even looked at the man who was helping her mother. Now, she realized she needed to thank him.

Turning toward him, Bethany caught her breath.

She recognized him right away. Those blue eyes would've been hard to forget. And, when their eyes met, she saw that he, too, recognized her.

The man from Yoders' Store!

Quickly, she averted her gaze, uncertain what to say to him. Without another word, Bethany propped up her mother's other side as she and John held Mary upright on what felt like an endless journey into the house.

"Where shall we seat her?" he asked.

Quietly, Bethany gestured toward the recliner in the back corner of the kitchen. It was the chair her mother always sat in after supper to read or crochet.

"Good choice," John said. "She can elevate her foot."

He helped Bethany get her mother to the chair and then stood back. With his arms crossed over his chest, his eyes seemed to follow Bethany as she hurried for something to cover her mother. Behind the sofa was a large basket of yarns, and on top of it was a threadbare quilt.

Taking it to her mother, Bethany laid the blanket over her mother's lap and gently repositioned her ankle on the footrest before covering it.

"Such a fuss," Mary said, resisting Bethany's attention.

But Bethany remained adamant. Her mother's ankle was swollen and felt warm to the touch. "Mayhaps you should see a doctor, Maem."

Mary dismissed her suggestion with a gentle wave of her hand. "*Nee*, Bethany. As I said, it's probably just a sprain. A little ice and a day or two off of it will help, I'm sure."

Bethany, however, wasn't so certain.

"What happened?" she asked for the second time.

This time, it was John who responded. "Maem said that she used a stepladder to reach something in the pantry and fell." He shook his head. "Seems the ladder's hinge wasn't locked properly."

Mary gave a weak laugh. "Edna told me to wait. I should've listened."

Kneeling down beside her, Bethany placed her hand on her mother's ankle, noticing that she winced at the touch. "*Ja*, Maem, you should've listened," she chastised in a soft voice. "Now you're injured."

"It'll be just fine by next week, I'm sure."

Bethany stood up, too aware that John was still watching her. His attention made her feel uncomfortable. She'd never been in a situation where someone scrutinized her so intensely. Her heart beat rapidly as she forced herself to look up at him.

"*Danke* for bringing my *maem* home," she managed to say.

"Anytime," he said at last, releasing her from the hypnotic spell she'd been under. His lips curved again, just a little at the corners. "Although I must confess that visiting under different circumstances would be preferable."

"Of . . . of course."

He took a step toward the doorway as if to leave. But he paused. "Mary, if you need anything, don't hesitate to have someone call us." His eyes flickered in Bethany's direction. "I'm happy to stop by."

While kindhearted, John's offer caught Bethany off guard. What need would her mother have of his assistance?

But Mary merely nodded, a look of genuine gratitude on her face. "*Danke*, John. I appreciate that. And do tell your *maem* that I'm terribly sorry. I'll leave her a message tomorrow, but I think she's right that I won't be able to help her on Friday."

"*Ja*, I figured as much."

He started to leave, hesitating just a moment longer to meet Bethany's gaze one last time.

"Good day, Bethany Ropp."

And with that, he left the house.

Chapter Ten

Thanksgiving was always a lively occasion.

Almost one hundred people crowded into the large kitchen of the Beachys' farmhouse. Some of the younger couples stopped in just to say hello before traveling somewhere else for the meal. But four large tables were set up with almost fifty folding chairs to accommodate two shifts of eating.

Family gatherings were always Edna's favorite. She loved seeing the children playing outside in the yard despite the cold air while the older men sat around the tables talking. They shared updates about friends and family who couldn't attend, as well as stories from when they were younger. Edna also loved working alongside the other women. She didn't even mind that Thanksgiving was never held at her house. While they had the space to accommodate large groups, Edna enjoyed not being the one in charge of entertaining so many people. For once, *she* did not have to oversee the cooking or the cleaning. Sometimes it was nice to be told what to do, that was for sure and certain.

"Henry told me that you've been booked solid through the holidays with feeding your tourist people," said her other sister-in-law, Mabel.

Edna handed her some dried plates to put away. Both Ida

and Mabel were older than she was, but they looked young and spry. She'd always gotten along with them, even though she didn't see them as often as she would have liked. Life was too busy for visiting frequently. Plus, they lived in different church districts, which made Edna wonder how on earth Mabel's husband would know about her business being so busy. Perhaps Elmer had run into him at a store and forgotten to tell her.

"*Ja*, I am." She wiped at another plate. "I've been working with a tour company in Ohio that really has been keeping me occupied."

"Ohio?" Mabel gave a little laugh. "Why, they have their own Amish there. Why would people want to come to Shipshewana?"

"For a change, I reckon." Edna handed her the plate. "Good for me, though. It's really helping us through a dry spell, if you know what I mean."

"And I also heard that Mary Ropp is helping you?"

She could only wonder how *that* news had spread so quickly. Mabel resided farther east, her house just over the border of Wilma's church district. Aside from Thanksgiving and the occasional summer picnic for the family, Edna rarely saw her. But she knew that Mabel's son Benjamin ran in the same group of friends as Wilma's *dochders*. Edna could only presume there was a connection there. If there was one thing Edna knew, it was that the roots of the Amish grapevine ran far and wide, with little need of fertilizer to spread quickly.

"You heard correct, Mabel," Edna said. "Although Mary fell yesterday and hurt her ankle. I doubt she'll be coming tomorrow or Saturday." And that certainly left Edna in a bind. She'd already made up her mind to ask John to help her. Being off for the week, he had the time. But she felt guilty because she knew how much he always looked forward to helping his father with farm work.

"She hurt herself?" Mabel caught her breath. "Oh help!"

"I do hope she's okay," Ida added. "That's such a shame."

"*Ja*, it sure was bad timing." *In more ways than one*, she thought. Edna laid the dish towel over the edge of the counter. "With the holidays and all," she added cautiously. "That will surely inconvenience her."

"Well, I bet Wilma would love to have her twins help you." As soon as Mabel said it, Ida snickered and turned away.

Edna knew that, even though they lived in different church districts, Ida and Mabel remained very close. Edna also suspected that they used the telephones in their barn for more than just business calls. Like many of the older Amish women, they enjoyed nothing more than sharing a little bit of gossip. And Wilma Schwartz definitely provided plenty of that.

"Oh, I bet she would, indeed." Edna tried to keep a straight face. "I'm just not so certain I'm ready for *that* kind of help."

Both of her sisters-in-law tittered, enjoying the fun banter that so often flew back and forth when families got together.

"And the boys? How are they?" Mabel scanned the room until she located Jonas and Jeremiah. "Have they calmed down at all?"

"If by 'calmed down' you mean started to think about courting," Edna said, not particularly liking the way Mabel had phrased her question, "then the answer is no."

"Such a shame."

"*Ja*, and John is such a *gut* man. I'm surprised he's not courting yet."

Me, too, Edna thought. "When he's ready, I suppose, it will happen. In God's time, not mine." But she sure did wish that His time would coincide a little closer to hers.

"Well, it's probably a good thing," Ida said. "After all, he's working at the auction *haus* and would probably need to live closer to town. And I just heard that Manuel Eicher bought an *Englische haus* and it cost a small fortune!"

"I heard that, too!" Mabel shook her head. "Almost a hundred and fifty thousand, wasn't it?"

Edna listened as her sisters-in-law shared information about the house, small with only one bathroom and not even enough land for a garden. But as terrible as that sounded to her, it dawned on her that John would probably have to move to a house like that one day. If he continued working in town, when he did finally settle down, it wouldn't be on the farm. Not if Jonas and Jeremiah stayed on with their father.

It was unfortunate and, frankly, unfair. But Edna knew that life wasn't always fair. With John being more responsible than his younger brothers, it had only made sense that he find employment elsewhere. The good news was that they had a lot to be thankful for: their health, their farm, and their ability to survive even when the economy wasn't in their favor. Still, as she glanced across the room and watched her eldest son, Edna knew that something needed to be done to help him find his way back to the farm.

If only she knew what that might be.

Chapter Eleven

Mary sat on the reclining chair at Verna's house, her leg propped up with the white cast jutting out from beneath her navy blue dress. Everything ached and she wanted nothing more than to return home, take her pain medicine, and go to bed.

But it was Thanksgiving, after all.

"Such a shame," Verna said, clucking her tongue as she handed Mary a teacup filled with black coffee. "I'm so glad Abram made you go to the hospital."

Mary glanced across the room to where her husband sat at the table, enjoying his own coffee while catching up with some of the other men. He must've overheard Verna, for he turned around and looked at Mary.

"How're you doing over there?" he asked.

Mary forced a smile. "Fine. Just fine."

His eyes moved to Verna. "And she thought it was just a sprain." He pressed his lips together and shook his head. "Wanted to wait and see."

"Well, you did the right thing, Abram."

Mary hated being the topic of discussion. She felt conspicuous enough sitting in the chair while the other women worked in the kitchen.

Verna must have cooked enough food for well over a hundred people, but only sixty had showed up. Mary suspected that her cousin was disappointed that more family members hadn't come. Two of Simon's family had canceled at the last minute due to illness, and Verna's brother begged off when his horse went lame. With its being a holiday, they couldn't hire a driver at the last minute.

"So much food." Verna shook her head. "You'll just have to take some home with you."

"Oh, there's no need for that."

"Nonsense." She took a few steps toward the kitchen. "Bethany, you make certain to set aside several plastic bags filled with turkey, mashed potatoes, carrots, and cranberry sauce. Whatever you need. And Myrna, you make certain she's not being bashful about the amounts."

Myrna nodded. "Will do, Maem."

Verna sat down in a chair next to Mary. "With you being injured and all, you'll need the food so you don't have to cook."

Mary stared at the leftovers that Myrna began piling up. "Land's sake, Verna! That's too much." With her small family of three, they'd never eat so much food before it went bad. Besides, Abram wasn't one to appreciate leftovers the way some other men did. "I wouldn't even know what to *do* with so much food!"

Myrna looked up as she finished filling a plastic storage bag with stuffing. "Make a few shepherd's pies and freeze them. That's what I intend to do."

"Of course! What a *wunderbarr* idea," Mary exclaimed. Why hadn't *she* thought of that?

Verna beamed as if the compliment had been intended for her and not her daughter.

Thirty minutes later, with all of the dishes cleaned and the extra tables put away, it was time for the other women to relax and catch up. Mary couldn't help but notice how differently Myrna carried herself. She was less abrasive and definitely calmer than she'd once been. Married life certainly suited her well.

"You're helping Edna, I hear?"

Mary hesitated. "I was, anyway." She gestured toward her leg. "Reckon I won't be able to help her anymore. I feel just awful about not being able to fulfill my promise."

Verna sighed. "I wonder what Edna will do now to cope with her Christmas rush and all."

Myrna scoffed. "Well, Wilma is always volunteering her girls. I'm sure they'll be able to fill in."

Verna stifled a laugh and quickly covered her mouth. "Myrna!"

"Well, it's true! It's a wonder Wilma didn't shove Rachel and Ella Mae on poor Edna in the first place."

Mary sighed. "Oh, she tried. Twice."

Verna leaned forward. "Three times if you count last spring. Remember? When we were baking?"

"Oh *ja*! I forgot about that."

"You mark my words," Verna said, jabbing at the air with her finger, "she'll get those two girls there one of these days."

Myrna made a noise deep within her throat as she sipped a cup of tea.

Setting down her teacup, the porcelain clattering lightly against the saucer, Myrna pursed her lips, clearly studying Bethany for a few long, drawn-out seconds. Mary couldn't help but wonder what her cousin's daughter was thinking. She'd always been very perceptive. It was a strength that, in the past, had masked itself as a character defect at times.

"Edna still has all three sons living at home, *ja*?" Myrna asked casually.

Mary sensed Bethany stiffen.

"*Ja*, she does," Mary admitted.

"The oldest is—what?—twenty-five or -six?"

"I believe so."

Myrna narrowed her eyes. "And the youngest isn't much more than twenty-one?"

Again, Mary concurred.

"Uh-huh." Myrna raised an eyebrow.

"What's that supposed to mean?" Verna asked.

"Nothing," Myrna answered, a light tone in her voice. The mischievous glow in Myrna's eyes told Mary that the young woman wasn't exactly telling the truth. In fact, from the looks of it, Myrna was up to no good.

"Just seems like an interesting setup for a young Amish woman to work in, don't you think?"

Mary was willing to let the remark pass without further comment, but Verna was not so inclined.

"Myrna Riehl!"

A forced look of innocence replaced the mischievousness on Myrna's face.

"What are you thinking?"

She faced her mother and smiled. "Nothing. Nothing at all." The old Myrna would have spoken her mind, not caring if she embarrassed someone. The new Myrna, however, remained silent.

It didn't matter, though. Mary didn't need any explanation. As soon as Myrna had mentioned Edna's sons, Mary understood exactly what thoughts had popped into Myrna's mind.

Truth be told, *she'd* had the same thoughts already, but she hadn't shared them with anyone. Perhaps it wouldn't be such a bad idea to see if someone could step in to help Edna, someone who wasn't one or even both of Wilma's daughters.

Her eyes traveled to where Bethany sat, her finger

tracing the rim of her own teacup, apparently ignoring the conversation or, perhaps, too deep in her own thoughts to be listening. With three young, unmarried men living at Edna's, it *would* be an interesting scenario to get Bethany over there. Surely *one* of them might show some interest in Bethany. After all, according to Edna, not one of them was currently courting—at least not that she knew of. And they *were* all of marrying age.

But Mary hadn't wanted to share her thoughts. Not with her friends, not with Abram, and most certainly not with Bethany. Not yet anyway.

The last thing Mary wanted was to introduce hope when it might lead nowhere. She had no idea if Bethany would be willing to help out Edna, and even if she did, who knew if she would favor one of the Esh boys? Sometimes, Mary thought, it was better to let God lead the way without holding any preconceived expectations of specific outcomes. That way, if things didn't quite work out, there were less chances of feeling disappointed.

Still, as the conversation drifted away from Edna and onto other topics, Mary couldn't help but pray that maybe—just maybe!—God might find a way to put Bethany into Edna's path, not only because she'd be helping the woman but because it might just bring her into the sphere of a possible future husband.

Chapter Twelve

After the Thanksgiving meal, Bethany couldn't wait until they returned home from Verna's house. It wasn't that she didn't care for Verna and her family. No, that wasn't it at all. But Bethany hadn't particularly liked Myrna acting like the matchmaker.

Oh, she'd overheard them all right. She'd just been too stunned to respond to the suggestion that she should help at Edna's, not because her mother was *injured*, but because Edna had three eligible sons.

Bethany had always gotten along with Myrna, even though other people did not particularly care for her overbearing personality. Myrna had always been kind to her, especially about her shyness. As a child, other people had teased Bethany about not wanting to attend youth gatherings. Myrna had always stuck up for her.

When Myrna had found a good match with Ezekiel, Bethany had been delighted for her cousin. Myrna certainly deserved her own happiness. But now that she was married it appeared that she was back to her domineering ways.

Well, Bethany was more than happy staying at home. And she certainly didn't need Myrna to plant seeds in her mother's head. It was unfortunate that her mother had injured her ankle and could no longer help Edna. However, that only meant her mother needed *her* more than ever at home. How would her mother get around without Bethany's help? And all of the responsibilities for the household chores would fall squarely on her shoulders.

"That was a nice Thanksgiving, wasn't it?" her mother said after Bethany helped her settle into one of the recliners. "So much food! And that turkey was just about the freshest I've tasted in I don't know how long." She glanced up at her daughter. "Did you know Ezekiel shot it himself?"

"*Ja*, you told me that twice."

"Did I?"

"Need anything, Maem?" Bethany took a blanket and covered her mother's legs so that she didn't catch a chill. "Tea, perhaps?"

Her mother reached up and patted Bethany's hand. "*Nee*, Dochder. I'm just fine. Besides, we're out of tea."

With her mother settled into her chair, Bethany unwrapped her black shawl from her own shoulders and hung it, along with her mother's, on the hooks by the door.

"Myrna looks happy, doesn't she?"

Bethany pursed her lips and frowned. "*Ja*, I reckon so."

"She's awfully good to Ezekiel's *kinner*, don't you think?"

Bethany took a deep breath. Her mother didn't have to spell out what she was thinking. Being the only child certainly presented its own share of difficulties. Now that she was older, her mother was certainly thinking about the future—and grandbabies. "She is, *ja*."

"I'm so happy for Verna," her mother continued, the sound of longing in her voice.

Bethany stood there, her back toward her mother, and shut her eyes.

"My one regret," Mary sighed, "is not having been able to give you siblings. If only . . ." Her voice trailed off.

Bethany suspected she knew where this conversation was leading. "I've never complained, Maem. And it's not your fault, anyway. It just wasn't part of God's plan."

"*Ja*, that's true." Her mother craned her neck to look at her. "You've always been the best *dochder* that I could've asked for. If only you might settle down though."

And there it was. Bethany pressed her lips together and took a deep breath. She never quite understood her mother. Some days, she'd declare that she hoped Bethany never married. Other days, she became teary-eyed thinking about Bethany having children. She imagined her mother's changeable thinking had something to do with her being almost fifty years of age.

"I'd so love to have a busier *haus*, wouldn't you?" Another wistful sigh. "Little ones running about. The laughter. The noise."

Slowly, Bethany exhaled. The last thing she wanted to do was to upset her mother, so she chose her words carefully. "Maem, if I *did* settle down, you know that I would most likely not live here. I'd have to live with my husband. So that means the *haus* wouldn't be busier, but *quieter*." She forced a small smile. "Did you think about that? Would you really want me to leave the *haus*? To live elsewhere? I sure wouldn't. I *like* living here. It's my home."

Slowly, Mary nodded her head. "You're right, Bethany. But you do have to live your own life."

"Mayhaps one day," Bethany said softly, just to appease her mother. There was no sense in alerting her to the fact that she didn't care if she never married or left the house. "But let's not make it today, *ja*?"

Her mother laughed. "Agreed. Not today."

Chapter Thirteen

Such a misfortune, Edna thought on Friday morning.

Just a few minutes ago, Jonas had run into the house, beckoning her to come to the barn: Abram Ropp was on the telephone. Edna had grabbed her shawl—the temperature outside had taken quite a turn recently—and hurried to the small room where Elmer kept the telephone he needed for business purposes.

"Abram," she had breathed into the receiver as she tried to catch her breath. "How's Mary?"

"Oh now, she's just fine."

"Such *wunderbarr* news! We were all so worried about her yesterday and last night. I'm so thankful that you called."

"Took her to the hospital Wednesday night."

Edna caught her breath. Why hadn't they called and left a message?

"Seems her ankle . . . it's fractured." Abram paused. "She's got a cast on."

Edna shut her eyes and leaned back, resting her head on the wall. Why hadn't he just said that from the beginning? She should've known better than to get her hopes up. It always took Abram Ropp three times as long as anyone else to get to the point of *anything*, especially when he was sharing important news.

"She won't be able to help out, I'm afraid. Best if she stays off her feet for a spell."

When Edna finally hung up the phone, she simply sat in the chair and stared at the old farm calendar that hung on the wall. She couldn't fault Mary for the inconvenience, but it truly was unfortunate timing.

Slowly, she headed back to the house.

While Edna prayed that her friend would heal quickly, she also prayed that she'd be able to survive without Mary's help. Perhaps one of the boys might help her serving food to the guests. Jonas always enjoyed interacting with them. But as soon as the thought crossed her mind, she knew that solution wouldn't work. He'd wind up joining them instead of actually helping her!

Sighing, she knew that she'd have to find someone else to help her over the next four weeks, but she didn't want to be saddled with Rachel and Ella Mae.

Once inside, Edna sat at the kitchen table and reviewed her schedule. She kept everything neatly organized in a notebook with a small calendar—updated, unlike the one hanging in Elmer's barn office—in order to keep track of upcoming reservations. Over a hundred people would be fed in her kitchen the following week, not including her own family. Had she finally bitten off more than she could chew?

Footsteps on the staircase interrupted her thoughts and she looked up to see John descending.

"You don't look happy," he said.

"I'm not." But she forced a weak smile. "But God will get me through this troubled time."

"What's wrong?"

"I just got off the phone with Abram. Seems Mary's ankle *is* actually broken. A small fracture."

John raised an eyebrow. "Really? That's not good."

"*Nee*, it's not. On many fronts."

The conversation ended abruptly when Jeremiah and Jonas burst through the kitchen door, laughing. Her eyes traveled to where they stood, kicking off their muddy boots.

"Maem, you should've seen Daed," Jeremiah laughed. "The cows broke through the fence into the back paddock. We were trying to get them back in and he slipped headfirst into the mud."

She gave him a stern look. "That's not something to laugh about."

But just as she spoke, her husband walked inside. He was covered, head to toe, in mud. He stood there, his arms at his sides, and only the whites of his eyes showing through the mud.

"What on earth . . . !"

Elmer frowned. "That darn Angus cow." He tossed his hat onto the counter. "She did it again."

Getting to her feet, Edna hurried to fetch him a towel. "You'd best strip there—no need tracking mud all over the rest of the house—and go take a shower right away. You'll catch your death from cold!"

Obediently, Elmer began unbuttoning his shirt. "Going to enjoy steaks when *that* one goes to the butcher."

From behind her, she heard Jonas chuckle. "Seems she'll have no fat on her, the way she likes running away from you."

"Boys!" But even Edna couldn't keep herself from smiling. She turned to Elmer. "That cow always has been a bit of a wanderer, wouldn't you say?"

"Hm." Elmer grunted as he took the towel and wiped the mud from his face. "Gonna need some boards from town. The ones we used to fix the fence won't hold for long."

John walked over to the refrigerator and opened it. Pulling out the pitcher of lemonade, he set it on the counter. "I can go for you, Daed. Save you the trip."

"*Danke.* That would be a big help."

Edna felt grateful for John's offer but, admittedly, a bit irate that neither Jonas nor Jeremiah had volunteered. It was unfair that John had to drive all the way to town on his day off from the auction house, especially since he was much more partial to farming than either of his two younger brothers.

"Mayhaps Jonas or Jeremiah might go in your place?" she asked, doing her best to avoid looking at the two young men. She didn't have to, for she knew that they were both making faces.

"It's all right, Maem," John said as he started to head to the door. "I need to stop at the harness store for a new trace. Mine's about shot. I'll take the hauling wagon for the lumber, Daed, okay?"

As John left the house, there was a collective sigh of relief from Jonas and Jeremiah. Edna frowned and gave them a sharp look. *One of these days*, she thought, *they'll learn that it's more important to give than to receive.* She just hoped it was sooner rather than later, otherwise neither one of them would ever attract a good Amish woman and settle down.

Chapter Fourteen

The cast on her right foot made her leg itch but there was no way to scratch it. Even though they had given her some pain medicine, the ache in her ankle hadn't improved. Thankfully, the following day wasn't a church Sunday, so she wouldn't have to go anywhere and could stay inside with her leg elevated.

"You must be one strong woman," the doctor had said after reviewing her X-rays. "It's indeed broken."

"Broken!" She couldn't believe her ears.

Beside her, Abram had made a soft noise. She looked at him and he shook his head, whether in irritation or wonder, she hadn't quite known. Having a broken ankle would definitely create more work for both Abram and Bethany over the next few weeks.

"Fortunately, it's just a small fracture. We'll put a cast on it and you'll need to stay off your feet for a few days. Nothing strenuous for several weeks," the doctor had said.

Now, back at home, Mary felt helpless, sitting down when there was so much work to be done. And she was supposed to go to town for her weekly food shopping. She usually went on Thursdays, but the pantry was practically empty; she hadn't gone the previous two weeks because she'd been helping Edna and then because of Thanksgiving.

Now they were out of so many things. Thankfully Verna had insisted on sending home leftovers the previous night or Mary would have no idea what to make for supper.

No, someone definitely needed to go to the grocery store and, with Abram working, the only other person who could possibly go was Bethany.

Mary shut her eyes and leaned her head back.

She hated asking Bethany to make that trip again. She'd been such a good sport about going the previous week when Mary asked. Now, because of her leg, Bethany would have to go one more time for a bigger order. Even before asking her, Mary knew that Bethany would not be happy about it, that was for sure and certain.

People always wondered about Bethany's aversion to meeting strangers. In truth, Mary didn't understand where her daughter's shyness had come from or even when it had started. In hindsight, she suspected it had something to do with Abram always protecting Bethany. He was overprotective by nature, but when it came to his only child, Abram had sometimes been a bit overbearing about insulating Bethany from the outside world.

Mary suspected *that*, in turn, had something to do with his own upbringing.

When he was growing up, his parents had a small store, and tourists often came to buy things. As a result, Abram had been exposed to many *Englischers* and had become shy himself. When he began courting her, Mary found that trait endearing. After all, many of the other young men were far too boisterous and rambunctious. Abram, however, preferred the simple things in life: long walks in the park, fishing at isolated ponds . . . anything that did not involve being around a lot of people.

And, of course, there had been the car accident involving his older sister.

By the time Bethany came along, they'd suffered years of distress over miscarriages and two stillborn babies. They'd both viewed Bethany as a gift from God and treated her as though she were a fragile figurine that might shatter.

Mary wondered if they should have insisted that she interact more with other children. When she had first turned sixteen, Bethany had attended youth gatherings. But now that she was a young woman, Bethany no longer attended them. She preferred to stay home, and as far as Mary knew, she had no one she could call a true friend. Peripheral friends, perhaps, but not a real confidant.

"You feeling all right, Maem?"

At the sound of her daughter's voice, Mary looked up and, upon seeing Bethany, smiled. With her dark hair and eyes, she always looked particularly pretty when she wore burgundy. "*Ja*, I'm fine. *Danke*, Dochder."

"Would you like some tea?"

But Mary knew there was no tea. That was one of the items on her list.

She shook her head. "We're out of tea."

"Anything I can do for you?"

At this question, Mary sighed. It was now or never. "*Ja*, there is. And I hate to ask it."

Bethany stiffened, clearly anticipating her mother's request.

"I know, Bethany, but I hadn't time to go to the grocery this past week and now . . ." She gestured toward her cast. "It would be better to go today than tomorrow, wouldn't you agree?"

She watched as her daughter swallowed, the color draining from her face. "I reckon so," she said in a slow, deliberate tone.

"I can ask your *daed* to pick up some items next week when he's coming home from work, but I don't think I have enough food to get us through the weekend." Mary knew they were out of much more than tea. Flour, sugar, butter, milk, and yeast were just some of the items that needed replenishment. But she also needed beef and chicken, as well as some fresh vegetables.

For a long moment, Bethany stood there, staring at the wall. Her lips moved but no words came out. Mary suspected that she was counting. It was a trick that she'd taught her daughter years ago to help collect her thoughts when she was feeling anxious.

Slowly, Bethany nodded. "I'll go." She walked over to fetch a pad of paper. She handed it to her mother. "Make a list then," she said with great reluctance in her voice. "I can ride my bicycle, I reckon."

"You're such a *gut dochder*," Mary said as she took the paper from her. "I promise I'll keep the list as light as I can."

But she could tell that Bethany wasn't listening. Instead, her lips were moving again as she stood there, her face turned toward the window while she stared outside and slowly began counting again.

Chapter Fifteen

On her way into town, as she approached the first major intersection, Bethany got off her bicycle and waited for the light to turn green. She'd heard the story a hundred too many times about how her father's older sister had been killed by a car. His mother had never quite been the same, her father always said when he warned her to be extra careful on the road.

Maybe that was one of the reasons she hated leaving the house so much.

Ever since she was a little girl, Bethany had loved nothing more than being at home. There was something comforting about the familiar sights, sounds, and smells. She liked being wrapped up in the familiar. She even loved gardening, although their garden hardly produced more than a few boxes of tomatoes, cucumbers, and beans each season. It was so small that weeding it only took her a few hours each week.

Once again, Bethany wished that they lived on a farm. She didn't like how close her family lived to town, just on the edge of the tourist area where traffic was heavier. And some of their neighbors were *Englischers*. Not that it mattered much. Bethany rarely saw any of them.

The light turned green and she guided her bicycle across

the intersection, triple-checking that no one was running the light from the opposite direction. As she made it to the other side of the intersection, a car pulled up alongside her. Bethany avoided looking at the occupants. From her peripheral vision, she saw that they were an older couple. Tourists, she thought, as she moved her bicycle to the side of the road and started to get on.

The car crept alongside her and, without thinking, Bethany glanced in their direction. A middle-aged woman leaned out the window, a camera in her hand pointed in Bethany's direction.

Immediately, Bethany jerked her head the other way, swerving her bike at the same time as if trying to get away from the invasive camera. But it was too late. The woman had taken her photo and the car drove away, leaving Bethany trying to regain control of her bicycle.

"*Ach!*"

The front tire hit a large rock on the shoulder of the road and before Bethany knew it, the wheel began to wobble.

She managed to stop the bicycle without falling, but a quick look told her all she needed to know: the tire was flat.

She pushed the bicycle to the side of the road where she could inspect it better. Leaning down, she checked the tire and saw that the rim had bent. "Oh help," she muttered as she touched it. Even if she could get it to one of those gas stations to inflate the tire, she still couldn't ride it.

With a frustrated sigh, Bethany stood up, shielded her eyes from the lowering sun, and looked down the road. She was closer to town than home. But if she continued, she'd have to push the bicycle both ways. And yet, if she turned around to return to her mother, she wouldn't have any of the groceries that were needed.

"Looks like you could use a hand."

Startled, Bethany stiffened at the sound of the man's

voice coming from behind her. She hadn't heard anyone approach. That familiar feeling of tightness clenched in her chest and she shut her eyes. *One . . . two . . . three . . .*

"I . . . I'm fine, *danke*," she managed to say.

"Looks like you've a flat there, *ja*?"

She recognized the voice as belonging to an Amish man. Glancing over her shoulder, she saw the horse and wagon-like buggy on the other side of the road. No wonder she hadn't heard it approach, for it had already been there, stopped at the intersection.

"*Ja*, that's a flat all right," the man said. "Traffic's too busy for you to be walking along the road," he said in a kind but firm voice. "Let me take you home."

The voice sounded familiar, but from where she stood, she couldn't see who it was. Who was this young man? Turning around, she squinted, trying to make out the face of the driver.

Immediately, she froze. "John Esh," she said in a whisper-soft voice.

"Bethany, right? Mary Ropp's *dochder*?" His eyes held hers, and she wanted to tear away her gaze, but she couldn't. There was something about this man that made her pulse quicken.

She couldn't speak but managed to nod her head.

"*Kum* now," he said and gestured toward the seat next to him. "Safer than walking."

"I . . . I have to go to the grocery for my *maem*."

He nodded in a thoughtful way. "I'll take you."

Inwardly, she cringed. Had he thought she was asking him to do that? As usual, she felt like a bumbling fool around this stranger. Something about his presence made her feel even more conspicuous than usual. While that wasn't an unfamiliar feeling for her, she was also worried about whether her hair had fallen from the bun at the nape of her neck or if her prayer *kapp* was askew upon her head.

That was definitely a new concern for her, and she felt the color rise to her cheeks as she averted her eyes.

"But my bicycle—"

"—can go in the back." Clearly, he wasn't taking no for an answer. Without waiting for her to counter his offer, he stepped down from the buggy and reached for her bicycle. He met her gaze and held it for a long moment.

"It . . . it's not that far."

The corner of his lips twitched as if he was trying not to smile. "You intend to push your bicycle to the store and then home?" He made a clucking noise. "If it were me, I'd accept the ride."

"I don't want to inconvenience you," she managed to say.

"No inconvenience for me at all." This time, he did smile. "In fact, I'd rather enjoy some company, if you don't mind stopping at the harness store with me on the way back."

Her resolve was wearing down. After all, he was right. It *was* safer if she rode in the buggy with him.

He tilted his head as he studied her with increased curiosity. "Besides, you really have no choice but to oblige me."

Her eyes widened.

Smiling, John continued, "My *maem* would have my *daed* take me behind the woodshed if she knew that I let you push your bicycle home."

Bethany's mouth opened just a little and then she frowned. "You're too old to go behind the woodshed."

He gave a little laugh, those blue eyes lighting up his face. "Get in now, Bethany, and take the reins so I can put your bicycle in the back."

Bethany nodded, feeling as if her heart would beat right out of her chest. What was it about this man that caused her pulse to quicken so?

Bethany had never been one to argue with anyone, even strangers. But John Esh wasn't *exactly* a stranger. She'd known him all of her life, although she hadn't seen much of him for a few years. When she had been younger, Bethany's mother and her friends often got together with their extended families, but those days were few and far between now. No wonder she hadn't recognized him at Yoders' Store the other week. The last time she'd spent any time with him, it had been at Edna's farm when the Eshes held a cookout. Bethany barely remembered it; she'd sat by her mother's side and avoided Myrna, Rachel, and Ella Mae. They were far too boisterous and loud, opinionated and argumentative.

But she'd only been ten or eleven years old.

Bethany knew that John was older than she by six or seven years. Unlike his younger brothers, John had never teased her or, in fact, paid any attention to her at all. Not once had she exchanged any conversation with him, that was for sure and certain.

Now, however, she found herself climbing into the buggy with him and felt her heart pounding as he quickly settled her bicycle in the back. It only took him a few minutes before he returned to sit beside her.

She saw him look at her, his blue eyes studying her face. When he didn't look away, she felt that familiar tightness in her chest.

"Is . . . is something wrong?"

"*Ja.*" He reached over and with his thumb, wiped at her temple.

Immediately, Bethany felt a shock course through her body. She'd never had a man other than her father touch her, and despite feeling uncomfortable, she also felt something else. "What was that for?" she whispered.

He turned his thumb around so she could see the dark smudge on the tip of his finger. "I imagine you didn't purposely put that on your face?"

Her mouth opened, just a little, and then she felt her cheeks grow warm. "Oh." Swallowing, she bit her lower lip. "*Nee*, I didn't put that there on purpose."

The corners of his mouth twitched as if he were repressing a smile. "That's what I thought." And then, he picked up the reins, holding them expertly in his hands, and clucked his tongue, urging the horse to move forward. The buggy jostled and she felt her weight shift, her arm brushing against his.

"Sorry."

She noticed that his lips moved, just a little. Was he smiling at her apology?

Suddenly her cheeks felt warm and she turned her head to look out the window. She'd *never* ridden in a buggy with anyone except her parents. But today she was seated beside a handsome young man with the most beautiful blue eyes and a comforting presence that, for some strange reason, made her feel safe.

Chapter Sixteen

Ever since Friday when Abram had notified her about Mary's leg, Edna had fretted about her situation. Somehow, she'd managed to keep everything together on Friday and again on Saturday, but that had only been because John wasn't working at the auction house. He'd volunteered to help her with serving the food and clearing the tables. He'd even rolled up his sleeves to wash dishes.

But he'd be returning to work this week, and Edna had to face the facts: she couldn't survive the next four weeks without help.

Slowly, Edna had come to the realization that she'd have no choice but to accept Wilma's offer, and *that* was not something she was looking forward to doing.

Once again, there were four groups of people coming that week. Edna knew she simply couldn't prepare food for everyone *and* clean the kitchen every day without help, never mind doing her regular chores, such as laundry and cleaning the rest of the house.

Now, she sat at the table, tapping her pencil on the edge of her calendar. The thought of calling the woman at Destination Amish and canceling some of the dinners crossed Edna's mind. However, as much as she wanted to do that,

Edna knew she couldn't. After all, she'd made a promise, and she'd no sooner break it than she'd tell a lie. Besides, she knew how much her family needed the extra income.

"What's the matter, Maem?"

Looking up, she saw John walk through the door, followed by her husband, Elmer. The last thing she wanted to do was cause either of them any worry, so she forced a smile.

"Nothing, John. Just looking over my calendar." *And worrying about how to manage the next few weeks*, she wanted to add but didn't. Edna knew that God would never give her more than she could handle. Perhaps working with Rachel and Ella Mae was part of His plan, and if so, she knew better than to question it.

Of course, after almost thirty years together, her husband saw through her. "Sure is a shame about Mary," he said as if reading her mind. He walked to the sink and turned on the faucet. After waiting for it to warm, he washed his hands. "You'll be needing other help while she heals, I reckon."

Edna sighed. She should've known better than to think that she could hide something from Elmer. "And on short notice," she admitted. "I didn't want to accept Wilma's offer, but I suppose I've no choice."

"Wilma's offer?" John handed his father a dry towel before he, too, began washing his hands. "You mean to have Wilma Schwartz help you?"

"*Nee*, John. Her *dochders*."

Immediately, he froze, an expression of dismay covering his face. "You mean the twins? Rachel? Ella Mae?"

Elmer chuckled and Edna shot him a sharp look.

"Wilma said they could help," Edna explained. "Mayhaps better than nothing."

"What's better than nothing?" Jonas tossed his straw hat on the counter and headed for the sink. His face and neck were covered in dirt and hay. With his hip, he nudged John out of his way and cupped his hands under the water before splashing it on his face.

"Having Rachel and Ella Mae Schwartz help me."

Jonas froze. "Rachel and Ella Mae Schwartz?" He enunciated their names as if just the sound left a bad taste in his mouth. He splashed the water on his face and then shut off the water and turned to face her. "I thought Mary Ropp was helping you."

"She was." Edna sighed. "But her ankle's broken."

"Bad luck, that." He reached for a hand towel and rubbed his neck. "But those Schwartz *schwesters*." Jonas made a face. "*Nee*, they would *not* be better than nothing. Why, those two aren't even in our church district and even *I* hear tell about how poorly they behave."

John raised an eyebrow. "That's a lot, coming from you."

Jonas threw the towel at him.

"Still, I have to agree with Jonas." John folded the towel and hung it over the edge of the sink. "Even I've heard stories about how difficult those two are."

"Since when do *you* listen to gossip, John Esh?" Edna scolded. Without help, she'd never survive. Between cooking for the tourists, preparing for the holidays, and baking cookies for Yoders' *and* worship, Edna had far too much work to handle on her own, even if she wasn't hosting the cookie club at her own house.

"It's not gossip if it's true," John retorted.

"Well, unless one of you boys wants to help out," Elmer said, leveling his gaze at Jonas, "we best be welcoming of Rachel and Ella Mae."

Jonas groaned.

"Besides, you never know, Jonas," Elmer continued. "Mayhaps you'll decide one of them suits your fancy," he teased his son.

Immediately Jonas held up both of his hands and backed away. "That's about as likely as Miriam Schrock not enjoying a bit of gossip."

Even Edna couldn't help but smile at Jonas's comment.

"Well, your *maem* needs some help, and surely neither you nor Jeremiah is suited for housework."

Edna choked back another laugh. But just as she was about to respond, John spoke up.

"There is another solution." He reached into the glass bowl on the counter and grabbed a red apple. For a second, he stared at it. "What about asking Mary's *dochder*? That quiet girl—"

Edna's eyes widened. "You mean Bethany?"

"*Ja*, Bethany," he said, nodding his head.

"She's so shy . . ." Truth was that it had been years since Edna had spent any time with Bethany. She remembered the girl as having been shy as a young child. From all of Mary's complaints—and Wilma's comments—Bethany's shyness had only grown worse. While she knew that Bethany was a fine baker and cook, she wasn't certain how the young woman would do in a chaotic environment with twenty or more *Englischers* needing to be served.

Surprisingly, John defended the young woman. "She seemed pleasant enough when I took Mary home the other day.

"Oh, she *is* pleasant, just so quiet. But I reckon she'd be more helpful than Rachel and Ella Mae," Edna said.

Jonas made a scoffing noise. "*Anyone* would be better than twenty Rachels and Ella Maes."

She shot Jonas another dark look, but she suspected that he was correct. "I reckon it's worth asking, especially since I really could use her help." One quick glance at the kitchen clock and Edna knew that calling the Ropp household would risk creating a delay. If Bethany or Elmer didn't check the messages right away, Edna wouldn't get a response in time to help that week. "Mayhaps you might ride over to ask, Jonas? See if she could start on Wednesday?"

From the corner of her eye, she saw John stiffen. "*Nee*, I'll go."

Edna leveled her gaze at Jonas. She wasn't about to let him off so easy. John was always the one to volunteer to run errands or go out of his way, while Jonas and Jeremiah rarely did so. "*Nee*, John. You travel enough to town, what with work and all. Besides, you ran errands for your *daed* on Friday. Jonas should go."

John shrugged. "I don't mind."

"Hallelujah!" Jonas didn't wait for his mother or father to state otherwise and darted from the room, practically skipping out of the house.

"My word," she mumbled and turned toward John. "That *bruder* of yours! You should've let him go. It's about time he steps up a bit around here."

"That's Jonas for you." John pushed off from the counter and started toward the door. "Best go harness the horse, then."

Chapter Seventeen

Mary sat in the recliner, her foot elevated, and stared out the window. She felt terrible. How on earth could she have let something like this happen?

With all of the groups coming to Edna's house over the next few weeks before Christmas, her friend needed help now more than ever. And, to make matters worse, Mary couldn't even help with the weekly baking of cookies for Yoders' Store. At least not until Abram said she could leave the house.

"Knock, knock."

Mary glanced up. "Wilma!"

Her friend filled the doorway, a concerned look on her face. "Hope you don't mind me popping in like this and all."

"*Nee*, of course not!" She gestured with her hand. "*Kum*, Wilma. Sit a spell. I've been bored out of my mind for two days now. You're a welcome distraction from all of my woes."

Wilma shuffled into the kitchen, dropping her large purse on the floor and placing a container on the counter. "Baked you some pumpkin bread this morning," she said, gesturing toward the container as she made her way over to the sitting area. Her eyes glanced at the cast on Mary's foot and she clucked her tongue. "Now, you tell me what on earth happened here?"

"Oh, it was so silly, really."

Wilma pursed her lips. "It usually is."

Mary managed a soft laugh. "Quite true."

A noise from the other side of the room momentarily interrupted the conversation. Mary glanced over and saw Bethany emerging from the cellar. Wilma followed her gaze and, upon seeing Mary's daughter, called out to her.

"Well now! If it isn't Bethany!" Wilma gestured wildly with her hand for Bethany to join them. "*Kum* sit with us. Tell me what silliness your *maem*'s been up to, getting herself laid up and all."

True to form, Bethany froze at Wilma's request.

"Hmph," Wilma mumbled. "That girl's always been plain scared of her own shadow."

Mary cleared her throat and averted her eyes. She didn't want to engage in a discussion about her daughter with Wilma Schwartz, that was for sure and certain. Truth be told, Mary much preferred her shy daughter to Wilma's competitive, argumentative two. But she'd never say such a thing. *Some things are best left unsaid*, she reminded herself.

Wilma shifted her weight and returned her attention to Mary. "So?"

"'So' what?"

Wilma frowned and pointed her finger at Mary's leg. "How'd you do it?"

"Oh!" Mary gave a nervous laugh. "I . . . well, I was helping Edna—"

"I knew that was a bad idea!"

Mary ignored the interruption. "—and I should've waited for one of her boys to help fetch that container on the top shelf, but I didn't." She sighed. "I fell from the stepladder."

Wilma made a loud noise, almost a sound of disbelief.

"Why, that Edna should've known better than to let you climb a stepladder!" Leaning back in her chair, Wilma gave a look of satisfaction. "Well, reckon now she won't be so quick to dismiss my girls' offer to help."

For the briefest of moments, Mary felt a strong desire to remind Wilma that neither Rachel nor Ella Mae had offered to help Edna. It was Wilma who had put forth their names. But she didn't want to appear argumentative or petty.

"Someone's here, Maem."

Upon hearing her daughter's announcement, Mary looked up. Two visitors? In one day? "Who is it?"

Bethany walked over to the door and peered through the windowpanes. The expression on her face did not change and Mary realized that her daughter did not recognize the horse and buggy.

Wilma started to get up. "If you're expecting someone, best I leave, then."

"*Nee*, stay, Wilma." She gave her friend a reassuring smile. "I'm sure it will be quick. Mayhaps someone from church. We don't get visitors often."

"When it rains, it pours," Wilma quipped drily.

By now, Mary's curiosity was too piqued to pay any attention to Wilma's comment. She hadn't thought to ask how Wilma had come to learn about her injury. Despite the late autumn weather, the Amish grapevine must be flourishing. If that was the case, it was most likely someone from church—perhaps the bishop's wife?—to check in on her.

She watched as Bethany waited in the shadows by the door for the inevitable knock. Mary's heart jumped at the sight. In the dim light, her daughter appeared extraordinarily beautiful. She wore her dark blue dress, a color that always made her skin appear like fresh porcelain. It dawned on Mary that Bethany was no longer just a girl. With her quiet demeanor and fetching features, Bethany had grown into the quintessential Amish *woman*.

She felt a surge of pride in her daughter, and yet that pride was bittersweet. How long would it take for Bethany to find her way in the world? Surely she'd never find it hiding at home, her only interactions with her mother and father.

She was a good daughter, that was for sure and certain. But there was so much more to life than just taking care of one's parents and home. It was time for Bethany to venture forth and find not just her way but herself.

If only God would show Mary how to peel back the years of overprotectiveness when both she and Abram had unknowingly blanketed their daughter from the outside world.

Her thoughts were interrupted by the sharp sound of someone's knuckles rapping against the door.

Bethany stepped forward and opened it. Mary waited, hoping that her daughter would greet the person so she would have a clue who had stopped by, but she heard nothing come from Bethany's mouth other than a soft *oh* sound.

"My *maem*'s in there," Bethany whispered after she composed herself.

When John Esh walked into the room, Mary almost caught her breath, too. He would have been one of the last people she'd have expected to visit her—that was for sure and certain. What on earth was *he* doing at her house?

"Good day, Mary," he said. His large dark eyes shifted from her to Wilma—to whom he politely nodded his head—and then to Bethany.

"John! What a surprise," Mary said. "Is everything all right at home?"

"Oh *ja*, sure. Right as rain." He reached up and grabbed his straw hat. Holding it before himself, he fiddled with it as though uncomfortable in the Ropps' kitchen.

Mary waited expectantly.

"I, uh, well, my *maem* asked me to stop by to see how you're doing."

That's odd, Mary thought. Surely Edna could have called instead of sending her son. "I'm fine, John." She gestured toward her cast. "A bit hindered from moving around but otherwise fine."

"Did Edna send you all this way just for that?" Wilma inquired.

He looked up as if surprised to see Wilma watching him. "Oh, uh, *nee*." He gave a nervous laugh. "She was, uh, wondering if it might be possible to have some assistance with her groups coming in this week." He paused.

"Assistance?" Mary frowned. She thought she had made it clear to Edna that she simply couldn't help her friend. She gestured toward her leg. "I'm afraid I can't be of any help, John."

Suddenly, Wilma became energized. "I'm surprised Edna sent you over here instead of to my *haus*. Unless, of course, you rode there first and one of my *dochders* sent you here."

"Oh, well, uh . . ."

Clearly perplexed as to how to respond, John's eyes flickered in Bethany's direction and, for the briefest of moments, lingered on Mary's daughter. Something lit up in his face, an expression that was not too hard for Mary to read.

And suddenly she had hope.

John cleared his throat and returned his attention to the two older women. "*Nee*, Wilma," John said at last. "Maem asked me to come here and inquire directly of Mary."

"To inquire what, exactly?" Mary probed.

"She was wondering if, mayhaps, Bethany could come in your place."

Wilma caught her breath and leaned back in her seat with a disgruntled huff. At the same time, Bethany stepped forward, her bare feet making a soft shuffling noise against the hardwood floor. Mary knew her daughter was about to reply to John's proposition.

Without giving Bethany the chance to speak, Mary quickly responded with a big smile. "Why, John, I think that's just a *wunderbarr gut* idea!" She ignored the horrified expression on Bethany's face, a look of shock sent in Mary's direction. "You tell your *maem* that Bethany would be *happy* to help out while I'm on the mend."

Chapter Eighteen

When she'd initially answered the door and had seen John Esh standing there, Bethany's first thought had been that, perhaps, he'd come to visit her. After all, he'd been so kind to her on Friday when he'd taken her to the store and then, after he stopped at the harness shop, brought her home. And, truth be told, she hadn't stopped thinking about him. With those piercing blue eyes and his quiet, soft-spoken sense of humor, John Esh was not someone that *anyone* could forget easily, she thought.

But when he asked, "Is your *maem* here, Bethany?" immediately she flushed, feeling foolish. What sort of silly girl was she to have even thought that he might come calling? After all, they didn't really know each other. His kindness the other day meant nothing. He was just a considerate man who had helped her when he'd seen she was in need.

Embarrassed that she'd even thought such a foolish thing, Bethany had lowered her gaze and gestured for him to enter the house.

She had remained standing in the shadows while John spoke with her mother. But when she heard the reason why he had come—to relay Edna's request for Bethany to work in her mother's place—Bethany almost lurched forward to decline.

But she didn't quite make it before she heard her mother accept on Bethany's behalf.

Her mouth opened, staring agape at her mother. Why on earth would her mother do something like that to her? Why would she commit Bethany to not only working outside of the house but to interacting with *Englischers*?

John slid his straw hat through his hands. "Maem will be right pleased," he managed to say.

"You know, Edna could've just called," Wilma snapped, clearly out of sorts that her daughters hadn't been asked.

"Ah, about that." John took a deep breath. "She was wondering if Bethany might come early Wednesday morning."

Bethany practically squeaked when she said, "*This* Wednesday?"

Once again, John looked at her, his eyes holding her gaze. "If you wouldn't mind."

She wanted to say no, but in her heart, she knew that she couldn't. And it wasn't just because John stood there asking her. It was because she knew how horrible her mother felt about not being able to fulfill her promise to help Edna. But the idea of working for Edna in a house filled with strangers petrified Bethany. If only she *could* say no.

And then it dawned on her that she had a way out. After all, her bicycle hadn't been fixed yet.

"Oh. I almost forgot. My bicycle. The tire's flat and the rim is bent." She glanced at John before she looked at her mother. "Reckon I can't help Edna after all, Maem."

John raised an eyebrow at her.

Surely he was wondering why she hadn't told her mother about the damaged bicycle tire. And if he realized that she hadn't shared that information with her mother, then he also knew that she hadn't told her parents about John rescuing her.

Bethany's heart fluttered as she remembered the time they had spent together, mostly in silence but with some light conversation, especially when he took her to the grocery store and even accompanied her inside. He'd pushed the small cart and waited patiently as Bethany put items into the cart. And then, after she'd paid, he had carried the box to his buggy.

No, she hadn't shared any of that with her parents. For some reason, she had wanted to keep it private, a sweet memory that she could revisit over and over again in her mind.

She thought she saw a hint of a smile at the corner of John's lips. "Oh *ja*? It's broken? Mayhaps I can take a look at it and get it fixed. In the meantime," he said, "I could pick you up in the morning and bring you back in the afternoon when I return from work."

"Oh!" She didn't know how she was going to get out of this one. "But that's too much to ask."

John's lips twitched. "*Nee*, Bethany. In fact, after a long day at the auction *haus*, it would be nice to enjoy some more pleasant company for a change."

Stunned, Bethany simply stared at him. She could look at it one of two ways: either John Esh was asking her to ride with him—something she'd never done before!—or he was merely being helpful.

When she realized that he was waiting for a response, Bethany pressed her lips together. Why did her mouth feel so dry? "Oh . . . I . . ." She glanced at her mother. "I'm sure that's too much of a bother."

"Bethany . . ." Her mother gave her a stern look. "We promised to help Edna," Mary said.

No, you *promised*, Bethany thought. If only she had the courage to actually say those words.

She didn't.

John grinned, his blue eyes sparkling. "Then it's settled. I'll come fetch you Wednesday morning, Bethany." The way he enunciated her name made Bethany suspect his request to provide her transportation was not merely to be helpful. "After morning chores." He backed toward the door. "Say eight?"

No words escaped Bethany's mouth. What could she say? Her mother had already committed her, not just to working for Edna, but also to accepting a ride from John.

"*Danke*, John," her mother finally said.

Bethany waited until he had finally left the kitchen—an act which took him much longer than she'd have thought possible. He kept smiling at her as he backed up until he bumped into the edge of the table. A blush covered his cheeks and he scooted to the side, continuing his retreat from the house.

Once the door shut and his footsteps faded down the porch steps, Bethany turned to her mother, not caring that Wilma was still there.

"Maem! How could you?"

Her mother's shoulders lifted in a soft shrug. "How could I what?"

"You should've spoken to me in private," Bethany cried out. "I'd have declined."

Wilma made a scoffing noise. "I can't believe it. She *does* talk," she mumbled.

Mary frowned at her friend and then turned to Bethany, an expression of satisfaction instead of regret upon her face. "I know that, Dochder. And that's exactly *why* I committed you."

Bethany slumped against the kitchen counter, her chin

practically touching her chest. She couldn't understand why her mother would do such a thing to her. Work at Edna's? With the *Englischers*? The idea of interacting with them terrified her. How many times had her father told her to avoid *Englische* tourists?

"You always kept me away from *Englischers*," she said at last, her voice soft and mild.

"When you were younger, *ja*, we did."

Somehow, she found the nerve to look at her mother. "And now you're asking me to help Edna serve them?"

Her mother patted the seat beside her, and reluctantly, Bethany crossed the room. Once she sat down, her mother reached out for her hand. She held it loosely in her own. "Bethany, Edna needs the help. The holidays are busy for everyone. You're doing her a big favor . . . and me, too."

Inwardly, Bethany wanted to groan. She *wanted* to help Edna, but she much preferred doing it from the comfort of her own home.

"And that John," Mary continued. "What a good-hearted man he is, offering to pick you up and bring you back. That'll make it easier on you."

Wilma made a funny noise and mumbled, "Mayhaps *that's* not the main reason for his offer."

Ignoring Wilma's comment, Mary added, "Besides, it's high time you began to interact with other young people."

She felt her mother give her hand a soft squeeze.

"It's only until the holidays. You'll help Edna Tuesday through Saturday, Bethany," her mother said.

"Five days?" Her voice practically squeaked. She'd never been away from her parents' house for so many days in a row. And who would do all of *their* chores? Surely not her mother, not with a broken leg.

"Oh, Maem! Please don't make me do it," she pleaded.

"It won't be so bad. Edna will do most of the talking, but

she needs help setting up, serving, and clearing the dishes. And baking, too. You'll be home every day before you know it."

But Bethany wasn't so easily convinced. She couldn't think of anything worse than having to serve people, especially *Englische* tourists.

Chapter Nineteen

There was an unusual energy in the Esh kitchen on Wednesday morning.

Edna first noticed something was off during breakfast. John appeared distracted and poked at his food. In fact, his quiet mood seemed to fill the entire kitchen. Jeremiah and Jonas ate in silence while John barely ate anything. Edna worried that something was wrong with her oldest son. Normally he'd be in a jovial mood, especially since he had taken off work that week to help his father with some projects. Today, however, something was clearly on his mind.

"I can't believe it's December already," she commented. "Before you know it, Christmas will be right upon us."

No one responded.

Sighing, she looked at John. "How fortunate that you're off work for another week."

He gave a slight nod and mumbled. "*Ja.*"

She raised an eyebrow. Something was definitely weighing on his mind.

Jeremiah, however, didn't seem to notice. He nudged his oldest brother. "I'll say it's fortunate. Now you can do my chores."

Instead of laughing or teasing his brother back, John remained silent.

If Elmer noticed anything unusual about how quiet everyone was at the kitchen table, he didn't comment. Instead, he focused on the things that needed to be done around the farm that day.

"After breakfast, I want to head out to the back pasture and clear those trees from the perimeter."

Jeremiah reached for another piece of toast and slathered butter across it. "Why?"

Edna sipped her coffee. She hadn't heard any discussion about clearing trees, so she, too, was taken by surprise.

"Need to cut them down, sell the wood, and prepare the soil for planting in the spring," was Elmer's solemn reply.

Edna's mouth opened. Her first thought was to comment about what a loss that would be to the farm. Those trees always provided a windbreak from the winter winds and summer storms. And they also shielded the farm from the new development on the other side. Elmer had always claimed that he'd never cut down those trees.

But she thought twice before speaking her mind. Clearly Elmer was thinking beyond the holidays and well into the future. More land meant more crops, and that meant more income. Saying what she truly thought—that it was a mistake—would only make Elmer feel worse about having made the decision at all.

"I'll need all you boys helping." Elmer pointed his fork at Jonas and Jeremiah. "And that means both of you."

"But John's here!" Jonas said. "He took off to help you. Why do you need us?"

John looked up and stared at his brother. Edna noticed the quizzical look on his face right away.

Elmer frowned. "Enough of that, Jonas. You'll help me

right after breakfast. Besides, John's going to fetch Bethany first, so don't think you're getting out of your chores."

Jonas grumbled under his breath.

Jeremiah, however, made a face. "Who's Bethany?"

"Mary Ropp's *dochder*. She's coming to help me, and she starts today," Edna explained. "And your *bruder* volunteered to pick her up and bring her back so she doesn't have to bicycle such a distance. It's getting colder out, you know."

Elmer shoved his chair back from the table, indicating that he was finished with the meal. "We've a lot of work to do, and the more hands, the better." As he stood, he smiled at Edna and gave a simple nod of appreciation for the meal. "Mayhaps a pot of coffee in a few hours? Warms a fellow up."

"Of course."

She watched as Elmer trudged to the door, pausing for his heavy coat and hat. His shoulders slumped, just enough for her to notice. She wondered how he was coping, carrying such weight on them.

Reluctantly, Jonas and Jeremiah stood up and followed their father outside.

To Edna's surprise, John lingered in the kitchen, even offering to help set up the long tables and folding chairs. The cows had already been milked and the horses fed. Yet John was clearly not as eager as usual to join his brothers and father in the dairy to clean the equipment or muck the manure.

"You always serve the same food to your guests," he commented.

"It's easier that way." She plopped the freshly peeled potatoes into the pot of salted water. "Although I do change it up a bit. Otherwise it would be boring for me to cook. Sometimes chicken, other times ham. Although most *Englischers* prefer the chicken. But the side dishes are usually the same: potatoes, chow chow, canned beets, and sliced bread."

He gestured toward the container on the cabinet. "Or rolls."

"*Ja*, rolls. *Englischers* sure do love their bread."

"No more so than we do, Maem."

"I reckon that's true." Plop. One more potato tossed into the pot. "Hard work needs a lot of fuel to refill the tank." She glanced at him. "I'd think you, of anyone, would know that."

"Hm."

Edna frowned. It wasn't like John to be so somber. Usually he was the one she could count on to make jokes and tease her. But not today.

"Everything all right?" she asked, hating to probe but her concern outweighing her usual commitment to her sons' privacy.

He shook his head. "*Nee*, just thinking."

"About?"

"Farming sure is a lot of hard work, don't you think?"

Edna froze. Had John overheard her conversations with Elmer over the past few months? Was he worried about the fact that the dairy market was in such poor shape? She knew that he had aspirations of taking over the farm one day.

"Well," she began slowly, choosing her words carefully. "I suspect that any job a person tackles is hard work."

"You were raised on a farm, *ja*?"

Edna couldn't help but laugh. "Oh, John. You know that to be true! Why are you asking me?"

He shrugged. "Just curious. I mean, if you hadn't been raised on a farm, would you have adapted okay?"

"We can adapt to any situation we want to," she replied.

He seemed to ponder that and then, satisfied with her answer, nodded. "*Ja*, that's what I thought." He glanced at the clock and then mumbled something under his breath before hurrying outside.

Not fifteen minutes passed before she heard the horse neighing in the barnyard, followed by the wheels of the buggy on the unpaved driveway. And from the sound of it, the horse was definitely trotting. She began to pull out a few pots and pans that she needed for making the soup. Within minutes, she forgot about John and the strange questions he'd been asking her. Instead, she focused on the task at hand: preparing the food for the week and getting ready to instruct Bethany how to best help her.

Chapter Twenty

Mary couldn't help but notice how Bethany kept pacing around the kitchen, her black sneakers making a shuffling sound against the linoleum floor. Back and forth. Back and forth. The noise was starting to get on Mary's nerves, but she thought twice about saying as much. Clearly Bethany was nervous enough without Mary adding to her stress.

"It'll be fine," Mary said softly.

"Hm?" Bethany stopped pacing long enough to look at her mother.

Mary gave her an encouraging smile. "Working for Edna. It'll be fine."

Without a word, Bethany began pacing once again.

If only Bethany were more open to trying new things, Mary thought.

At her daughter's age, Mary had been shy, too, but nothing like Bethany. In fact, Mary had enjoyed going to singings with her small group of friends. She loved singing hymns, especially when the boys tried to sing them faster than they were sung at church. It seemed risqué at the time, which, in hindsight, made Mary laugh to herself. How could singing a song faster be a sin?

Of course, at the time, it *had* been frowned upon by the bishop and preachers. Her own parents had warned her about singing fast hymns, and for two months, she had been forbidden to attend any youth gatherings. Being so obedient, Mary had complied without making a fuss.

In truth, she hadn't minded, for at the time, she had started courting Abram, who, rather than risk his own righteous reputation, also stayed away from the singings.

"Why don't you sit a spell?" Mary gestured toward the rocking chair. "Worrying won't make John arrive any faster . . ."

Instead of commenting, Bethany made a soft noise. She moved over to the window and peered outside. In the reflection from the light, her skin appeared almost translucent, not one blemish upon her cheeks.

Mary sighed. "My, how you've grown," she whispered.

"What was that, Maem?" Bethany turned her head and looked at her mother.

"Come sit while you wait."

Reluctantly, Bethany left her post by the window and joined her mother in the sitting area.

"I can hardly believe that it's so cold out, can you? Seems like summer only just ended. But here we are, already in December."

"And soon Christmas." Bethany managed to smile. "The children's pageant at the school *haus* is my favorite."

"It always has been," Mary agreed, glad that the change of subject had distracted Bethany from her anxiety. It was a tactic she'd learned to use long ago when her daughter appeared anxious. "Even when you were a little girl."

The memory of Bethany standing in the front of the school with her peers, singing hymns, reciting Scripture, and reenacting the Nativity scene warmed Mary's heart. Afterward, there were always desserts for the children and their parents: cookies, cakes, pies, even homemade candy. Sometimes the older widows made little presents for the children: a crocheted bookmark, little houses made from old Christmas cards, or store-bought candy canes. It was never anything extravagant; just a token of love for the youngest generation of Amish, who would continue sharing their love for God and Jesus with the next.

Bethany glanced at the calendar and exclaimed, "Why, it's less than a month from now!" Forgetting about her apprehension, Bethany's face lit up. "December twentieth, I believe."

Mary nodded. "The Friday before Christmas, *ja*."

Clasping her hands together, Bethany seemed lost in her memories. "I'll make gingerbread cookies, I think. We don't make those enough." She looked at her mother. "Mayhaps I'll make a small bag for each student. Do you think Teacher would mind?"

This time, Mary laughed and shook her head. "*Nee*, Bethany. I doubt *anyone* would mind."

For a few moments, silence fell over the room once more. Mary worried that Bethany would begin fretting again and tried to think of something to say to her.

To her surprise, Bethany broke the quiet by asking, "I never did inquire as to what *you* are doing today."

"Oh, I'll be just fine. Don't you worry about me."

Bethany nibbled on the edge of her thumb in a nervous sort of way. "Mayhaps it's not such a good idea for me to leave you alone after all."

"I said I'll be fine, and I will be," Mary responded. "Besides, I won't be alone. Wilma and Verna are coming here."

Bethany appeared puzzled. "I thought you and your friends baked the cookies for the store on Wednesdays at Verna's or Wilma's."

"That's true, but they left a message that they would bake them here this week." She smiled. "To keep me company."

The sound of an approaching buggy interrupted their conversation. As the rhythmic noise of the horse's hooves grew louder, Bethany's face paled. Mary watched her, almost afraid that she might back out at the last minute. A few years ago, that would most certainly have happened. But Bethany was no longer a young teenager. She was an adult and, as such, knew better than to break her promise. Long ago, both Mary and Abram had taught her that promises were meant to be kept and breaking them was akin to lying, and *that* was something God most certainly frowned upon.

"Well, I'd best get going, then," Bethany said in a voice so low that it almost sounded like a whisper. Standing up, she started to cross the room toward the door.

Mary waited until Bethany had taken her black shawl from the peg and tossed it over her shoulders.

"Bethany?"

Her daughter paused, her hand lingering on the doorknob.

"*Ja*, Maem?"

Mary gave her an encouraging smile. "*Danke* for helping Edna."

Bethany swallowed and nodded her head. And then, with a twist of the doorknob, she pulled open the door and disappeared through the opening.

Alone in the house, Mary waited until she heard the sound of the horse's hooves clattering once again on the driveway, pulling the buggy away from the house, before she breathed a sigh of relief and actually believed that Bethany would, indeed, follow through on her promise.

Chapter Twenty-One

Bethany felt awkward in the buggy beside John. Try as she might to sit apart from him, his arm kept brushing hers, and twice his leg touched her thigh. She couldn't scooch any farther away unless she could melt into the side of the buggy.

"Was awful kind of you to help out my *maem*," he said, his hands jiggling in time with the walking horse. He glanced at her and waited for a response. "She's really been needing an extra pair of hands."

"Oh?"

He nodded. "I think having your *maem* helping the past two weeks really made it obvious."

She wasn't certain how to respond to that so she remained silent.

For the next few minutes, Bethany stared out the window, too aware of John sitting next to her. What was it about him that made her feel so nervous? It wasn't like her typical shyness. No. This was definitely something different.

He was nice enough, that was true. And he certainly was handsome. But there was something else about John Esh that made her heart pound and her pulse quicken.

"Bethany?"

Startled from her thoughts, she quickly turned her eyes from the window. "Hm?" She noticed that he was watching her, and she felt her cheeks grow warm.

"I asked if you're looking forward to helping my *maem*."

"Oh." Folding her hands, she rested them on her lap. "I enjoy helping other people, *ja*."

John slowed the horse to a halt at a stop sign. After looking both ways, he urged the horse to move forward again. "I sure am glad you could do it," he said. "If you'd said no, she might have asked Wilma's *dochders* to help." He chuckled. "You know those two, *ja*?"

The Schwartz family was in her church district, so she knew the two young women well enough. Bethany nodded, but said nothing. Oh, she knew Rachel and Ella Mae's reputation for being difficult and argumentative, mostly with each other. But she wasn't about to comment on such a thing. Even though she *had* personally witnessed such behavior, she knew that it was not her place to judge anyone, even Wilma's daughters. They had to answer to a higher authority about their conduct, not her.

"Interesting young women," he said.

Bethany gave a little shrug. "None of us are perfect."

He chuckled. "That's one way to look at it."

She wondered why the trip was taking so long. Although she wasn't certain of the time, she knew that she was most definitely late. It was well after eight o'clock, and that was when she was supposed to be there. Perhaps if he'd urge the horse to trot instead of slowly amble down the road.

"It's getting late," she said at last, hoping that he'd take the hint and speed up the horse. She was feeling increasingly anxious and wanted to get to the Esh farm. "Your *maem* will be wondering why I'm not there yet."

He gave the reins a little slap on the horse's rump and

urged it forward. “Come on now, girl,” he called out, and the horse immediately picked up a trot.

Within minutes, they arrived at their destination. Once John stopped the buggy, Bethany quickly slid open the door and started to climb out. Then, thinking better of it, she turned back to him.

“*Danke* for picking me up, John.”

He nodded once in acknowledgment. “My pleasure, Bethany.”

Without waiting for him, she hurried to the front porch and into the kitchen.

“My word,” Edna said as her eyes darted toward the clock. “I thought he must’ve gotten lost fetching you.”

Quietly, Bethany removed her shawl and hung it in the mudroom.

“I set out the plates and utensils on the one table. If you wouldn’t mind covering both tables with the cloths and then setting them, that would be a good start,” Edna said as she stirred something on the stove.

“Okay.”

From just inside the mudroom, Bethany’s eyes scanned the kitchen. Two large tables had been set up in the sitting area of the kitchen. Unlike her parents’ home, the Esh house had large rooms. Clearly a wall had been taken down at some point—or perhaps an addition had been built, for Bethany had not seen a house with such an accommodating kitchen and sitting area.

Bethany took a deep breath as she smoothed down her apron and then reached up to make certain no stray hairs had fallen from beneath her prayer *kapp*. Only then did she tell herself that she was ready.

When she entered the kitchen, she realized that Edna stood there, her eyes trailing her. How long had she been watching her?

"Is . . . is everything all right?" Bethany asked, suddenly nervous that she'd done something wrong already.

But Edna merely smiled and shook her head. "*Nee*, Bethany. Everything is just right."

Strange, Bethany thought, but said nothing. Instead, she focused on what she was supposed to do: work.

Chapter Twenty-Two

It was all Edna could do to keep herself from staring at the young woman as she worked. Without doubt, Bethany was one of the prettiest Amish women she'd seen in a long time. And it wasn't just her physical looks. Sure, her dark brown hair, deep-set brown eyes, and high cheekbones made her look like one of those *Englische* models. But it was more than that. There was an air about her, not of confidence or superiority, but of servitude and righteousness.

She was just beautiful—inside and out—a godly person. Edna knew that right away.

It was just after ten thirty when the timer dinged.

Bethany jumped. "Oh! What's that for?" She opened the oven. "Nothing's baking."

Edna laughed. "*Nee*, nothing is baking just yet. I already precooked some of it and we'll finish baking it prior to the guests' arriving at noon."

She shut the oven door. "Then why did the timer go off?"

Pointing to the stove top, Edna explained. "I promised the men I'd take some coffee out to them. They're cutting down trees in the back field, and it sure was chilly this morning."

Something changed in Bethany's demeanor. It was a

subtle shift, but Edna noticed it right away. "Shall I take it to them?"

"*Nee*, but *danke*. You wouldn't know where they are, I suppose." Edna opened a cabinet and withdrew four coffee mugs by the handles. "I'll go."

Without being asked, Bethany took a dish towel and picked up the coffeepot. "I'll take this for you, then."

Edna didn't need Bethany's company; surely she could handle taking four mugs and a coffeepot outside by herself. But she figured it wasn't a bad idea to have Bethany accompany her. That way, in the future, Bethany could take it out for the men, which would free up Edna to continue working inside.

A few minutes later, they approached the back field. Edna noticed that Elmer and John were hard at work while Jeremiah and Jonas talked by the mules and flat wagon.

Edna frowned. *Isn't that the way it always is?* she thought. Even on John's week off from the auction house, he was working harder than his two other brothers combined. She made a mental note to speak to Elmer about it—again!—later that evening. It just wasn't fair to John that he worked so much to help the family while Jeremiah and Jonas often only did the bare minimum.

"Hot coffee!" she sang out as they neared the men.

Jonas looked up and, upon seeing her and Bethany, walked away from Jeremiah. He smiled as he met them halfway. "Just in the nick of time," he said, his words directed toward Edna but his eyes on Bethany. "You ready to go home? I'd be happy to take you."

Edna frowned at him. "You know it's not even noon yet, Jonas. Stop teasing."

He feigned a look of exhaustion. "Just being polite, that's all. Besides, I'm about tuckered out from working so hard!"

Edna raised an eyebrow. "Must be exhausting talking to your *bruder* so much while your *daed* and John are cutting down the trees."

"What?" Jonas made a face, glancing over his shoulder at his father and brother. When he turned back toward his mother, he jerked his thumb in the direction of the trees. "Who do you think took down all those other trees?"

"Oh, I'm quite certain I know who took them down," Edna said, not trying to hide her disapproval of his comment.

"Why, I was just taking a break, that's all!"

Elmer walked up behind him and clapped his hand upon his son's shoulder. "That's right. Taking a break all right." He laughed and winked at Edna.

Jonas bristled as he reached for the mug of coffee that his mother offered him. "I *was* working hard," he mumbled.

Edna noticed that he avoided looking at Bethany as he took a step away, separating himself from the small group.

"Coffee!" John joined them and gave Bethany a small smile. He nodded his head in a silent greeting, to which Bethany responded in kind, the color flooding her cheeks. "Warms a man up, drinking hot coffee in this weather," John said, lifting the cup to his lips and sipping at it.

Edna surveyed the woods, noticing that only a dozen or so trees had been cut down. She exhaled, wondering how much work lay ahead for her husband. "It'll take you weeks to cut all these trees."

"*Nee*, not weeks. I'm hoping it's all finished before Christmas," Elmer said as he held out his coffee mug for more.

She was happy to oblige. As she refilled his mug, she gave a slight shake of her head. "I don't see how."

"I believe in Christmas miracles!" Elmer teased.

"Hm." Edna knew God was in the business of miracles, but she wasn't certain that helping Elmer cut down those trees, remove the stumps, and fertilize the soil was at the top of the Almighty's to-do list. "Well, mayhaps His first miracle will be getting Jonas and Jeremiah to exercise their arms and not their mouths," she quipped.

From behind them, Jonas scoffed and set his coffee mug on the wagon before disappearing in the direction of the trees.

Jeremiah laughed, clearly unfazed by his mother's comment. "He's embarrassed to be rebuked in front of a certain person," he whispered in a loud voice and then gestured toward Bethany with his head. "Mayhaps he's *ferhoodled*."

She didn't have to look at the young girl to know that she was uncomfortable with Jeremiah's comment. Edna would have been, too, and she hadn't been a shy young woman. "Now, Jeremiah," she scolded in a sharp tone. "It's not nice to poke fun at your *bruder* like that, nor is it kind to say such things at all!" She glanced at Bethany and saw that, indeed, Bethany stood stiffly beside her, her eyes staring at the ground. As Edna returned her attention to Jeremiah, she noticed that John focused on Bethany, an intense expression on his face. *Leave it to John to be the only one of my three sons to display any sense of compassion*, she thought.

"That's right, Jeremiah." Elmer gave him a look of reproach. "Your lack of manners is unacceptable."

The reprimand from his father appeared to do the trick. Jeremiah dipped his head and mumbled an apology.

"Now get back to work." Elmer gestured toward the trees. "You and Jonas need to pick up the pace. No more dillydallying," he snapped.

Disgusted with her two younger sons, Edna collected the four coffee mugs and started walking toward the house. The more distance she put between herself and the two boys the better. "Come along, Bethany. The guests will be arriving shortly."

As they headed away from the woods, Edna noticed that John lingered by the wagon, his eyes locked onto Bethany. It warmed her heart that at least one of her sons had inherited enough compassion and sensitivity to make up for what was lacking in Jonas and Jeremiah.

Chapter Twenty-Three

As usual, Wilma was making a mess. Flour covered her hands, arms, even portions of her face. Mary had never quite understood how anyone could make such a wreck of a kitchen just from baking cookies.

"Land's sake, Wilma! You're wearing more flour than we used in the dough! We should just sprinkle you with pumpkin spice and bake you!" Verna said sharply, clearly thinking the same thing as Mary.

"Oh hush yourself now!"

Verna scowled. "And you *will* help me clean this up, Wilma Schwartz. No sneaking off to the bathroom like you normally do."

"I have a weak constitution," Wilma cried out in self-defense.

"Weak constitution, my foot!" Verna gave the cookie dough one last pat. "There! Now I think we're ready to start." Lifting the bowl, she carried it over to where Mary sat. "I'll fetch the baking sheets if you want to start rolling them into one-inch balls."

Mary gave Verna a warm smile of gratitude. How thoughtful of her cousin to include her in the cookie-making process! Others would just do it themselves. It was often easier that way. But Verna knew Mary well enough to suspect that she was feeling left out and helpless. Having a task, even one as simple as rolling cookie dough into small balls, alleviated those feelings.

"I do wonder how Bethany's doing at Edna's." Mary set down a dough ball on the baking sheet.

"She'll be just fine, mark my words." Verna joined her in the sitting area. Reaching into the bowl, she grabbed some dough and rolled it between her two palms. "She's a fine young woman, Mary. Just needs a bit of exposure, that's all."

Wilma scoffed.

"What's *that* supposed to mean?" Verna asked, her tone sharp and upbraiding.

Coming over to join them, Wilma was more than happy to respond. "That girl will surely get exposure at Edna's." She plopped onto the sofa next to Verna. "Why, she'll have downright culture shock, if you ask me!"

"No one asked you."

Wilma wagged her finger at Verna. "You sure did. Just now. You asked me what I meant."

"Oh help." Verna rolled her eyes.

Mary, however, wondered about Wilma's words: "culture shock."

When Mary had first encouraged Bethany to work for Edna in her place, she hadn't thought about the possible negative impact it might have on her daughter. Instead, she'd only prayed that it would help Bethany come out of her shell. In hindsight, Mary realized that Bethany's exposure to all of those *Englischers* might have a reverse impact. As sheltered as Bethany had been for so many years, would she be able to handle working at Edna's? Had Mary made a mistake in asking her daughter to step in?

Suddenly, Mary felt her chest tighten as her anxiety increased.

Verna leaned over and placed her hand upon Mary's leg. "Are you all right?"

"I . . . I hadn't thought about that," she whispered. "What Wilma said. Do you think Bethany will be able to handle so many strangers? All together? At once?"

Her cousin patted her knee. "Now, now," she reassured Mary in a soothing voice. "Bethany will be just fine. Despite what Wilma said"—she cast a stern look at the other woman—"Edna would never let anything happen to Bethany. She'll ease her into working among those *Englischers*. Besides, you were there. You said yourself that it wasn't so bad, that the tourists mostly talked among themselves."

Wilma clucked her tongue. "You act as if you've sent her to market!"

Mary glanced at Wilma. "I suppose market would be *much* worse." It was true. If she'd forced Bethany to work at a market, where people came and went in droves, it *would've* been worse. At least by working with Edna, Bethany was still somewhat sheltered and, as Verna had pointed out, wouldn't have to interact too much with the guests.

"I suppose you're both right."

Verna gave her one last pat. "Of course we're right. Besides, it's high time that Bethany began to experience the outside world, even if it's only at Edna's *haus*. Otherwise, how will she ever meet anyone to get married?"

This time, it was Wilma who mumbled "Oh help" and rolled her eyes.

"Why, just think, if we hadn't put our heads together and found that job for Myrna, well, where would *she* be today?" Verna reached for more dough. "She'd not be married to Ezekiel, that's for sure and certain."

"And we wouldn't be hearing about it every single time we're together," Wilma mumbled.

Verna snapped her head around, glaring. "What did you say?"

"Nothing." Wilma forced a benign smile to mask her unkind comment. "Nothing at all."

"Hmph." Verna squished a cookie dough ball onto the baking sheet. "Somehow I don't believe that!"

Mary fought the urge to scold the two of them. Sometimes they behaved like schoolgirls instead of middle-aged women. She didn't fault Verna. There were times that Wilma's attitude was too overbearing and domineering. She was always quick to overtake the conversation and often made derogatory comments. But scolding her friends wasn't Mary's style.

Wilma turned her attention to Mary. "You know, I was thinking—"

"Dangerous thing," Verna quipped.

Wilma shot her a look before continuing. "—and mayhaps this is a bit far-fetched, but . . ." She paused.

"But what, Wilma?" Mary urged.

"Well, when John Esh came over the other day—what was that? Monday?—he sure struck me as a righteous man." Wilma glanced at the other two women. "And he sure did look at your *dochder* a lot."

Mary froze. She couldn't deny that she'd noticed John's attention to Bethany, but she hadn't realized that Wilma had been paying such close attention, too. "What are you saying, Wilma?"

"Well, wouldn't it be something if . . . well . . . you know."

Verna gasped. Her eyes grew large and a smile broke onto her face. "Oh, Wilma!" she interjected. "I agree!"

"Are you two saying what I think you're saying?" Mary clucked her tongue and gave them a stern look. "I thought we agreed not to do any more matchmaking."

"Mayhaps it's more like match-hoping instead of matchmaking," Wilma said in a teasing tone.

"Well, whatever it is, I reckon we'll just let nature take its course."

Wilma adopted an air of indifference and gave a little

shrug. "I don't see where guiding them along a bit would hurt. I mean, if it were my *dochders* . . ." Her voice trailed off and she left the sentence unfinished.

She didn't have to complete her thought. Mary knew exactly what Wilma would do if it involved Rachel and Ella Mae. In fact, it dawned on Mary that Wilma had suggested having the twins help Edna for a particular reason: the Esh boys.

"Hmph." She pursed her lips. Though she might secretly hope that Bethany would find a special friend while helping Edna, Mary wasn't about to interfere. Fortunately, the timer went off.

Saved by the bell, she thought.

"First batch of cookies is done," she announced, grateful for the opportunity to change the subject.

She watched as Verna and Wilma hurried over to the kitchen. Using hot pads, they removed four baking sheets of cookies, setting them on the cooling rack before putting another four sheets of unbaked cookie dough back inside the hot oven.

"It's amazing how much money we've raised from selling cookies at Yoders' Store to increase Amish Aid." Mary returned her focus to rolling more cookie dough in her palms.

Verna nodded. "I heard that the cookies are selling out before the weekend starts! And the bishop of our district said we've raised well over five thousand dollars so far for our three church districts."

"Mayhaps we should try to make more for the weekend," Mary said. "Drop off another batch on Friday morning."

Wilma made a face. "I don't have time to make more. Plus, we're going to Edna's on Friday morning to make cookies for church."

Mary sighed, knowing that she couldn't go. She would

miss being there with all of her friends. "Mayhaps Bethany and I could make them tomorrow evening."

"If she's not too tired after working at Edna's." There was a trace of sarcasm in Wilma's voice, which Mary chose to ignore.

"I'll be thankful when Edna can rejoin us." Mary placed a ball of dough onto the baking sheet. "It's so nice when it's the four of us. Feels like something is missing without her here."

Wilma scoffed. "Something? You mean 'someone,' and it doesn't *feel* like someone's missing, because Edna *is* missing."

Verna clucked her tongue and rolled her eyes. "Oh, you know exactly what she meant, Wilma Schwartz!" And then, under her breath, she added, "Always so argumentative about everything."

"What did you say?"

Smiling, Verna repeated Wilma's words from just a few moments earlier. "Nothing. Nothing at all."

Chapter Twenty-Four

Bethany finished washing the last plate, shook it over the sink to free any remaining drops of water, and then set it onto the drying rack. *Finished*, she thought with a small feeling of satisfaction building inside her chest. Her first official day working outside of the family house! And she'd survived with only a few mild panic attacks.

"My word, Bethany!" Edna exclaimed as she walked out of the pantry room. From the look on the older woman's face, she was clearly pleased. "This room is so clean and tidy that it looks as if I'm ready for Sunday worship."

Bethany couldn't help but smile at the compliment.

"And so early, too!" Edna set down a container on the kitchen table. For a moment, the older woman stood there and surveyed the room. "And to think we'll do it all again tomorrow," she said with a slightly deflated sigh. "You'll be coming back, *ja*?"

Bethany stopped working. "Coming back?"

"Tomorrow." Edna sat down in a chair at the kitchen table. "Or did they scare you off? All those *Englischers*."

Ah, Bethany thought, realizing that Edna was teasing her. She gave a soft laugh. "*Nee*, Edna, they didn't scare me off."

"What do you think, then?"

Bethany tilted her head. "About?"

Spreading her hands before her, Edna gestured toward the room. "Today. The guests. The work. Everything."

"Oh!" She felt her cheeks warm up. She should've known what Edna meant. "It . . . it really wasn't so bad."

A laugh escaped Edna's lips. "Not so bad, indeed. This was a particularly fine group of women. Last week, however"—she clucked her tongue disapprovingly—"they ate so much that your *maem* and I worried we didn't have enough!"

"She told me."

"That's right. You and Mary made me all those apple pies to serve to the weekend group. I sure did appreciate that."

Demurely, Bethany looked away.

"Usually I have leftovers for my family to eat at supper. I'll doctor them up a bit, so that they aren't always eating the same food—add ham or meatballs, *ja*?—but it sure does make extra work for me when the guests devour everything in sight."

She could only imagine! She was amazed at how much *this* group had eaten. She couldn't fathom how anyone could have eaten still more.

Taking a deep breath, Edna glanced at the clock. "Well, it's earlier than I anticipated, but if you're done, you're done." She smiled at her. "Reckon I should fetch one of the boys to take you home."

Bethany watched as Edna walked to the mudroom and opened the door that led onto the porch. A few seconds later, a loud bell rang out. Once, twice, three times. When Edna returned, she explained. "I told Elmer I'd ring the bell when I needed Jonas to take you."

Bethany returned to drying the dishes and then stacked

them on the counter. She wasn't looking forward to being driven home by Jonas. She'd seen through his attempts to hide his laziness earlier that day when she and Edna had brought out the coffee. And a man who didn't value hard work certainly did not impress Bethany one bit.

Not ten minutes later, Bethany could hear the sound of a horse outside the house. Edna walked over to the window and peered outside. "Ah, the buggy's almost ready. Why don't you collect your things and go on out? And one of the boys will pick you up at the same time tomorrow, *ja*?"

Bethany nodded.

As she walked into the mudroom and reached for her shawl, she felt herself beginning to grow anxious. Quietly, she walked outside and stole across the small patch of grass between the house and the turnaround in front of the barn. She could see Jonas adjusting the brake lines, and without speaking, she climbed into the buggy.

With the sun starting to set already, the air was brisk and cold. She shivered and pulled her shawl tighter around her throat.

"Cold?"

Startled, Bethany looked up. John? "Oh!" She had been expecting Jonas! The change was definitely preferable to her.

"Something wrong?"

She stumbled over her words. "*Nee*, not wrong. It . . . It's just that your *maem* said Jonas was taking me."

John raised an eyebrow. "Shall I fetch him? He'd be more than happy to do so."

Appalled, Bethany flushed.

Leaning against the buggy, John took a deep breath. "Look, Bethany, do me a favor, *ja*? I've worked hard all day and, well, I could use a little break. So if you don't mind, mayhaps it'd be all right if I, not Jonas, took you home."

Had she offended him? Her stomach churned and she felt her heart begin to palpitate. She needed to correct this wrong, and quickly. But her throat felt dry as she fought the panic.

Speak, she willed herself. *Say something. Anything!*

Swallowing, she shook her head. "*Nee*, John. I . . . I simply meant that I'm so sorry you were inconvenienced by taking me." She paused and moistened her lips. "*Especially* because you worked so hard today."

A hint of a smile touched his lips. "I'm not."

"You're not . . . ?"

He turned to look at her. The expression he wore was solemn and serious as he said, "I'm not sorry, and I'm definitely not inconvenienced."

Her mouth opened, just a little.

"In fact," John continued, returning his attention to the horse, double-checking the brake lines, "it's rather nice. A fellow gets tired of always being with just his *bruders* or coworkers."

Bethany felt her heart skip a beat. Was he trying to tell her that he wasn't courting anyone? "I . . . I can imagine that would be rather . . ."

He waited for her to finish. When she didn't, he smirked. "Rather what, Bethany?"

She struggled to find the right word so that she didn't offend him. "Monotonous, I reckon."

He laughed. "If by 'monotonous' you mean dull and tedious, then you are more than correct."

"That's not what I meant!" She felt her cheeks heat up, embarrassed that he had interpreted her word choice in such a negative manner. "I mean, I don't know your *bruders* or coworkers to say if they *are* dull and tedious!"

His laughter subsided, but there was a bright sparkle in his blue eyes as he looked at her. "Well, I can assure you that they are," he said in a playful tone, "which is why I am more than happy to take you home, Bethany Ropp. Unlike them, you are neither dull nor tedious. In fact, I find *your* company to be rather refreshing after a long day of work."

Chapter Twenty-Five

On Thursday morning, Edna was bustling about the kitchen when she saw the buggy emerge around the corner of the barn.

John must be returning with Bethany already. She smiled to herself, content with how smoothly things had run the previous day and how John had volunteered to fetch her. In fact, he seemed quite happy to help out by picking her up and taking her home.

As she opened the oven door, a wave of dry heat hit her face, and she quickly slid in the bread pans. The kitchen was warm, thanks to the extra help from the oven. She'd always preferred the cold weather that came with winter to the heat of summer. There was something cozy about lazy winter days. With fewer outdoor chores, winter definitely meant time to focus on baking in the kitchen or crocheting in the sitting area. But recently, despite the cold weather, her kitchen always seemed extra warm.

Footsteps behind her interrupted her thoughts. She turned in time to see Elmer walk over to the kitchen window and peer outside. She hadn't heard him come downstairs. Once again at breakfast, he'd been unusually quiet. Even now, he remained silent for a minute, his eyes following something.

"What is it?" she asked, her curiosity piqued.

"John and Bethany."

Hearing Elmer say the two names together, Edna straightened. *John and Bethany. Why, those two names sound just about right together*, she thought. She joined him at the window.

Bethany was standing beside John as he unhitched the horse from the buggy. At one point, he said something and the young woman hurried over to take hold of the horse's bridle while John held the left shaft. After setting it upon the ground, he took the horse from Bethany and the two of them disappeared into the barn.

"Oh my," she whispered. Was it possible that Bethany and John might be interested in each other? The possibility definitely intrigued her, and she wished she hadn't asked Jonas to take Bethany home later that afternoon. She wouldn't make that mistake again, that was for sure and certain.

"Oh no!" Elmer wagged his finger at her. "I know that look on your face." He pushed away from the counter and walked over to the coffeepot. It was empty. Without hesitation, he began to refill it with water and then put fresh grinds in the basket. "What're you up to now, Edna Esh?"

"Nothing," she said, hoping that her husband couldn't see through her.

"Don't be getting any ideas there, *fraa*." He wagged a finger at her. "I *know* you."

Edna put her hand on her hip and faced him head-on. "Now, Elmer! I have no idea what you mean."

"Uh-huh." Clearly he didn't believe her.

"I mean, just because John *was* a little extra cheerful this morning," Edna started, "doesn't mean anything, right?"

"I noticed that, too," Elmer said as he set the pot onto the stove. "But don't go getting your hopes up."

She placed her hand on her chest. "Me?"

"*Ja*, you!"

She feigned being insulted. "Hmph."

When the kitchen door opened, Edna leaned backward, craning her neck to see whether or not it was Bethany who walked through first. The young woman stopped and looked around the room, her eyes brightening as she gave Edna a quiet smile, then removed her shawl and hung it on a peg in the mudroom.

"*Gut martiye!*" Edna sang out when she saw Bethany. She wasn't too surprised to see John right behind her. Sure enough, his face beamed. He leaned against the kitchen doorframe, his arms crossed over his chest with a special brightness to his blue eyes.

Elmer made a noise, and she glanced at him.

"Okay then, maybe you can hope a little bit," he whispered and winked at her before turning to his son. "*Kum*, John, get some fresh coffee. Enjoy it now before we head back outside to cut more trees."

After fetching his coffee, John lingered in the kitchen, leaning against the counter by the stove with his mug in hand. His eyes trailed Bethany as she crossed the floor toward the sink. Without being asked, she began to wash the dirty pans, letting the water run for a few minutes so that it warmed up. John took the opportunity to open a drawer and withdraw a fresh dish towel, which he proceeded to set upon the counter next to Bethany.

Edna observed this gesture with mild curiosity. John had always been her thoughtful son, the one who went out of his way to help out without being asked. It pleased her that he continued displaying such considerate manners to Bethany.

Loud footsteps pounding down the staircase preceded

Jonas's appearance in the kitchen. He glanced over at Bethany and grinned.

"Back again, eh?"

She flushed and looked away.

He laughed and hurried over to grab a cup of coffee. John barely moved to make room for him.

"Hey, there's a singing tonight," Jonas said, clearly directing the comment to Bethany. "Over in Bishop Mast's district. You know anyone there?"

She kept her back to him. "*Nee*, I do not."

"Really?"

Bethany gave a little nod.

"Say! I've got an idea!" Jonas gave her a bright grin. "Why don't I take you home after you're finished and we can stop at the youth gathering?"

Edna noticed that John stiffened, but he didn't speak up. Bethany, however, immediately stumbled over her words, clearly uncomfortable with the forward way in which Jonas had asked her to go with him.

"Oh, I . . ." Her eyes looked first at Edna and then shifted over to where John stood. "I don't go to youth gatherings."

"What about when they have singings?"

She shook her head. "I don't go to singings, either."

Jonas frowned. "You *never* go to singings?"

This time, she shook her head. "I don't particularly care for them. Besides, I prefer to stay home in the evenings."

Edna could tell from the expression on Jonas's face that he was growing frustrated. "No youth gatherings. No singings. What *do* you do for fun?"

Before Edna could chastise Jonas for his impolite question, John pushed himself away from the counter and clapped his hands, the sharp noise cutting the tension in the air. "Best get to work now, Jonas. Daed's waiting for us."

Jonas held up his mug. "I just got my coffee!"

"Take it with you." John walked toward his brother and placed his hand upon his shoulder, turning him around so that Jonas had no choice but to follow John out of the house.

"I'm so sorry about that," Edna said to Bethany. "I'm afraid Jonas is just not used to having young women around."

Bethany gave a little shrug. "It's all right."

Edna left the subject alone, suspecting that this was one of those situations where less said was soonest mended. But she made a mental note later to have a firm discussion with Jonas about how he spoke to Bethany. The last thing she wanted was for Bethany to get scared off and quit because of his antics.

However, the way Bethany bounced back made Edna realize that the young woman hadn't been too perturbed by Jonas's uninhibited question. She was definitely stronger than Mary gave her credit for. And, knowing Jonas, he'd soon give up trying to pursue the young woman.

But John?

Edna had never known John to go to singings or youth gatherings. He focused mostly on his work, both off and on the farm. The way he lit up around Bethany definitely spoke volumes about his interest in the girl. If only she could know better what Bethany thought of John. She was far too stoic and reserved, which made her a hard read for Edna.

While she couldn't be certain about it, Edna had to admit that the idea of John and Bethany secretly courting did not displease her. Of course, only time would tell whether or not a match might, indeed, be made.

Chapter Twenty-Six

Mary hummed to herself as she sat in the recliner, working on a new blanket. She might be confined to her chair for a few days, but that didn't mean she should use it as an excuse to be lazy. Instead, she had spent her time reading Scripture, catching up on her correspondence, and now working on a blanket. Her fingers moved quickly, the yarn sliding between her thumb and pointer finger as she crocheted. With Bethany working yesterday and today, Mary had already halfway finished a new blanket that she intended to give her daughter for her hope chest.

She worried about her daughter and said a silent prayer with each row that she crocheted. The previous evening, Bethany hadn't said much about her day at Edna's. Mary fretted that the work was overwhelming for her. After all, she'd been so sheltered for most of her life.

Earlier that morning, once again, Mary had noticed how Bethany seemed extra apprehensive, adopting her place in front of the window, occasionally pacing the floor until the horse and buggy pulled down the driveway.

"Don't forget we need to bake more cookies for Yoders' Store. Wilma said they ran out before the end of last week-end," Mary had called out when Bethany had reached for her black shawl and swung it over her shoulders.

"*Ja*, I remember," Bethany replied.

"Your *daed* will drop them off in the morning."

But the door was already shut by the time Mary finished speaking.

Oh, how she had wished she could hurry to the window! She'd have loved watching John Esh help Bethany into the buggy. She couldn't remember the last time her daughter had gone anywhere with anyone! But she knew better than to get up. Always a stickler for following the rules, Abram had insisted that she stay off her feet, just as the doctor had instructed.

Now, however, it was close to three o'clock. Surely Bethany would be returning soon. Mary hated to admit it, but it was nice to be home alone for a few hours each day. She hadn't been alone in the house for more than an hour or two since Bethany had attended school. Ever since then, the only time Mary could savor any solitude in her own house was when she sent Bethany on short errands.

Despite having enjoyed the peace in the house, Mary was anxious for her daughter's return. Being alone was refreshing, true, but not for too long. It wasn't as if Bethany was troublesome. Quite the contrary. She was quiet and helpful, never one to complain or naysay. And she certainly didn't gossip, not like Wilma or that Miriam Schrock!

After two long days alone, Mary was ready for some company.

When she finally heard footsteps on the porch, Mary anticipated that Bethany would enter the house. To her surprise, it was Abram.

"Home so early?" Her eyes darted toward the clock. He usually didn't get home for another hour.

"*Ja*. Looks like snow so they let us leave early."

Abram crossed the room and stopped in front of the sink. After flipping on the faucet, he bent forward and splashed water on his face and neck. "Figured I'd go fetch Bethany," he said after he shut off the water.

"Mayhaps you should wait before you ride to the Eshes'."

He rubbed a kitchen towel across his damp skin. "Wait? Whatever for?"

Mary continued crocheting as she spoke to her husband. "I think John is bringing her home."

"Again?"

Mary nodded.

"I don't mind getting her. Could save him the trip," Abram said and laid down the towel in a crumpled heap on the counter.

"Mayhaps you wouldn't be doing such a favor." She gave him a sly look, hoping that he didn't probe further. Abram might not be as approving as she of a special friendship forming between Bethany and John. *Correction*, she thought, *Bethany and* anyone. Abram certainly would not approve of any matchmaking attempts on her part.

But Abram caught the hidden meaning beneath her comment. "Now, Mary—"

She set down her crochet hook. "What?" She hoped she sounded innocent, but one look at his face and she knew he'd seen through her.

He wagged his finger at her in a reproachful manner. "Now, don't you go meddling."

Immediately, Mary held up her hand as if holding him at bay. "I can assure you, Abram, I am not meddling."

Giving her one of *those* looks, he didn't seem convinced by her words.

"Honest!"

He scoffed at her declaration of innocence. "Your women friends were here yesterday, your little cookie club—"

Mary's eyes widened.

"—and I know how you women plot and scheme. Always

matchmaking. You probably already have the poor girl married off to one of those younger Esh boys!"

"Abram Ropp! We've done no such thing!" Mary would have been less offended by her husband's accusation if they had actually discussed such a possibility. But the truth was that, while she had hopes of something between Bethany and John Esh, she certainly hadn't voiced that secret dream to anyone.

Abram took a deep breath and exhaled slowly. "Good, because Bethany's far too young to be thinking about courting anyone. I won't have it." He glanced at the clock and then at the bedroom door. "Well, if I don't have to get Bethany, I'm going to take advantage of the time and take a little nap. Wake me in an hour, *ja*?"

He didn't wait for an answer.

Mary stared after him, still hurt by his accusation, as well as his declaration about Bethany being too young to court. She was, after all, nineteen and more than ready to walk out with a special friend. Mary knew her husband had always been overly protective of their daughter, but he'd never vocalized such opposition to Bethany courting anyone. That worried her, for, if her suspicions about John and Bethany were even remotely true, what would happen when Abram found out?

Chapter Twenty-Seven

The clock was striking three when the kitchen door opened. Bethany had just finished putting away all of the plates, silverware, cups, and platters. She shut the cabinet and turned around, moving toward the table at the same time. But she stopped abruptly when she bumped directly into John.

She felt his hands on her arms, firm but gentle, as he steadied her, holding her where she stood, close before him. He towered over her, his chin practically on top of her head.

"Easy there," he murmured, his voice low and his breath warming her ear.

Embarrassed, Bethany tried not to look up. She started to take a step backward, but he still held her. Curious, she tilted her head enough so that she could raise her eyes and meet his gaze.

"You okay?"

She gave a single nod.

"Sorry about that," John said and relaxed his hands. "Didn't mean to sneak up behind you."

She took a deep breath. There had been something comforting about being so close to him, her cheek practically resting against his shoulder. "I should've looked where I was going."

Still, he didn't release her and remained standing, silently staring intently into her face. His eyes narrowed as he studied her.

"What's wrong?"

Slowly, John leaned over, lifting up one hand and running the backs of his fingers across her cheek. "You splashed water on your face."

Instinctively, she reached up and touched her cheek where he had. "Did I?"

"It's gone." Finally, he released his grip and took a step away from her, giving her some space. "Surprised to see you still here."

She blinked.

John smiled. "I meant you haven't gone home yet." He pursed his lips and glanced toward the window. "Sun's going to start setting soon. I'll harness up the horse and take you home if you're ready."

Her eyes widened and her pulse quickened. Earlier that morning, Jonas had made a comment about taking her home. She hadn't been particularly partial to that idea and felt more than a little relieved that John, not his brother, would be the one driving the buggy.

He must have mistaken her silence for apprehension. "I mean, if that's all right with you."

Before he could say anything else, Jonas rounded the corner from the other room, where he'd stacked the chairs for his mother. Bethany felt his presence long before she heard him. His feet froze and he stood, silent, in the doorway for long enough that Bethany suspected he was surprised to see his older brother in the kitchen.

"Hey now," Jonas called out, a cheerful tone to his voice that, when Bethany looked at him, was not reflected in his expression. "Daed said I'm to take you home now."

"Oh!" Bethany wasn't certain how to respond.

Fortunately, John spoke up. "*Nee*, Bruder, I already told Bethany that I would take her home."

"But I—"

John leveled his gaze at his brother. "You can help Daed with the milking."

Jonas stared at Bethany as if anticipating that she might speak up on his behalf. But Bethany merely averted her eyes.

"You sure about that singing tonight?" he asked at last, breaking the uncomfortable silence that hung in the room.

"I have to help my *maem* bake more cookies for Yoders' Store."

"Hm. Mayhaps I'll stop by to check, just in case, on my way over there."

Stunned at his presumption, Bethany looked up and stared at him. There was nothing she would dislike more than attending the singing, except, perhaps, having Jonas come calling on her. His persistence was exasperating. "Truly, there's no need. Singings aren't for me."

"You might change your mind."

Bethany knew that there was no chance of that happening.

Fortunately, John saved her from having to respond. "Jonas, Daed's waiting for you."

With a heavy glare at his brother, Jonas stomped out of the kitchen, pausing just once when he got to the door. He glanced over his shoulder at Bethany. He mouthed the words *I'll stop by later* to her and then slipped through the door.

Horrified, Bethany wondered if John had witnessed that last silent communication from Jonas.

"I'll go harness the horse, then," John said, giving no indication that he'd seen it.

When John walked out of the house, Bethany exhaled. It felt as if she had been holding her breath. Something would have to be done about Jonas, but she didn't want to hurt his feelings. While she was flattered by his attention, she had absolutely zero interest in Jonas Esh. There was something too abrasive about his manner that would never suit her.

Turning around, she leaned against the counter and stared out the large window over the sink. She could see John already at the barn, leading out the dark bay horse. She watched him as he deftly harnessed the horse to the buggy, pausing every so often to pat the mare on the neck.

While she might have no interest in Jonas Esh, she realized that the same couldn't be said about his older brother, John. He was gentle and soft-spoken, caring and attentive. Even more importantly, he wasn't overbearing like Jonas. And while she remained hopeful that he might return her interest, she couldn't be certain. Perhaps he was just being kind and polite. She prayed that his attention to her was more than that, but she just wasn't familiar with the whole courtship process.

Besides, she reminded herself, she barely knew him. And he was so much older than she was. Bethany didn't know if he was courting someone else. Surely at twenty-six years of age, a man like John Esh would have a special friend.

Still, she couldn't help but remain hopeful. He had, after all, volunteered to take her home, even after Jonas had said he wouldn't mind doing so.

Time will tell, she told herself as she went into the mudroom to collect her shawl.

"Edna?" she called out. "I'm leaving now."

The footsteps that came from the cellar grew louder as Edna hurried upstairs. As she walked through the doorway, she smiled at Bethany. "I'll see you on Friday, *ja*?"

Bethany nodded.

A few minutes later, she sat beside John, listening to the musical rhythm of the horse's hooves on the road. Despite the silence in the buggy, she felt comfortable in John's presence. Unlike his brother, John didn't feel the need to occupy every moment with words. It was as if he, too, appreciated the peace of just being. If only, she thought, he was appreciating the peace of just being particularly because he was with *her*.

Chapter Twenty-Eight

On Friday morning, Edna eagerly greeted Wilma and Verna when they walked through the kitchen door. She'd already set up the tables for her guests, who were to arrive at noon, and the ingredients for baking the cookies were laid out on the counter.

Wilma dropped her large black purse on the floor. It landed with a loud thump.

"My word, Wilma!" Edna laughed. "What on earth do you have in there? The kitchen sink?"

"Everything but!" Wilma glanced around the large room, her eyes widening as she stared at the two large tables. "Are those a permanent addition to your kitchen?"

"Sure feels that way." Edna reached into a cabinet and pulled out several large mixing bowls. Elmer had actually offered to build a dedicated room for her lunches next spring, but she didn't want to share that information. Wilma would have too many questions, and *that* was something she didn't have time to deal with. "Best get started with the cookies. I don't have much time for visiting today, I fear."

Verna clucked her tongue and gave a slight shake of her head. "Mayhaps we should be doing our worship cookies at my house until your busy season ends."

With her back toward her friends, Edna froze. She'd worried that such a suggestion would slip past one of her friends' lips. And it was the last thing she wanted to do. For so many years, her three best friends had been coming to her house to bake cookies every other Friday for their respective worship services. Edna enjoyed the consistency and fellowship of their schedule, but she had still other reasons for always wanting to host their gatherings.

Her house needed life. *Female* life.

She was the only one of her friends who did not have a daughter. When her friends came over, Edna felt complete. It was nice to have laughter and teasing in her own kitchen—one that was normally so quiet—that could only come from women enjoying each other's company. And not just women, but *friends*.

"Oh, everything's been right easy," Edna said slowly, carefully choosing her words. "I've a little routine now, and, of course, Bethany's been an amazing help."

At the mention of Bethany, Wilma scoffed.

Verna rolled her eyes and made her way to the counter. She didn't wait for any instructions but dove right in to making the cookies. "I'm so glad that's working out for you."

Edna caught Wilma making a face.

"And not just for you, of course, but for Bethany."

"Pshaw!" Wilma waved her hand, clearly irritated by the direction of the conversation. "Girl's just coddled too much."

Verna cast a dark look in Wilma's direction. "Funny, isn't it? You said as much to me about Myrna right before she began working for Ezekiel last spring."

Edna pressed her lips together. *Uh-oh*, she thought. It was going to be one of *those* days.

Wilma merely raised her eyebrows and coolly replied,

"And see how loosening your apron strings helped her finally land a husband?"

Edna could see Verna bristle at the remark, so she quickly jumped in between the two women. Plastering a smile on her face, Edna gestured toward the ingredients on the counter. "Let's get started, shall we? We've only a little bit of time before I need to tidy up for my guests, so no sense wasting it, *ja*?"

Half an hour later, the cookies were baking in the oven, and the women sat around the kitchen table, a pot of fresh coffee situated on a hot pad before them.

"So, I've some interesting news," Verna announced as she picked at the cinnamon buns that Edna had set out for them to enjoy with their coffee.

"Oh *ja*?" Edna smiled at her friend.

Wilma waved a piece of her bun in the air. "Let me guess—"

But Verna didn't give Wilma a chance. "Myrna and Ezekiel are expecting."

Wilma slapped her hand on the edge of the table. "I knew it!"

"That's *wunderbarr*!" Edna felt genuine joy for her friend. Oh, to have a baby in the house again, even if only for visits. "How's she feeling?"

Wilma shoved the piece of bun into her mouth. "Took long enough."

Verna ignored Wilma's comment. "Just fine. A bit tired and all. But that's to be expected. Although she sure was busy when I saw her yesterday, cleaning the *haus* and tending to Ezekiel's little ones."

"When is the blessed event to happen?" Despite her joy for her friend, Edna couldn't help but feel a bit of sorrow. When would it be *her* time to share such good tidings?

"She's due in February, God willing. She made me promise not to say anything, of course, until now."

Wilma's mouth opened, hanging agape.

Verna gave her a smug smile. "Seems it didn't take them so long after all, eh?"

"Hmph."

With a satisfied sigh, Verna returned her attention to Edna. "Now that Myrna's all settled into married life, it's time for our next project, don't you think?"

"Project?"

Verna laughed. "Well, you *do* have three eligible sons, Edna. It's high time we find one of them a young woman to court."

"Oh, that." Edna pressed her lips together. She didn't want to say anything about John and his apparent interest in Bethany, at least not until she was certain that it was reciprocated. And the Lord only knew whether or not Bethany shared John's sentiments. "In due time, I suspect."

Loud footsteps on the porch interrupted their conversation. Jeremiah walked inside, pausing to kick off his boots. Despite the cold temperature outside, they were still caked with gooey mud.

"You seen John, Maem?" he asked, nodding his head in acknowledgment to Wilma and Verna.

"You know he went to fetch Bethany."

Verna clucked her tongue and tried to hide her amusement. "Mayhaps a project in the making?" she whispered to Wilma, but loud enough so Edna could hear.

Edna felt the color drain from her face. "Now, Verna . . ."

"Oh, don't you 'now, Verna' me," she retorted in a playful tone. "What a good match that would be. Don't you think so?"

She *did* think so, but she wasn't about to admit it.

"Besides, isn't it about time you had little feet running

through the *haus* again?" Verna gave her a broad smile. "Surely you don't want me to be a *grossmammi* by myself!"

Edna picked up her coffee mug and sipped at it. "Honestly, Verna," she said lightly as she suppressed a smile, "I have no idea what you're talking about."

Chapter Twenty-Nine

Bethany impatiently waited for the moment when the horse and black buggy would turn down the short driveway and stop in front of her house. For the past five minutes, she had been standing at the door, her black shawl already over her shoulders, as she waited. Behind her on the wall, the clicking of the clock echoed in the quiet kitchen.

She disliked being late. For anything. It stressed her out, increasing her anxiety, whenever she wasn't on time. So, she had positioned herself to stare out the window so that she didn't keep John waiting.

"Oh my." Her mother limped out of the bedroom. She'd gone to fetch a sweater, for the house was colder than usual. "I hope that heater kicks in soon."

Bethany glanced over her shoulder. "Daed forgot to turn it up this morning. I did it, though, so I reckon it'll warm up soon enough."

"I sure hope so. Makes it even colder when you can't move around so much." Her mother sank down into the recliner and raised the footrest. "It's just been a week and I'm already tired of this cast."

"I'm sure." Bethany wasn't surprised that her normally cheerful mother was complaining. Being restricted to a chair was definitely no fun. She returned her attention to the window. She wanted to be ready when the horse and buggy arrived.

Behind her, Mary sighed. "I'm going to miss going to Edna's today to make cookies for worship."

Bethany felt for her mother. It had been over a week since she had broken her leg. With the exception of Thanksgiving, she'd been confined to the house. And Bethany knew that her mother didn't like being idle. The highlight of her week was always baking cookies with Edna, Wilma, and Verna. But Abram said it was too soon for Mary to be away from home for so long.

Truth be told, Bethany hadn't remembered that her mother's friends would be at Edna's baking cookies. It made her feel worse knowing that her mother would be alone all day.

"Don't forget to bring home cookies for us to take to worship."

Bethany frowned. "Wilma will bring some for church."

But Mary insisted. "Just bring some anyway, Bethany. You know I don't like showing up empty-handed."

This time, Bethany gave a soft laugh. "We never show up empty-handed."

There was a long silence that filled the room, broken only by the clock. Bethany had almost forgotten that her mother was still in the room when she heard her sigh once again.

"Oh, how I wish I could go along with you."

"Well, that wouldn't be good for your leg, Maem," she said softly. "Remember, the doctor said to stay off it for a week or so."

"It's been over a week."

"Only just. Better to be safe than sorry, don't you think?"

Bethany knew that her mother couldn't argue with that advice.

"Be certain to send my regards to all of them. And let

them know that Abram dropped off those cookies this morning at Yoders'."

"I will."

She heard her mother rustling some papers, most likely that week's *Budget* newspaper. Both her parents poured over the newspaper each week, sometimes reading it two or three times before the next week's issue arrived.

The sound of the horse's hooves and buggy wheels caught her attention. "He's here," she mumbled and hurried out the door.

The cold air made her catch her breath. It clung to her lungs as she made her way to the buggy. Winter was her favorite time of year, but only when she didn't have to leave the house.

The door slid open and a hand reached through the opening.

"Hurry! It's warmer in here."

Bethany took his hand and put her foot on the step. Once inside, she slid the door shut behind her.

"Smells like snow."

Bethany shivered. "Oh *ja*? I never really thought about snow having a smell."

He reached behind the seat and retrieved a worn quilt. She wondered how many generations of Esh children had slept under it.

"Here, Bethany. Use this to cover your lap."

As she started to take it, his hand brushed hers, and Bethany felt that increasingly familiar jolt. Her eyes fluttered upward and she saw that he watched her, his own blue eyes curiously studying her reaction. What was it about John Esh that brought crimson color to her cheeks and set her pulse racing?

"Can't have you catching a cold now, can we?" he said, his voice low and comforting. "Maem would have no choice but to enlist the help of the Schwartz *schwesters* then, and we all know that wouldn't work out so well."

There was something about the way he said that—the Schwartz *schwesters*—that made her giggle. Just a little one, and she quickly covered her mouth with her hand, hoping that he hadn't heard.

But he had. She could tell by the way he chuckled under his breath.

For the first few minutes, as the horse guided the buggy along the road away from Shipshewana, they didn't speak. The silence began to grow uncomfortable, and Bethany wondered if she should say something.

"*Danke* for coming to get me," she heard herself say.

John glanced at her as if contemplating whether or not to say something in response. Perhaps John hadn't wanted to make the drive to fetch her. Perhaps Jonas hadn't, either. Suddenly Bethany felt her chest tighten, a constriction that so often came with her panic attacks. Had she burdened the Esh family? Perhaps she should've just insisted upon fixing her bicycle. She'd need it for other things, anyway, like going to town and running errands.

When John cleared his throat, Bethany felt as if she might jump out of her skin.

"I told you I would," he started slowly. "Actually, Daed suggested that Jonas pick you up this morning. Reckon he felt I didn't care for driving all the way out here twice a day, especially since I usually go this way to the auction *haus*." He paused and moistened his lower lip. "But I don't mind, and I hope *you* don't mind that I came in his place."

She swallowed. What, exactly, did *that* mean? "I . . . I . . ." She wasn't certain how to respond, and once again, she felt her cheeks heat up. "That's fine, John."

"Is it?"

Those two words, so short and succinct, caught her off guard. She couldn't keep herself from lifting her gaze to look at him. She wasn't exactly surprised to realize that his eyes had not ceased watching her. And yet, unlike her reaction when she was around other people, there was something comforting about John's attention. He wasn't pushy or forward. Instead, he seemed to be as reserved as she was.

When she realized that he was waiting for a response, Bethany bit her lower lip. How should she respond without appearing too eager? What if she was misreading the message behind his words?

"I . . . I enjoy your company," she whispered.

If she had worried that she might appear too brazen, the expression of relief that washed over his face reassured her that her words had been perfectly chosen. For once, Bethany felt comfortable in the presence of a man who was not family.

Chapter Thirty

Mary could have been knocked over by a feather when Verna and Wilma surprised her with a visit on their way home from Edna's house.

"Dropping off cookies for you!" Verna sang out as she swept into the room and dropped a container onto the counter.

"Oh, how thoughtful! I thought Bethany would bring some home, but this is ever so much better!" She tucked the blanket around her propped-up leg and gestured toward the chairs. "Sit for a while. Please." It might have only been a week, but Mary suddenly realized how lonely and bored she'd been sitting in the recliner day in and day out. Aside from her friends' visit on Wednesday, she hadn't seen anyone but Bethany and Abram. She'd especially missed baking cookies with her friends at Edna's house.

"How was everything at the Esh farm today?" she asked, although she cared more about how Bethany was making out than anything else that was going on at the farm.

Verna gave her a reassuring smile. "The *haus* was set up right nice already, and Edna seems to get on really well with Bethany."

Mary beamed. "Oh?"

"*Ja*, for sure and certain. Your *dochder* sure is a hard

worker. Mind you, we left just before the guests arrived, but she never once stopped bustling about the kitchen, cleaning up after us and making certain everything was ready for Edna's people."

The compliment pleased Mary. She was certainly thrilled to hear that Bethany was such a hard worker. Despite her joy, she knew better than to look at Wilma. Mary was fairly certain that such kind compliments about *her* two daughters rarely—if ever!—made their way to Wilma's ears.

"I'm telling you," Wilma said as she worked on the scarf she was making. "There is love in the air, you mark my words." She pointed one of the needles at Mary. "Your *dochder* will be an Esh or my name isn't Wilma Schwartz!"

"Oh?" Mary feigned ignorance, but she certainly suspected she knew that Wilma was referring to John. While Mary found the thought of such a union wonderfully pleasing, she did her best to hide her enthusiasm. She'd said nothing to Bethany about her own suspicions; she certainly wasn't going to say anything to her friends.

"That John is such a nice young man," Verna added. "And I know that Edna's been worried about him for a while. It would be nice if he'd find someone to settle down with."

Now Mary's curiosity was really piqued. "Did she say something, then? About John?"

Verna shook her head. "*Nee*, she did not. But you know how private she is. Unlike some others." She looked at Wilma when she spoke.

"Ha! I could say the same for you," Wilma teased back. "But I will concur with Verna. John definitely seems to have eyes for Bethany."

"Now, Wilma," she said in a gentle but reproachful tone, "you really mustn't speculate. That's how feelings get hurt if things go sour."

"Only thing sour in that household was the milk she

used for making biscuits!" Wilma retorted briskly. "Why, that girl practically floated into the house after John brought her over."

Verna leaned forward and added, "He kept hanging around the house, too."

"Hm." Wilma returned her attention to her knitting. "There's a Christmas courtship happening right before our eyes, that's for sure and certain."

Mary laughed. "You're putting the buggy before the horse, I fear. She's only just started working for Edna."

Still, the idea that her daughter was finally enjoying the attention of a young man pleased her. And a Christmas courtship would most certainly be fun for both of them.

"I think we could do a little more to put those two together, don't you think?" Verna smiled in a conspiratorial way. "Mayhaps a few extra errands to run together?"

If Wilma had suggested such a thing, Mary wouldn't have been surprised. But to hear it from Verna shocked her. "Why Verna! That's—"

Wilma interrupted. "—brilliant!"

"That wasn't the word I was going to use!"

Verna adopted an innocent look. "I don't see anything wrong with helping them along a bit."

But Mary did. "I will not interfere in my daughter's life."

"It's not really interfering . . ."

"Verna!"

Wilma jumped to Verna's defense. "I agree with Verna."

Mary's mouth dropped.

"Now listen, Mary," Verna said. "A little nudge or two wouldn't hurt, would it? They still have free choice to make up their own minds—"

"—which look made up already, mind you."

"Right, Wilma!" Verna smiled and Wilma nodded. "We're just helping to expedite the decision-making process."

"That's all."

Mary narrowed her eyes and scowled at them. "'That's all,' she says."

"Well, Bethany *is* rather shy, and John is quite conservative," Verna continued. "A little encouragement might help them to open up to each other."

Mary didn't like this idea one bit. It was exactly what Abram had warned her about. "That's meddling."

"So?"

"Meddling is wrong."

Verna and Wilma exchanged a look.

"I'm not so certain I want to meddle." She pointed at each one of them. "And neither should either of you."

Chapter Thirty-One

"Maem," John said as he walked into the kitchen on Saturday afternoon, "I need to stop in town. Helping a friend with a project. Need anything?"

Bethany pretended to focus on washing the dishes, but inwardly her heart raced and her blood felt as if it was on fire.

"*Nee*, I don't, but *danke* for asking, John." Edna was busy counting money at the table, making a small pile of bills of various denominations. "Mayhaps, however, you could take Bethany home."

Standing up, Edna took the pile of money and walked over to the young woman. "Thank you for all of your work, Bethany. Here's for the past week." She smiled at her. "I don't think I could've done it without you."

She felt awkward taking the money and slipping it into her pocket.

"Now, I can finish here and you go on home, then."

Bethany's eyes flew first to the clock and then shifted to John. "It's still early though . . . Are you sure there isn't something else that needs doing?"

Gently, Edna placed her hand on Bethany's arm. "You've worked hard all week. And most of the cleanup is finished. Besides, if you don't accept John's ride, you might have to wait another hour or so until Jonas is finished."

Satisfied, Bethany nodded and hung the dishcloth over the edge of the sink. She gathered her things and followed John outside. A light dusting of snow covered the walkway, and she held the railing as she walked down the porch steps.

"Careful now," John said. "It might be slippery—"

No sooner had the word slipped through his lips than Bethany felt herself sliding off the last step. She reached out with her hand as if to protect herself from hitting the ground, but she found herself in John's arms, her hand pressed against his shoulder and her face against his chest.

"Oomph."

She tried to escape his grasp, but he held on to her.

"You all right?"

All right? Yes. Embarrassed? Definitely.

"*Ja*, I . . . I'm fine."

"Look at me."

She looked up.

"Oh, Bethany." He made a face and shook his head.

"What?"

"Snow. You have snow on your face." He placed one of his hands on her shoulder and, with the other, reached up to touch her forehead. "There. All better now."

"Oh help!" She freed herself at last and quickly lifted her hands to her face, rubbing her fingers across her cheeks and eyes.

Watching her, he laughed. "I told you it's gone."

She felt foolish. John, however, appeared most amused.

Ten minutes later, she rode silently in the buggy, her eyes straight ahead but her heart beating rapidly.

He was quiet for the first part of the trip, and that made Bethany feel nervous. Once again, she began to have self-doubts. Had she misinterpreted his intentions? Was he merely being a nice young man and helping out his mother? Surely he would talk to her if he was interested? Jonas, after all, had done nothing *but* talk to her whenever he had the chance.

Clearly, however, John Esh was nothing like his younger brother.

As they approached the outskirts of Shipshewana, he cleared his throat. "I need to stop in town," John said, his eyes focused on the road ahead of them. "I could drop you off first, or"—he glanced at her—"mayhaps you might want to accompany me."

She hesitated. She'd have liked nothing more than to spend more time with him, but she didn't want to appear overly eager. Quickly she tried to think of how to respond. "I don't want to put you out of your way."

"I'd like the company."

Bethany caught her breath. Had he truly just said that? "Oh, well, I don't mind, I reckon."

He raised an eyebrow, an amused look in his blue eyes and a hint of a smile on his lips. "You didn't ask where I was going."

Embarrassed that she'd accepted his invitation without inquiring further, she felt the heat intensify on her cheeks. "I did not."

"You trust me so much?"

The truth was that she *did* trust him. She couldn't quite understand what the difference was between Jonas and John, but the feelings she had about the former were most certainly not the same as what she felt for the latter. "I suppose I do," she whispered.

He cleared his throat. "I thought to stop for a cup of coffee. Mayhaps a piece of pie, too."

She fought the urge to smile. "*That* was your errand in town, then? Your friend's project?"

He turned his head and met her gaze. "*Ja*, Bethany."

While she admired his creativity in asking her out on a

date, she found herself concerned that he had deceived his mother. "You lied to your *maem*," she said in a soft, reproachful tone.

Immediately, he rebutted her accusation. "*Nee*, I did not lie."

"Having coffee and a piece of pie is *not* helping a friend with a project."

"The friend is myself—we should always be our own best friend, don't you think?—and our friendship is the project." He waited as if gauging her reaction. When she said nothing, John took a deep breath. "I would not want to presume anything, Bethany Ropp, about you. I would, however, like to learn more. And I do not think *my* interest in you is something that I want *others* interested in. It is better to mislead my mother than to embarrass either one of us, wouldn't you say?"

There was wisdom to his words. Bethany felt that familiar tickle inside her chest, her heart feeling as if it skipped a beat at the way he had opened up to her. While she might interpret his words in a variety of ways, she realized that, indeed, he was navigating the waters of courtship with her. Like many of the older Amish folks, he preferred to do it in secret, a way of preserving reputations and saving face. She appreciated that and better understood why he had misguided his mother as to his true business in town.

"I understand, John Esh." She shifted her eyes from his face back to the road. "And I think having a cup of coffee and a piece of pie sounds right *gut*."

Half an hour later, she sat across from him at a coffeehouse along Van Buren Street in Shipshewana. She could count on one hand the number of times she'd been at a restaurant in town, and she felt conspicuous, too aware that other people—*Englischers!*—were staring and smiling at them. Surely they suspected that John and Bethany were courting.

"How's your coffee?"

She'd forgotten to taste it, but John's question prompted her to do just that. "*Gut.*" She set down the mug. "Hot."

He chuckled. "That's *gut*, because iced coffee is best served in the summer."

Uncertain what to say, Bethany took another sip of the coffee. She wished she knew what to talk about. Had she been with Jonas, that wouldn't have been a problem, because Jonas loved nothing more than to talk. She could've just sat there, nodding her head and saying an occasional "*ja*" as she pretended to listen to him. But with John Esh, Bethany would never do such a thing.

"You work near here, then?" she asked.

"*Ja*, I do." He gestured over his shoulder, but not at anything in particular. "Down the road that way. Not far from here."

She nodded, even though she didn't know exactly where he was indicating. "You like it?"

Immediately, she noticed that the jovial gleam in his eye faded. Just a bit. "*Nee*, Bethany, I do not."

She raised her eyebrows, surprised at both his candor and his confession. "Then why are you working there?"

"I have to." He played with the paper napkin under his coffee mug. "The truth is that I'd like to be a farmer, but right now, my family needs my income." He glanced at her as if to make certain she was paying attention. "My *daed*'s a dairy farmer, and the dairy market isn't so good these days."

Bethany wasn't certain how to respond. She knew that much was true from listening to her father talk about it. But she hadn't paid much attention. After all, her father worked in town, and they had no family who would be impacted by the downturn in the dairy industry. "But if you want to farm, why don't you just help your *daed* at *his* farm?"

John gave a little shrug. "He has enough help with Jonas and Jeremiah."

From the way Jonas talked, Bethany didn't think he much cared about being a farmer. She couldn't help wondering why Jonas didn't find a job outside the farm so that John could follow his dream.

"Perhaps one day it will work out," she said, wishing she had stronger words of encouragement for him. "After all, God has plans for us, and He doesn't always reveal those plans when we want, but when *He* wants."

John raised his mug of coffee to his lips, peering at her over the rim. His blue eyes seemed to dance behind the steam. "That's a right *gut* way of looking at it, Bethany."

Chapter Thirty-Two

On Sunday, Edna found herself fighting sleep as the preacher stood before the congregation, speaking about supporting the community and giving back. With the upcoming holiday season, Edna didn't have time to give more to the community, even if she wanted to. Besides, with all of the weekly baking for Yoders' Store, the proceeds of which were donated to Amish Aid, she certainly felt as if she was doing her part to help the community.

Sometimes when the preacher gave his sermon, his voice seemed to drone on, and Edna couldn't help but shut her eyes. Just a little. With so many people crammed into the shop over the Rabers' barn where worship was being held that day—it was larger than the room in their house—the air was warm, and Edna wished one of the men would open a window for a small breeze. But no one else seemed bothered by the warmth.

Taking a deep breath, Edna sat up straighter, blinked her eyes rapidly, and tried to focus on the preacher's words, hoping to fight the weight of sleepiness that fell over her.

Stay awake, stay awake, she told herself.

The previous day had been a hectic one. The large group of women had been more needy than usual, and Edna had done her best to run interference so that they didn't bother

Bethany. Fortunately, John had come into the kitchen just in time to help Edna serve the women so that Bethany could stay in the kitchen.

Exhaling, Edna scanned the room until she found John, seated on the other side with the other unmarried men. How handsome he looked, she thought, watching as he stared at the preacher, his eyes never wandering. He seemed to absorb every word, unlike her; she wasn't finding the sermon particularly interesting this morning. She wasn't alone, however. John's companions fidgeted a little or glanced over to where the young women sat.

At twenty-six, John was the oldest of the unmarried men in their church district. Like the older women and men, the unmarried members of the church sat together, and in the order of their age. Whenever the unmarried men entered the worship service room, it was John who led them, followed by twenty-three-year-old Peter Herzberger, who sat to his right. Rumor had it that Peter was courting Hannah Schrock, and if the Amish grapevine spoke the truth, they were likely to be married over the winter. That would leave John seated next to his brother Jonas, the next youngest of the unmarried men.

If John didn't get married soon, he would most likely make the decision to publicly announce his status as a bachelor. He'd grow a beard, even though he wasn't married, and sit with the married men at church. Most young men who weren't married by twenty-six or so did just that. It wasn't terribly common, although she remembered John Stoltzfus from her youth. He'd never married. Instead, he had made the silent—but public—declaration of his perpetual bachelorhood by growing a beard and sitting with the married men one day. Years later, he had died unexpectedly, still a bachelor and living at home with his elderly mother.

Edna felt a wave of panic. She wasn't certain how she'd feel if her John made such a declaration.

At least she could take comfort in knowing that regardless of his marital status, John was a devout member of the church. *That* was something that gave her secret pride: all of her sons had taken the kneeling vow. She couldn't imagine how she'd have felt if one of her children had refused to become a baptized member of the church.

Automatically, her eyes shifted to Susan Schwartz, who sat toward the front of the room among the other elderly women. Fifteen years ago, three of her six children had left the Amish faith, two refusing to be baptized and one leaving the church *after* being baptized because he fell in love with an *Englische* woman. Even worse, it had all happened in rapid succession over a six-month period of time.

For several years after her sons' decisions, Susan had been depressed, her heart broken about what she viewed as her failure to raise her children properly. Edna knew that many people whispered behind Susan's back, wondering aloud about the reasons half of her children had left the faith. Edna hadn't been one of them, but she had felt tremendous compassion for the older woman.

For Amish parents, there was no pain worse than a child who refused to join the church.

Someone nudged Edna.

"Quit your daydreaming!" the woman seated next to her hissed.

Edna blinked and looked around. Everyone was getting to their knees to pray. She, however, had been so lost in her thoughts that she hadn't realized it.

Quickly, Edna turned around and scrambled to her knees. She folded her hands and rested them on the bench, lowering her forehead against them. Despite her best efforts to pray for her family, friends, and community, she kept thinking about John.

She loved all three of her sons, but she was proudest of John. He was kind and conscientious, always thinking about other people's needs before his own. And his loyalty to the church, God, and his community made him especially endearing to her. Why, just yesterday he'd offered, again, to drive Bethany home, even though there had been a recent snowfall.

She hadn't objected, because she secretly hoped that he was making that drive for other reasons.

Such a good man deserved a good wife. If only he might find *someone* to suit his fancy, especially if that someone was Bethany.

Chapter Thirty-Three

"And I heard," Wilma said as she leaned across the table so that no one could overhear her, "that Timothy Metz heard from the bishop about the miserable state of his mules."

Mary pursed her lips and shook her head. "Such a shame. I always wondered why no one said anything to him. It's just not right."

"A man who can't take care of his animals has no business farming," an elderly woman chimed in. "That's what my *daed* always used to say when I was growing up."

Without saying so, Mary secretly agreed. Timothy Metz was a very conservative Amish man who, with his family, lived just on the border of their church district and the neighboring one. She'd always thought that it would have served the Metz family better if the district lines had gone around them. They were one of the few farming families in their church district, and that created its own problems.

"Those mules need some more groceries, that's for sure and certain," Wilma said in a terse tone. "Bishop made a comment about the *Englische* authorities catching sight of them. Apparently, someone already complained once."

Mary gasped. "No!"

"*Ja*, that's true." Wilma nodded. "And Bishop doesn't think it's good for the community to have *Englischers* complaining about animals."

It was true that some people liked to cause trouble for the Amish. And the church leaders often spoke about how they needed to give the *Englischers* no reason to make accusations. All of the Amish farmers that Mary knew took wonderful care of their animals. But all it took was one bad apple to ruin the bunch, and that was definitely what Timothy Metz was doing.

Another elderly woman spoke up. "I feel for those farmers," she said with a long, drawn-out sigh. "It's not like it used to be when everyone farmed and could live a good life doing so. There's just so little money in farming anymore."

"So true." Wilma gestured toward Mary. "You know that Bethany's working at Edna Esh's place." She paused when the two other women frowned as if trying to recall whom Wilma was referring to. "Elmer's Edna? She runs the tourist business from her farm?"

"Ah, *ja*! Edna Esh."

"She does that because of the poor price of dairy," Wilma stated in a matter-of-fact tone.

"It's a wonder they can survive," one of the women said.

"But it sure is fortunate that Edna's bishop permits such businesses in the home," said the other woman. "Why, my sister made dinners for tourists in her home, but when the church district lines were redrawn, her new bishop forbade her to conduct business like that. Can you imagine?"

"Oh help!" Mary clucked her tongue. "Such a shame."

"Reckon Edna doesn't have to worry about that," Wilma said. Then, with a sly look at Mary, she added, "Mayhaps she'll turn that business over to Bethany when she marries John Esh!"

Stunned, Mary's mouth dropped, and she sat there, speechless.

But the older women reacted with joy. "Is that so? Bethany's to marry?"

"Oh, I know nothing about any such thing," Mary said quickly. It was the truth. The only thing she knew was that Bethany surely was happy about something, but she hadn't confided in Mary as to what, exactly, was making her so joyful.

"But are they courting?" the other woman asked.

"Does he come calling at the *haus*?"

Mary frowned at Wilma for having started the scuttlebutt. She certainly hoped that Bethany didn't overhear the women talking. She'd be completely mortified if she thought people were gossiping about her. "It's best not to speculate about such private matters, don't you think?"

A satisfied smile crossed Wilma's lips.

Irritated by her friend taking such pleasure in her discomfort, Mary quickly changed the subject.

"With the holidays coming up, we should be thinking about other things anyway." She turned away from Wilma. "I was thinking of making some knot quilts to donate to the Mennonite church for the homeless."

Both of the older women gave a nod of approval.

"Since I'm laid up for a while and all," she added.

"I imagine you could start getting around soon," Wilma quipped.

Mary raised an eyebrow. "You're right, I'm sure. Mayhaps I could get Abram to bring me to your *haus* to make those quilts." She put her finger to her cheek as if thinking. "In fact, mayhaps Verna could join us, too. A fun quilting bee, and I'm sure that Rachel and Ella Mae would love to help out."

Wilma's eyes widened.

"It being for charity and all," Mary concluded, trying to hide her own satisfaction at Wilma's reaction.

"I'd be happy to donate some fabric," one of the women said. "In fact, I could cut the pieces into six-by-six squares tomorrow."

Clapping her hands, Mary couldn't hide her grin. "That's so *wunderbarr*. Perhaps others would do the same, and then Wilma, Verna, and I could piece them together while Rachel and Ella Mae tie the knots!" She turned toward Wilma. "Mayhaps Friday would be a *gut* day to start this project? And Bethany could join us after she's finished at Edna's. I'm sure she'd love to help, too."

From the expression that Wilma wore, Mary felt certain that she wanted to reach out and throttle her. Of course, Wilma would never do such a thing, nor could she back out. But the look on her face said it all. Wilma had never hosted such a gathering, and to do so with only one week's notice would certainly keep her busy.

Mary didn't particularly mind if Wilma was uncomfortable. She had, after all, shared Bethany's secret without any regard for her daughter's—and John's!—apparent wish to keep their budding friendship private.

Besides, while any time of year was good to give back to others, the holidays were one of the best times to undertake charitable projects. It was high time that Wilma remembered there were more important things in the world than gossip, Mary told herself.

"I reckon Friday's just fine," Wilma said in a slow, deliberate tone.

"*Wunderbarr!*" Mary beamed.

The only problem, however, was how on earth would she get there?

Chapter Thirty-Four

It was three o'clock when Bethany began walking home from the worship service. She knew that her parents would be visiting for a while longer, and frankly, she wanted a little time alone to breathe in the crisp air and catch up her thoughts.

There was something special about that John Esh, something that made her feel light and happy whenever he was around. Just one look into those blue eyes made her feel lost and complete at the same time. It was a true conflict of emotions, that was for sure and certain.

The still air stirred, a cold wind pushing at her back. She tightened the shawl around her shoulders and clutched it at her throat. In the distance, she saw that the sky on the horizon had turned gray. A dark gray that indicated snow might be headed toward Shipshewana.

"Bethany!"

Startled, she looked up to see John Esh slowing down his horse and buggy as he approached her.

"John!" She couldn't help but feel that God had guided her to walk home alone, something she rarely did after worship. Perhaps God had wanted her to run into John.

The horse stopped a few feet in front of her.

John held the reins in his gloved hands, trying to steady

the horse as it fought the bit in its mouth. He glanced at the sky. "Feels like snow, eh?"

Shyly, she nodded.

"Heading home, then?"

Bethany could hardly look at him. Those eyes always felt as if they saw right through her. Did he know that she thought him the most handsome man she'd ever met? Did he suspect that she felt safe in his presence? Was it possible that he could read her mind? If so, she had cause to blush.

"Let me give you a ride. Getting too cold for you to walk."

Immediately, her mouth opened. "But you've just come from that direction!"

His lips turned up at the corners, a hint of a smile lighting up his face. "And I can easily go back that way, too."

"The horse—"

"—needs the exercise, trust me." He stepped on the foot brake and dropped the reins onto the floor. Carefully, he climbed out, and after issuing a stern warning to the horse, he reached for Bethany's arm. "Come now," he said, his voice soft but commanding. "Can't have you getting sick now, can we?"

She wanted to tell him that the cold didn't make people sick; germs did. But she didn't want to appear argumentative. Besides, she couldn't think of anything nicer than warming up in the small buggy seated next to John Esh.

"Settled in?" he asked as he sat next to her and slid the door shut.

She nodded. "*Ja.*"

"All right then." He picked up the reins and jiggled them while clucking his tongue. Immediately, the horse began trotting down the road.

"Oh!" Bethany turned her head, peering behind them as she realized that John was continuing east on the road, while her house was back toward the west. "But the farm is—"

John cut her off. "I know." He kept a tight hold on the reins, not permitting the horse to trot too fast. "If you don't mind," he said without looking at her, "I'll take the longer way home."

If it was cold outside, Bethany no longer remembered. She knew that color had flooded to her cheeks, and she pressed her lips together so that she wouldn't give way to the smile that wanted to brighten her face. "I don't mind," she managed to say and settled back into the velvet-covered seat next to John.

For at least a mile, they rode in silence. Bethany had never been one to explore the roads around her parents' home. In the past, if she needed to go somewhere, she'd always taken the most direct (and fastest) route possible. It just felt safer that way.

Today, however, riding with John, she experienced a whole new way of looking at her community. He drove along the back roads, expertly guiding the horse with voice commands as well as the reins. There were few cars out, and Bethany found herself feeling secure beside John. She looked at the different farms, saw clusters of buggies at different houses, and occasionally lifted her hand when another buggy passed.

"You ever been out this way?"

She faced him. "I haven't."

"It's a pretty area."

She gave a little nod. "*Ja*, it is."

The horse trotted for a little while longer before John spoke again. "I'll be working again this week," he said.

"Oh?"

"*Ja*, at the auction *haus*, you know."

She did know.

"But I don't work there on Saturdays. Just Tuesday through Friday."

She couldn't help but wonder why he was telling her this.

"I'd hate to be presumptuous, but"—he glanced at her—"mayhaps next Saturday I might pick you up and bring you home like I did yesterday." He cleared his throat. "If you wouldn't mind, that is."

She prayed he couldn't hear her heart beating. "I . . . I wouldn't mind at all."

"And, well, mayhaps we might go into town and have some supper afterward?"

Now she definitely knew he could hear her heart. It pounded so hard that her ears throbbed. "You . . . you mean like on a . . ." She stopped short, embarrassed that she had even uttered those words.

He laughed. Just a little. "*Ja*, I mean like on a . . ." He, too, stopped short, and then he turned his head to look at her. He winked. "*Just* like that actually."

The breath whooshed out of her lungs and she felt as if she couldn't breathe. A date. He was asking her out on a *date*! Her mouth felt dry and her palms felt clammy. She knew that she was perspiring. How on earth was it possible that someone like John Esh might actually be interested in someone like *her*?

"Well?"

Torn from her thoughts, she realized that he was waiting for an answer from her.

Fighting the urge to smile, Bethany averted her eyes as she said, "*Ja*, John, I would like to go into town and"—she paused, her heart pounding as she realized what she was agreeing to—"have some supper with you." Lifting her gaze, she met his and, in a teasing tone, added, "Like on a . . ." She cut herself off and then let the smile brush across her lips. And then, without another word, she turned to look out the window, hoping that he didn't see her smile broaden as she did so.

Chapter Thirty-Five

For two and a half days, Edna found herself looking forward to Friday. Oh, she couldn't wait to get out of the house!

When Bethany had arrived on Wednesday, she had relayed a message about the quilting bee from her mother, and immediately, Edna volunteered to help with the knot-tie quilt project. *What a wonderful idea from Mary*, she thought.

On Thursday evening, she went into the basement, using the LED flashlight to help locate a box of fabric. John carried it up the narrow staircase for her and even helped her sort through it, keeping her company while she made three piles: definitely use, maybe use, and toss into the rag basket.

Now that her Friday guests had departed and the kitchen was back in order, ready for the next day's group, it was time to leave for Wilma's house.

Outside the kitchen window, Edna could see Jonas harnessing the horse. All week Jeremiah had been picking up Bethany in the morning and Jonas bringing her home in the afternoon. With John back at work, Bethany's transportation depended on the two boys. Jonas was still sulking, clearly disappointed that he wasn't going to drive Bethany home. In fact, when he'd come into the kitchen to see when Bethany would be ready to leave, he'd practically pouted when

Edna informed him that she, not he, would take Bethany home that afternoon.

Curiously enough, Bethany hadn't displayed any emotion about the announcement.

Edna admired how composed Bethany always appeared whenever Jonas was around. Her son, however, was the complete opposite, usually acting more animated and livelier in the young woman's presence. She was glad that John wasn't around to witness it. He'd probably have taken his younger brother outside to share some harsh words with him.

After sliding her arms into the coat sleeves, she began to button the front. It was much warmer to wear a coat than a shawl, especially since snow was in the forecast. "Ready, Bethany?"

"*Ja*, I am."

"You'll catch your death of cold in that shawl." Edna opened the door and, as if to prove her point, shivered. "It must be thirty-five degrees!"

But Bethany said no more. Instead, she quietly followed Edna toward the awaiting buggy.

Jonas gave her a long look, his eyes appearing distressed. "You sure you don't want me to take you, Maem?" he asked, but his gaze remained fixed on Bethany. "I could run some errands and come back to fetch you."

"Don't be silly." Edna climbed into the buggy and situated herself on the seat. "Besides, your *daed* needs your help with the evening chores anyway."

He shuffled his feet and made a face as he began to walk away.

For the first few minutes of the drive, Edna said nothing. Her mind was whirling with all of the things she needed to do. The holidays were always such a busy time of year. Besides her catering business, she also needed to help cook for the school pageant, which was in two weeks. There would be the large family gathering on Christmas, which, fortunately, fell on a Wednesday this year. The dinner was being held at Mabel's house this time, so at least Edna didn't have to worry about cleaning her own house.

And, of course, she would help Verna, Wilma, and Mary with baking cookies again for Yoders' Store and for worship service.

She couldn't wait to get back on a regular schedule.

About halfway into their journey, she heard Bethany sigh.

"It's been a long few weeks for you, *ja*?" Edna asked. "I must admit that I can hardly imagine how I ever made do without your help."

The young woman gave a modest smile. "*Danke*, Edna, but I'm sure it's no more than anyone else would do."

"Have you enjoyed yourself?" Edna asked the question before she thought better of it.

When Bethany hesitated before answering, Edna braced herself. Over the past two weeks, Edna had changed her opinion of Bethany. The young woman didn't appear to be as deathly shy as her mother always made her out to be. Instead, Edna had observed that Bethany was merely very quiet in her manner. She preferred avoiding change or unusual situations and people. In fact, Edna had come to appreciate Bethany, admiring her hard work ethic and focus on task.

She'd been considering asking the young woman to continue helping her in the spring.

But when Bethany didn't respond right away, Edna feared the worst.

She was, however, pleasantly surprised when Bethany finally responded.

"I have, Edna," she admitted. "More than I thought I would."

Inwardly, Edna breathed a sigh of relief. "I'm so glad,

Bethany. I know that it can be extra hectic around the holidays, so I truly appreciate your help. Knowing that you're enjoying yourself makes me feel much better about having asked you for help in the first place." She slowed the horse to a stop at an intersection and glanced at Bethany. "I was worried you'd hate all the commotion."

"It *is* rather chaotic," she said, "especially when they all talk at once."

Edna laughed.

"But they've all been rather nice, and I like hearing about the things they are doing for the holidays. Like Christmas parties with friends and family. Singing carols and visiting. That sounds like such a festive thing to do."

Suddenly, Edna had an idea. "Why don't we have a holiday party like that?"

Bethany frowned.

"*Ja*, just like the *Englischers*. Why! We could have all of our families come to my *haus* for a large supper, and we could sing hymns." Edna grew animated with excitement. "Oh, Bethany! That's just a *wunderbarr* idea."

"It was your idea, not mine."

"But you *gave* me the idea!" She almost felt giddy with delight. It had been years since the four families had done anything together. Sure, the women baked cookies every week, but that wasn't the same thing as having their entire families gather for fellowship and visiting. "Mayhaps we could do it on Christmas Eve. That would put all of us in the mood for Christmas, don't you think?"

For a moment, Bethany didn't respond. She appeared to be mulling over the idea. She pursed her lips and frowned. "Would *all* of the families be invited?"

"I don't see why not."

"Do you think they would go?"

Such questions, Edna thought. "I imagine they would.

Mayhaps not the older ones who are married and don't live nearby, but the others surely would."

And then, Bethany gave a soft smile. "I think that's a fine idea."

Quietly, Bethany turned her face toward the window, watching the landscape pass by, the smile still lingering on her lips. Edna raised an eyebrow, wondering at the young woman's reaction.

Chapter Thirty-Six

Mary sat at Wilma's kitchen table, piecing together the squares that had been donated for their efforts. Her needle and thread slid through the fabric with ease. She loved sewing, and piecing simple quilt tops was particularly enjoyable because she didn't have to think too much. Unfortunately, the sewing was taking longer than she'd expected.

She'd hoped that they'd be able to finish twenty quilts, a feat that would require each woman to piece four tops, a hefty goal to attempt. Under different circumstances, it might have been attainable, but not with Wilma's two daughters. They were having quite a hard time matching the different squares in an acceptable pattern so that the quilt tops were pretty enough to meet their standards.

"That's a terrible pattern," Ella Mae snapped from the other side of the room.

Wilma had set up a folding table so that her daughters could create the quilt tops for the women to piece. Unfortunately, Ella Mae and Rachel couldn't seem to agree on anything, and it was a wonder that *any* of the tops were being pieced at all.

"Yellow and green look ugly together," Ella Mae continued.

Mary looked up in time to see Ella Mae swipe Rachel's

proposed pattern so that the fabric squares fell off the table. Neither one of them bent down to retrieve the fabric.

"Girls!" Wilma shuffled over to the table. "You're making a mess and getting nothing finished."

"It's Rachel's fault," Ella Mae said, pointing to her sister.

"You're far too picky," Rachel retorted. "It's for charity. Those folks should be thankful for the quilts and not care about whether or not the colors match."

Mary glanced at Verna, who responded by shutting her eyes and shaking her head.

"Let me help." Bethany walked over to the table and made a quick assessment. "Mayhaps it would help if the squares were stacked and organized by color, *ja*?" She began to collect the squares and set them in small piles on the table. Within minutes, there was a rainbow-colored organization to the chaos that had been the result of Rachel and Ella Mae's efforts.

Then, Bethany began to pick up the squares, choosing different shades of the same color, and laid them out on the table. "That should be nice enough, don't you think?"

Mary watched as Rachel and Ella Mae tensed, clearly not appreciating Bethany's taking over what they deemed "their" job.

Edna, however, walked over to look at what Bethany had done. "Why, that's just *wunderbarr*," she exclaimed. "I do believe you have a knack for this, Bethany." Without waiting for anyone to comment further, Edna collected the squares and headed over to the table, situating herself opposite Mary, so that she could begin piecing the squares together. "Now, your *maem* is almost finished piecing, so why don't you get another one ready for her while Rachel and Ella Mae get ready to attach the backing and begin knotting, hm?"

Despite her best efforts, Mary couldn't help but smile. *Leave it to Edna*, she thought, *to resolve the problem at hand.*

They'd only pieced four quilt tops so far, not nearly the number that Mary had anticipated. But Wilma had insisted that Rachel and Ella Mae were the best suited for organizing the squares. Now that Edna had arrived, the situation had been remedied, and hopefully without any hard feelings.

As Edna settled herself at the table, pulling out her bag of sewing supplies, she looked over at what Mary was doing. "That seems fine enough."

It was a masked compliment, and Mary nodded in response.

Edna began threading her needle. "Bethany and I had an idea on the way over here."

"It . . . it was *your* idea."

Edna dismissed her with a hand wave. "Bah! You gave it to me."

Mary smiled at the casual banter between her daughter and Edna. How much Bethany had changed over the past two weeks! Being around Edna was surely helping her come out of her shell. "What's the idea, Edna?"

"A holiday party!" She practically glowed as she announced it. "For our families. On Christmas Eve, to put us in the Christmas spirit."

"You mean like the *Englischers* do?" The scowl on Wilma's face made it clear *exactly* what she thought of that.

"I'm always in the Christmas spirit," Verna countered.

But Mary liked the idea. "I think that's a right *gut* idea, Edna. When was the last time we had the families together with all of the *kinner*?"

Wilma scoffed. "They aren't *kinner* anymore, are they now?"

"Oh, Wilma!" Verna clucked her tongue. "Don't be so difficult."

Mary ignored them and leaned toward Edna. "Would you be willing to have it at your *haus*, Edna?" She hated to put that burden on her friend, especially since she was always entertaining people at her house. But this was different. This was for friends, not *Englische* tours. "You do have the biggest gathering room, as well as all those tables and chairs."

A broad smile broke onto Edna's face. "Why, Mary, I'd love that."

"Truly? After all of your work with the tours?"

Edna nodded. "Oh *ja*. I'd love to have everyone over at the *haus*. It's been far too long since we've done a family gathering." She glanced over her shoulder at Bethany, who was already finished collecting squares for a second quilt top. "Besides, your *dochder* has made it so easy for me to do my job that it hardly felt like work these past few weeks."

Mary beamed at the compliment directed toward Bethany. Hearing those words from Edna was all the Christmas gift *she* needed that year.

Chapter Thirty-Seven

All week long, Bethany had been increasingly anxious as Saturday approached. The quilting party at Wilma's hadn't helped ease the feeling of butterflies in her stomach.

During the week, she hadn't seen John. However, when she was at the Eshes' house, she had felt a warm sense of comfort in knowing that John had been there just hours before. When she returned home at night, she knew that he'd be passing near her house on the way home from his job in town. And at night, she could hardly sleep as she tossed and turned, thinking about John Esh and those piercing blue eyes that seemed to sparkle whenever he spoke to her.

For the past three days, she'd had to endure riding with Jeremiah and Jonas. Jeremiah wasn't as bad as Jonas, who continually talked about himself. On Wednesday, he'd spent the entire journey boasting about all of the wood he had cut since his father had started them chopping down those trees last week. On Thursday, he'd shared with her that he was the fastest milker in the family—although, like the wood chopping, she doubted his tale.

The only good thing about his stories was that she could

merely tune him out, nod her head, and give an occasional "*ja*" while she enjoyed her own thoughts of John Esh and their upcoming date on Saturday evening.

And yesterday, of course, Edna had driven both her and her mother home.

Now, today John had promised to fetch her and she was ever so excited.

"Your red dress?"

Bethany jumped at the sound of her mother's voice. "You frightened me!"

Her mother frowned, a curious expression on her face. "I noticed. You must've been awfully deep in thought not to hear me."

The truth was that Bethany *had* been deep in thought. About John.

"You're wearing your red dress to Edna's?" The bishop had only just approved the new color of fabric a year ago and it had taken almost that long for her mother to convince Bethany to make a new dress from it. "You've never worn it before."

"I haven't?" Bethany tried to think. Was this truly the first time she'd worn it? "Oh, well, I thought I'd wear it today." She gave her mother a soft smile. "It feels a little festive, don't you think?"

But that wasn't the whole truth. She had wanted to wear it for her date with John. Secretly, she thought the bright color contrasted in a nice way with her brown eyes and hair. Besides, she was tired of always wearing dark colors like navy blue or hunter green. Deep down, ever since she'd begun working for Edna, she'd started to feel different. And while she might not always be able to speak her mind, she could express herself in other ways. Wearing a bright-colored dress was a good start.

"Well, I think you look quite nice," her mother said. She turned her head toward the window, even though she couldn't see out of it from where she stood. "Oh! I hear a buggy. I think Jeremiah is here for you."

Please be John, please be John, Bethany prayed as she fetched her shawl and purse before hurrying out the door.

The cold air hit her as she hurried down the porch steps. She shivered as she approached the buggy.

"Hurry, Bethany!" From inside the buggy, John leaned over and slid open the door for her.

Immediately, her heart felt as if it flip-flopped. She climbed inside the buggy and smiled. "*Gut martiye,* John Esh!"

His blue eyes practically danced at her cheerful greeting. "I see the cold weather agrees with you."

She shook her head. "*Nee*, I only like winter when I can stay inside. It's too cold and dreary otherwise. In summer I love gardening in the mornings. Makes me more cheerful. At least that's what my *maem* says. And I despise the snow."

He clucked his tongue and jiggled the reins, urging the horse forward. "Well then, I reckon I'd like to see you in the summer." He glanced at her. "If you're even *more* cheerful then."

Leaning against the seat, Bethany stared out the window. The truth was that she felt more cheerful these days than ever before. She suspected that she knew the reason why: John. What was it about him that made her feel light-headed and tingly inside? There was something about him that just gave her goose bumps and made her daydream whenever she was apart from him.

For the rest of the trip, they rode in silence. That was one of the things she increasingly appreciated about John. Unlike Jonas, he didn't feel the need to fill every second with talk. In the afternoons when Jonas had taken her home, she often got a headache from his constant chitter-chat.

As the buggy turned down the driveway, John broke the silence. "Speaking of snow, it's supposed to snow later."

She looked at the sky. "It is a bit gray, isn't it?" She sighed. "Ugh."

"Hopefully it won't hinder Maem's people from coming."

Bethany didn't think it would, but she didn't want to sound argumentative, so she said nothing.

"Maem says we're having a Christmas Eve holiday supper." He glanced at her. "Said it was your idea."

Bethany's mouth opened and she gave a slight gasp. "It was *her* idea."

John pressed his lips together and shook his head. "She said it was definitely your idea." He paused as if thinking. "In fact, she said, 'That Bethany had the best idea when we rode to Wilma Schwartz's *haus*.' She seemed rather impressed with your enthusiasm."

"I didn't say anything about it!" Bethany felt the heat rising to her cheeks. Would John think that she had suggested such a thing so that she could spend more time with him? Just the thought was scandalizing to her. "I truly didn't!"

He laughed and nudged her with his arm. "I'm teasing you."

It took her a long moment to realize what he'd said. And then, she smiled. "Oh, John! You had me scared there for a minute."

"Scared? About what?"

"Well, I . . ." She paused. She didn't know how to explain it without embarrassing herself. "I . . . I'm just not that forward, that's all."

"I know that, Bethany." He gave her a reassuring wink. "That's one of the many things I admire about you."

One of the many things. Bethany had that familiar light-headed feeling. It was a feeling she was getting used to whenever she was in John's company.

And she liked it very much, indeed.

Chapter Thirty-Eight

When the buggy pulled into the driveway, Edna was standing at the sink, washing the pans she'd used to make fresh bread. She peered out the window in time to see John emerge from the driver's side and walk around to help Bethany climb out.

Shutting off the faucet, Edna continued watching, her curiosity piqued.

After getting out of the buggy, Bethany stood outside, helping John unhitch and then unharness the horse. During the week, when Jeremiah had arrived after picking up Bethany, she'd hurried right inside to get started with work. Edna hadn't thought much of it before, but now, as John said something and the young woman smiled, she realized that a friendship had, indeed, formed between them.

After they put away the horse, John once again escorted her to the house. They walked slowly, their heads bent together as they talked.

Turning away from the window, Edna leaned against the counter, her mind whirling. Was it possible that her hopes were coming true?

"*Gut martiye,*" Bethany said softly to Edna as she slipped her shawl from her shoulders. John was right there to take it from her.

"It's supposed to snow later," he whispered. "You really need to wear a warmer coat."

Bethany gave a small nod and the color rose to her cheeks at his caring rebuke.

Edna's heart began to race. Anyone with a pair of eyes could see the chemistry between the two. The way he watched her and spoke in such a kind, tender tone. The way her cheeks pinked up and she looked away demurely but listened to him with such respect.

"Coffee?" She didn't wait for their answers as she poured two mugs. She was eager to see more of their interactions and didn't want to shoo John away too quickly.

"*Danke*, Maem." He sipped at the coffee as his eyes scanned the room. "You all set in here? I could fetch more chairs if need be."

"We should be okay, I believe." Just to be certain, Edna looked around. Twenty-two people were coming that day. With only one week left until the official end to her season, Edna knew her remaining schedule by heart. "I just need to finish the soup and bake the dessert, but they're ready."

John glanced at Bethany. "Mayhaps she doesn't need your help at all, then," he said. "Mayhaps I should just take you back home already."

Bethany's eyes widened, just for a brief second, and then she realized he was joking. Her eyes lit up and she tried to hide her smile.

"Now, John," Edna said, "don't tease her so." But it was clear that Bethany was not offended in the least. In fact, Edna hadn't seen either Jeremiah or Jonas speak so intimately with her. Most of the time, Jonas merely spoke about himself, while Jeremiah said nothing at all. "Besides, I'm just not certain how I could do any of this without Bethany anymore. I'm hoping, come spring, she might consider helping me permanently."

The room fell silent. John avoided looking at either one of them as he finished his coffee and seemed to contemplate something inside the cup. Finally, he tore his eyes away from it and stared at the wall behind Edna. "*Ja*, I can see where something permanent might be a right *gut* thing." He glanced at Bethany when he added, "I mean, if such an arrangement would suit Bethany."

She appeared to catch her breath, the color draining from her cheeks. For a moment, she chewed on her lower lip as she met his gaze. "I reckon that might be something to pray on."

Immediately, Edna felt a wave of excitement. She suspected that there was something more to what met the eye when it came to John and Bethany, and frankly, the idea excited her. Bethany would be a wonderful wife for any man in the community, and Edna would welcome her into the family with wide open arms. Their personalities matched, and from the way John peered at Bethany, her son was head over heels in love with her.

Suddenly, an idea came to her. "Mayhaps you could take Bethany to the chicken coop and fetch me some eggs. I want to make deviled eggs to put out on the tables." She'd never done that before, but it sounded like a good idea, especially if it meant that she could continue observing the two young people.

John raised an eyebrow at her, most likely as a result of her strange request. But Edna continued acting nonchalant.

"You wouldn't mind, would you, John?"

He set down the mug on the counter and shook his head. "Of course not, Maem." The look he gave her, however, suggested that he suspected what his mother was doing. "Mayhaps Bethany could borrow your coat." He looked at the young woman. "It's warmer than your shawl."

Edna merely nodded and watched as, obediently, Bethany followed John to the mudroom where he helped her put on the jacket and then held the door open for her to pass through.

Edna stood there, leaning against the counter as she tried to collect her thoughts. A smile broke onto her face as she realized that the quiet manner of John was mirrored perfectly in Bethany. What a sound match they would make!

Chapter Thirty-Nine

Mary sat at Wilma's kitchen table, sipping at a cup filled with lukewarm coffee. Abram had dropped her off at the Schwartzes' just an hour ago so that she could finish working on the knot quilts. Now, with eighteen quilts finished, folded, and set upon the counter, Mary had time to relax and visit with Wilma.

"Where are the girls?" she asked as if she suddenly had realized that they weren't there. Truthfully, she'd noticed their absence when she'd first arrived but had said nothing. It was far more pleasant to work quietly without their constant bickering.

Wilma gave a small shrug. "I'm not certain. Maybe visiting friends. I was putting away laundry when they left."

Mary frowned. She'd *never* let Bethany leave the house without knowing where she was going. What if there was an emergency? What if she needed to find her? But that was clearly not how Wilma was raising her two daughters.

"Well, I'm sure glad that we finished these quilts." Mary meant it. She'd been feeling rather useless these past few weeks. Making the quilts had started to help her feel more cheerful. She ran her hands over the top of a quilt and sighed. "I can only imagine how happy the homeless people will be to wrap themselves in something warm at the shelter."

Wilma made a noise deep within her throat.

"What?"

"Nothing."

Mary persisted. "*Nee*, Wilma. What is it?"

"I reckon I'm not feeling the holiday spirit as much as I should be."

Uh-oh, Mary thought. *That* was not like Wilma. She might complain a lot, but it was almost always good-natured and not truly serious. The confession she'd just made put Mary on high alert. Something was wrong with her friend.

"Do you want to talk about it?" she asked.

Again, Wilma shrugged, but within a few seconds, she spoke. "It's just that I'm feeling poorly, Mary." She raised her head and met Mary's concerned eyes. "It's the girls."

"What about the girls?"

Wilma sighed, her shoulders drooping just a little. "Yesterday, with everyone here, especially Bethany—"

"Bethany?" Mary interrupted. The reference to her daughter caught Mary off guard. Had something happened yesterday that Mary had missed? "What about her?"

"—it became clear to me. Rachel and Ella Mae, well, mayhaps they have some . . ." A hesitation. ". . . some troubles."

"Oh my," she whispered.

For the past few years, she'd grown so used to Wilma complaining about the twins and how argumentative they were, especially with each other. It had been a long time since Mary had spent much time with them. It appeared that, as everyone's children grew, they went their own ways, and it was hard for all of the families to get together. Mary had gathered that Rachel and Ella Mae were a bit difficult to handle, but, despite everyone's jokes, she had always thought Wilma was embellishing her stories just a touch.

Now, she realized that poor Wilma was starting to get the blues, just as she had six years ago when the twins had turned sixteen.

Wilma wrung her hands and avoided meeting Mary's concerned gaze. "I know it's high time that they settle down, but after I saw how Bethany behaves compared to my two *dochders*, I realized that no one will *ever* want to marry them. Not like they are now."

If Rachel and Ella Mae always behaved as they had yesterday, Mary would certainly agree with her. But she was reluctant to admit so much. "That's not necessarily true—"

"*Ja*, it is," Wilma interrupted. A tear fell from her eye, and she swiped at it. "You know one of the reasons that I'm always pushing Rachel and Ella Mae on Edna?"

Mary frowned. "Because it would do the girls good to do some hard work outside of the house."

Wilma waved her hand at Mary. "*Ja*, *ja*, there's that. But also because Edna has those boys! I surely thought that one of my girls might strike the fancy of one of her boys. But Edna chose Bethany over my twins and now *she's* courting John—"

This time, it was Mary who interrupted. "Stop right there, Wilma Schwartz."

Clearly startled by Mary's strong tone, Wilma blinked at her.

"You said this the other day, too, and I just want to prevent more baseless gossip. We don't know whether they are courting, and I don't want to presume anything." She was growing weary of repeating herself. If Bethany chose not to talk to her about her friendship with John, Mary had to assume there was a reason why. "I respect her privacy, and so, Wilma, should you."

Wilma's mouth opened and she sat there, dazed, for a long moment.

Mary took advantage of the silence to continue. "Besides, if your *dochders* have troubles, it's no good to just marry them off. You need to address those issues and resolve them. Otherwise, they'll never make anyone a good *fraa* and most certainly they won't have a good marriage."

Finally, she shut her mouth and pressed her lips together. How dare Wilma think that she could just pawn her two unruly girls off on Edna and, hopefully, two of her sons!

"Land's sake, Mary Ropp!" Wilma blinked twice. "I've never heard you speak in such a tone in all the years I've known you."

Immediately, Mary's irritation vanished and she felt guilty. She shouldn't have spoken so sharply to Wilma. Her friend was feeling poorly, and instead of supporting her, Mary had snapped at her. She couldn't even remember the last time she'd allowed her emotions to dictate her words.

"I'm . . . I'm sorry, Wilma."

But Wilma stopped her by holding up her hand. "*Nee*, you're right. It's not my business to speak aloud about Bethany's special friendship. And my *dochders* do need some fine-tuning before I send them over to Edna's."

Mary sighed and gave her head a little shake.

"Or anywhere else," Wilma added quickly.

Rather than continue berating Wilma, Mary decided to shift the conversation. "Mayhaps you should focus on other things than your *dochders*. Their time will come, I'm sure. Let's talk about the school pageant on the twentieth and our holiday supper on the twenty-fourth. Those are *wunderbarr gut* things to do before the holidays, don't you think?"

Reluctantly, Wilma nodded. "And I was invited to a cookie bake."

Mary raised an eyebrow. "Really?"

"*Ja*, in my cousin's church district."

"Well, that sounds like fun, too. So, you have plenty of things to do that can take your mind off of Rachel and Ella Mae."

Now, if only Mary had something that *she* could focus on in order to stop wondering about Bethany and John Esh.

Chapter Forty

The snow began falling around two o'clock, and by the time she'd finished cleaning up after the *Englischers*, Bethany saw that almost two inches had already accumulated.

She stared out the window that overlooked the fields to the east of the Esh farm. Everything looked so beautiful blanketed in white. While Bethany didn't particularly enjoy the cold of winter, she did love a good snowstorm.

"Enjoying the view?"

She started at the soft voice beside her ear. He stood so close to her that she could feel his warm breath on the back of her neck. She continued staring out the window, smiling, even though she knew that he couldn't see her expression. Outside the window, a red cardinal swooped down and landed on a fence railing.

"Look at that," he said, reaching out to point, his arm brushing against hers. "It's the same color as your dress."

He'd noticed! Bethany felt giddy. "It . . . it is, isn't it?"

As John withdrew his arm, his hand paused and pressed against her arm. "You wear it better than the cardinal," he said in a soft voice.

She smiled to herself, knowing that her cheeks grew pink at the compliment. Uncertain how to respond, she changed the subject. "It's starting to feel like the Christmas season, isn't it?"

Withdrawing his hand, John took a deep breath and exhaled slowly. "*Ja*, it sure is. Christmas is a *wunderbarr* time of year. A time to remember what's truly important in life."

"God's gift."

She sensed that John nodded. "*Ja*, that's right, Bethany. God's gift to the world. His only begotten son. Any other gift pales by comparison, don't you think?"

She couldn't have agreed more. But as she stood there, watching the white flurries drifting downward from the sky, she knew that she didn't have to answer in words. Seeing the beauty of God's hand painting the winter scene before her gave Bethany a particularly strong sense of peace.

John remained standing behind her, close enough that she could feel the energy emanating from his body. The fact that he could stand there in quiet observation without filling the air between them with endless—and meaningless—words made Bethany feel warm and set apart from the rest of the world in a happy, joyous way. The bliss she felt in his presence was a new emotion to her.

And then, he leaned down and whispered, "I'd best take you home, don't you think?"

Shutting her eyes, she felt as if every nerve in her body was on fire. "I reckon that's a good idea," she whispered, her heart pounding.

Suddenly, she realized that he hadn't mentioned taking her for supper. She hoped that he hadn't forgotten or, even worse, changed his mind. A wave of panic washed over her. What if he *had* changed his mind? Or was he simply no longer interested in her? What if he never had been? Was it possible that she had misread him?

She felt weak as she went to collect her things. She'd never courted anyone and, frankly, hadn't ever really expected to. And then John had happened along. But Bethany had no idea how to court or what to expect. She had no siblings or close friends who might share their stories with her, guiding her through the unspoken world of courtship.

John waited for her at the door and, once again, helped her with her shawl. "You might borrow my *maem*'s jacket if you'd like."

She caught her breath. "Oh no! I couldn't! She might need it herself."

He frowned. "Well, let's make certain you wear a heavier coat next time, *ja*? It's gotten too cold out for just a wool shawl."

Her mother had always told her that, too. But Bethany preferred the shawl, for it wasn't as constricting as a jacket. "It keeps me warm enough, I suppose."

"Hm."

He helped her into the buggy, his hand holding hers as she put her foot on the round step. When she sat down, John still held her hand, his touch lingering seconds longer than it should've.

Bethany didn't mind, but she couldn't help wondering why he hadn't said anything about supper. Had she imagined that he had asked her about that last Sunday?

"You settled?" Only when she nodded did he release his hold on her hand and then slide the door shut.

Bethany took the quilt that he'd laid on the seat and spread it over her legs. It was warmer in the buggy, but that didn't mean much, considering it was in the low thirties outside.

"Oh *gut*," he said as he climbed in next to her and noticed she'd already wrapped the blanket around her legs. "You make certain you stay warm under there."

"You . . . you want some, too?"

He seemed to contemplate it, but then he shook his head. "*Nee*, it's better for you to use it. I want you to be warm. Besides, I'm okay."

He picked up the reins and guided the horse backward before he turned it around and headed out of the driveway.

The horse trotted along the roadway, its dark mane flowing in rhythm with the beat of its hooves. Still John remained silent as he drove the horse.

Bethany felt that rising fear again. Perhaps he was sorry he had asked her. Perhaps she *had* imagined it. Lord only knew how often she had daydreamed about him over the past weeks. Had one of those daydreams been so real that she'd confused it with reality? She wanted to ask him, but she was too nervous to do so.

Finally, John stopped the horse at an intersection, and rather than continue straight toward her parents' home, he turned left.

He must have sensed that she looked at him, for he gave a hint of a smile. "Figured we'd go into town for something to eat, if that's still okay with you."

Bethany released her breath. She hadn't realized she'd been holding it. "That's fine," she said softly. She'd have gone *anywhere* with John Esh.

"And . . ." He paused. "Well, I thought that I might pick you up tomorrow. Around six thirty?"

She tried not to smile. Tomorrow was an off Sunday; there was no worship. If he wanted to pick her up to go into town, then he definitely was calling on her. After all, Sunday evening visits were almost always reserved for courting. "Oh?" she said softly.

"Unless, of course, you have plans already."

"Oh *nee*," she gushed. "I . . . I don't have plans."

He gave a little laugh and she wondered if he had been teasing her.

"Well then, you do now. Just be certain to wear boots."

That was a strange request! "Boots?"

He nodded. "*Ja*, I have somewhere special to take you, but you need boots." He glanced at her shawl. "And a warmer coat."

"What's so special about tomorrow?"

He stared straight ahead. "I was thinking that mayhaps we might go to a singing."

Stunned, Bethany could only repeat the word while she collected her thoughts. "A singing?" That was the last thing she wanted to do. She disliked singings. The young women stood on one side of the room and the young men on the other. She wasn't close enough to any of the other girls to feel comfortable standing in a small group. And then, from what Bethany remembered, they gossiped and talked about the men, especially the ones they liked.

No, a singing was definitely not something Bethany was interested in attending, but she was afraid to say that. Instead, she swallowed. "If . . . if that's what you'd like."

He laughed. "I'm teasing you, Bethany."

She gave him a quizzical look. "Teasing me?"

"*Ja*, teasing. If you're anything like me—and I think you are—singings are the last place on earth you'd want to be."

This time, she understood what he meant. A sigh of relief escaped her lips. "I'm so glad you feel that way. I'd have hated to disappoint you."

Something softened in his expression. "I doubt there's much about you, Bethany Ropp, that could disappoint me."

Clutching her hands, she shifted her eyes to stare out the buggy window. Her breath felt heavy and labored as she realized that she needn't have any doubts about John

Esh and his intentions. It was time to shelve her fears and embrace the fact that God had led them to each other. She felt a mixture of apprehension and excitement at that thought. Was it possible that John Esh felt the exact same way about her as she felt about him?

Chapter Forty-One

Edna had been sitting near the propane heater, crocheting a scarf, when she heard the soft shuffling of feet on the staircase. It was Sunday evening and, after a long but leisurely day at home, Edna was almost ready for bed.

It was John.

One glance at the clock on the wall and Edna realized that it was too late for any last-minute chores. So he was either coming to sit with his parents for a little bit—something he rarely did at this hour—or he was going out. That, too, was unusual for John, who often preferred a good night's sleep to leaving the farm after dark.

"Going somewhere?" she asked.

He froze. "Oh, uh . . ." He paused as if trying to think of something to say. Clearly, he hadn't expected to find her sitting there. He must've been deep in thought not to have noticed the light coming from the back corner of the room.

"John, are you going out again tonight?" She frowned. "You didn't get home until late last night. Surely you're too tired."

In truth, *she* was the one who was most likely too tired. The previous night, she hadn't been able to sleep until she heard him come home around nine. He'd left shortly after three thirty to take Bethany home, and then he hadn't returned. Had that been Jonas or Jeremiah, Edna would have expected it. Those two always went out on the weekends. But it wasn't like John to just disappear for over five hours. So, she had worried, alone, until his return.

She'd been surprised that no one else had seemed to notice his absence. After supper, Jonas had borrowed Elmer's buggy and left the house. Edna wondered if he was courting someone, because he usually went out with his younger brother. But Jeremiah had bundled up and left on foot alone, most likely to go out with friends. And Elmer had fallen asleep in his chair, the *Budget* newspaper on his lap and his reading glasses perched on the tip of his nose.

Only Edna had paid attention to the quiet in the house and the absence of her oldest son.

Tonight, however, was different. Elmer had already gone upstairs, and both Jonas and Jeremiah had been gone all day. Now, with the sky so dark and the house so quiet, the last thing Edna had expected was to see John walking down the stairs at such an hour.

And dressed in his nice clothing, too.

He was *definitely* going out.

"I'm not tired," John said. "And it wasn't that late. Before nine o'clock, anyway."

But that *was* late for John.

"It's just not like you to"—she sought the right words—"disappear like that. I was worried. And now again? Two nights in a row?" Edna paused, wanting to inquire where he'd been, but knowing it was best to respect his privacy. "Will you be out so late again tonight?"

He glanced at the clock, and Edna did the same. It was almost six. Surely if he was going to fetch Bethany, he would be home even later. At least he didn't have to work at the auction house the following day. But Edna knew that Elmer still needed his help. The men hadn't finished cutting up all that wood yet, although they'd managed to bring most of the logs into the barn before the snow fell.

John merely gave her a blank look, a stoic expression on his face. "Not sure."

Sighing, Edna gave up. He was, after all, a man. Besides, if he was, indeed, courting Bethany, Edna knew that, as his mother, she needed to give him the space to do so. After all, John had always been a very private person. And Edna knew that nothing good ever came from a mother getting too involved with her son's trying to make such an important decision.

"Well then, just be careful driving, because I'm sure not all of those back roads are cleared yet." She tried to busy herself with her crocheting, but she couldn't focus. Her fingers fumbled and she could barely fit the hook through the slip stitch. "I really do worry about you, you know."

To her surprise, she heard him cross the room and then, even more surprising, she felt his hand on her shoulder. It was a comforting, if unexpected, gesture. She couldn't remember the last time he'd done such a thing.

"I know, Maem," he said. "But there's no need for concern."

She reached up her hand to cover his and managed to crane her neck enough so that she could peer up at him. His face looked bright, his eyes sparkling in the glow from the propane light. "I'm sure, John," she said and managed to find a smile to bestow upon him. "I . . . I'm glad you're going out. Truly."

She meant it. However, the realization that her prayers might finally be answered caused her a moment of panic. What would life be like in the *haus* if John did marry? Where would he live with his bride? Surely not at the farm. Just the thought of John moving away made her realize that sometimes the answer to a prayer gave birth to new worries.

John smiled back at her. There was a gentle expression on his face, one of understanding and love. "I know that, too, Maem." And then he withdrew his hand and quietly walked out of the room.

His words touched her heart, and Edna suspected that they were the closest he would come to admitting the truth. Not surprisingly, being more conservative than his brothers, he chose to court in private. If he didn't want to share his private life with her, she would respect his wishes.

Chapter Forty-Two

Mary could hardly believe her eyes. It was past six o'clock, and Bethany was standing near the door.

"Are you going somewhere?"

At the sound of her mother's voice, Bethany jumped. "Maem! I didn't see you come in the room."

Mary shut the bedroom door behind herself and hobbled over to the kitchen table. Resting her hand on the back of a chair, she leaned against it. "You frightened me, Bethany. I thought I heard something out here."

"I'm sorry if I startled you."

Mary stared at her daughter, who was lingering near the door with her shawl draped over her shoulders. She wondered if John had asked Bethany to ride with him this evening. After dark.

And that worried her.

"It's also a little late for going out, don't you think?" Mary didn't particularly like the idea of John taking her daughter out in the evening.

Bethany pursed her lips. "I . . . I suppose so."

"And the roads might be icy."

"I saw them spreading salt on the roads earlier."

"Hm." Mary still didn't feel comfortable with her daughter

going out tonight. "Salt melts the ice, but the cold might freeze it again."

Bethany took a deep breath and exhaled slowly. It wasn't like her to appear vexed, and that, too, bothered Mary. "Maem, I . . . I'm just going out for a short spell. I hadn't said anything because I didn't want to cause you any concern." A strained smile softened her expression. "Honest, I'll be fine."

The sound of the horse and buggy approaching filled the kitchen. Mary didn't like this. Not one bit. But she knew that she couldn't stop her daughter. Bethany was almost twenty and, as an adult, permitted to make her own decisions. Besides, Mary knew that she should be happy her daughter was courting someone, although she was more than a little disappointed in Bethany's decision to be so secretive, especially with her. She was, after all, Bethany's mother and, from what she could tell, her best friend.

Suddenly, it dawned on Mary that, perhaps, her own mother had felt the same way during *her* courtship with Abram. They, too, had been secretive about seeing each other. In fact, her parents hadn't even known that she was seeing anyone at all, never mind Abram Ropp! When she finally told her parents that the bishop was announcing their wedding at the upcoming church service, they'd actually inquired who was the young man she intended to wed.

As Bethany slipped outside, Mary stared after her. Her daughter was out with someone, and Mary was certain it was John. While she trusted John, she still worried. Her daughter hadn't socialized very much and certainly hadn't spent time in the company of young men.

And here was John, picking her up after dark on a Sunday night. Where on earth could he be taking her?

Sighing, Mary shuffled back to the bedroom, knowing that she'd be worried sick until she heard her daughter's footsteps on the kitchen floor later that evening. It was bound to be another long, sleepless night.

Chapter Forty-Three

He stopped the buggy in the cleared-out parking lot of a small park. The snow reflected the moonlight, and the trees almost looked dark blue instead of dark gray. There was no one there, and as luck would have it, no one seemed to have visited the park that day, for the bank of snow was unmarred by footprints.

Bethany looked around. "What are we doing?"

"I know you said that you favor summer," he said, "but I wanted to take you for a walk in the snow. See if I might change your mind about being outside in winter."

While she found *that* possibility highly improbable, she was certainly willing to give it a try. At least, if John asked.

"Is that why you told me to wear boots?"

He held up his hands. "Guilty as charged. You're onto me."

She smiled at him. "I should've suspected something."

Once outside, John tied the horse to the hitching post by the lead he'd attached to a halter placed over its bridle. He patted the horse's neck and whispered "Be right back" into its large, brown ear.

"Do you always talk to animals?"

He laughed. "Perhaps the better question is, don't you?" He helped her down from the buggy, his gloved hand holding hers for a moment. When she thought he might release it, he didn't. Instead, he gave it a soft squeeze. "Is this okay?"

It took her a second to realize that he meant to keep holding her hand while they walked. Growing up, her mother had always told her that holding hands and kissing were meant to be saved for marriage, and then only in private. Bethany stared at her hand engulfed by his and wondered about her mother's advice. Surely it couldn't be a sin to hold hands, could it?

"I . . . I reckon it's okay," she responded, her voice shaking.

Apparently sensing her discomfort, John leaned over to whisper, "You aren't wearing gloves, so this will help keep your hand warm."

She looked up at him. "Then what about my other hand?"

He blinked.

She held up her hand and wiggled her fingers at him. "This one will stay cold. I don't think that's fair, do you?"

He tried not to smile and then stood before her, taking hold of her other hand. "We can't let that happen, can we now?"

It felt awkward, standing in the middle of the parking lot, facing each other and holding hands. Behind him, the horse stood patiently at the hitching post, its breath poofing out of its nose in a white mist. But, despite the cold, Bethany felt warm inside.

"There's something about you, Bethany Ropp," John said softly. "I . . . I don't know how to explain it."

She tried to look away, but his gaze held hers.

"Do . . . do you know what I'm talking about?" he asked.

She swallowed and slowly nodded. "I . . . I think I do."

He took a step backward, gently pulling her with him. When she followed, he took another step and then another, until she heard the snow crunch under his feet.

"I feel as if I've known you for a very long time," he said, carefully holding her hands so that she wouldn't stumble in the snow.

"Well, technically, you have." She smiled up at him. "We've known each other since we were small *kinner*."

He laughed. "That's true. But that's not what I meant."

He kept walking backward, gently pulling her along. Finally, he stopped and then turned to stand beside her. He wrapped one arm around her back so that he could hold her right hand while he held her left hand at his side.

"I wanted you to see this." He nodded toward the frozen lake before them. The wind must have blown the snow from the surface during the day, for the moonlight reflected off of it. "Isn't it beautiful?"

Bethany could hardly tear her eyes from the scene. It was nature at its best. With the trees on the far side of the lake and the white snow on its banks, the lake looked truly majestic in the moonlight. Everything glowed the strangest color. She couldn't tell if it was yellow or blue. But the moon illuminated the scene in that beautiful color.

"Oh!" she breathed. "It's . . . it's glorious."

"Have you ever seen anything like that?"

She shook her head. There was no memory that could compare to the sight before her eyes.

"*Gut!* I wanted to share it with you. To be the one to show you something so magnificent." He squeezed her hand. "And I hope to show you many other things just like it."

Bethany felt a strange sensation. It started in her very core and radiated out to the tips of her toes and the top of her head. The feeling was warm and wonderful. She suspected it had something to do with the fact that she stood there, in the snow, her hand being held by John Esh as she looked at this beautiful example of God's majestic creation.

And it was certainly fed by John telling her that he hoped to show her many other things in the future.

At that moment, that idea sounded like the most wonderful possibility in the world.

As they stood there staring at the frozen pond, Bethany lost track of time, not knowing whether five minutes or ten passed by before John broke the silence with a long sigh.

"Well, best go back to the buggy. Can't have you freezing out here."

"I'm not that cold."

In the darkness, she saw him smile.

"Neither am I, but let's not take any chances. If you caught a cold, my *muder* would be very unforgiving." He released one of her hands and led her through the snow, back toward the buggy. "It seems she's grown quite fond of you." He paused. "And your help."

Bethany followed him, trying to step in his footprints in the snow. "She said she wants me to work there in the spring."

John didn't answer right away. They neared the buggy, and only then did he respond. "I think you'll be helping her in the spring, for sure and certain."

He helped her into the buggy before he unhitched the horse from the post.

As he drove away from the park, she let her eyes linger on the pretty lake. No, she wasn't a fan of the cold, that was true, but John had certainly delivered on his promise to change her mind about disliking it so much. For the rest of her life, she'd never forget standing on the bank of the lake, John's arm wrapped around her as she absorbed the heat from his body while she admired the majestic vision of God's work before her.

Chapter Forty-Four

"Where were *you* last night?"

Edna froze.

It was Monday morning and she was standing at the stove, making pancakes for breakfast. The table, covered with a simple green and white checkered tablecloth, was already set. But she hadn't finished cooking yet when Jonas and Jeremiah walked inside, kicking off their boots in the mudroom, at the same moment that John walked downstairs.

John walked over to where Edna was standing and reached for the coffeepot. "Out."

"You never go out," Jonas said, his voice a mixture of curiosity and irritation. "And you didn't get up to help with morning chores."

"Got in late."

Jonas scoffed. "How late? Seven?"

Jeremiah laughed.

"Boys." Edna didn't want to hear bickering, not so early and especially not between John and Jonas. She was used to Jonas and Jeremiah teasing each other and, occasionally, having a disagreement. But John usually stayed neutral. Both of the other boys left him alone. She didn't like Jonas challenging him. "Best call your *daed* for breakfast, Jonas," she said, hoping that she might redirect his attention.

Jonas gave his older brother a stern look before he went onto the porch and rang the bell that hung there.

Edna took the opportunity to look at John. He didn't look particularly well rested. There were dark circles under his eyes. But she'd heard him arrive home, and it hadn't been terribly late at all.

"Everything go well last night?" she asked. "You weren't gone very long."

He sipped at the coffee. "Told you I wouldn't be out for long."

Edna waited. Where could he have gone at that hour and for such a short period of time?

He met her concerned gaze. Despite his somber exterior, John was clearly pleased. His eyes sparkled. "Nothing to worry about, Maem," he said. To her surprise, he leaned over and planted a soft kiss on her cheek. "And *ja*, everything went well," he whispered before moving over to take his seat at the table.

Edna almost caught her breath.

Despite being vague, John had just confessed the truth. He trusted her enough to confide that he *was* courting someone—and she simply knew that someone was Bethany Ropp!—and things were going well.

After having spent so much time with the young woman, Edna couldn't be more pleased. Bethany was a good woman who valued hard work, obedience, and loyalty. Unlike many of the other unmarried Amish women Edna knew, Bethany truly shunned worldliness. Even her *rumschpringe* had been without any issues, at least according to Mary.

Yes, Bethany Ropp would make the perfect wife for John.

The noise of Elmer and the other two boys clambering into the mudroom interrupted the moment.

Edna tried to wipe the smile from her face. The last thing she wanted to do was to reveal John's secret to the rest of the family. In due time, she told herself, he'd share the information, but only when he was ready.

"Where were *you* this morning?" Elmer asked as he sat down.

John rolled his eyes.

"He went 'out' last night," Jonas said, answering for his brother. "He's finally found himself a girl."

John rolled his eyes.

"Definitely that old *maedel* from Benjamin's district," Jonas quipped.

Edna carried the plate of pancakes and placed them in front of Jonas. "Eat before it gets cold." Perhaps if he had a mouthful of food, he'd stop tormenting John.

She sat down and waited for Elmer to join them. Only then did they all bow their heads to say the before prayer. She waited until Elmer looked up before she gestured for Jonas to start serving.

"I've a busy week," she announced, hoping the change of subject would distract Jonas. "I'll be cleaning today and doing laundry. So no tracking mud into the *haus*." She directed *that* comment to both Jonas and Jeremiah. "And I'll need help setting up the tables and chairs tomorrow night." She looked at John. "You'll be able to help with that, *ja*?"

To her surprise, he shook his head. "Mayhaps Jonas and Jeremiah could help."

A heavy silence fell over the room. Edna couldn't remember the last time that John had excused himself from helping her with *anything*.

What's this about? Edna thought.

Even Elmer stared at John, waiting for his explanation.

"I have plans," he said at last.

"Plans?" Edna frowned.

"With old *maedel* Bessie again, I bet," Jonas teased.

John ignored him. "I'll be back later in the evening, if you can wait. I could help then, but I know you like setting up in the afternoon."

Edna observed John, wondering where he might be going on a Tuesday night. With work the next day, surely, he would want a good night's sleep. In fact, she couldn't remember John *ever* going out on a weeknight when he had work in the morning.

Perhaps Mary had invited him over for supper, she thought. But then why wouldn't she have said anything when they were all gathered at Wilma's *haus* on Friday?

Oh, the secrets of courtship! Edna remembered how she, too, had been reticent to share any information about Elmer calling on her with anyone. She hadn't told her parents, or even her sisters, not until Elmer had proposed. But Edna had thought that things were changing a bit in more modern times, that the youth were a bit more open about it. Apparently not.

"*Nee*, that's all right," she said. Let him have his secrets. At least Edna was certain that, whatever plan her son had, it was with Bethany Ropp. "Your *bruders* can do it."

Jonas rolled his eyes. "Thanks, John!"

Elmer reached over and nudged Jonas's arm. "That'll do, Jonas. Your *bruder* is doing more than his fair share of work supporting this family."

Jonas scoffed but didn't reply.

Edna looked at her husband, and when he met her gaze, she raised an eyebrow. He gave a little shrug and then picked up his knife and fork. When he cut into his pancake, everyone's attention fell away from John and focused on the food. Edna, however, couldn't keep herself from watching him. She'd wanted this for John for so long. But now that it was here and appearing to be happening, she realized that he'd most likely be moving away whenever he did marry.

And *that* realization tainted the joy of knowing her son was courting such a lovely young Amish woman.

Chapter Forty-Five

It had been nice to have Bethany at home all day, Mary thought as she folded the laundry, her daughter standing beside her as she helped.

For as long as Mary could remember, she always did laundry on Mondays and Thursdays. Growing up, her own mother had done the wash three times a week, but she'd had more children, and that meant more clothes.

Mary had adapted her mother's schedule to suit her smaller family.

But it had rained yesterday, so they'd had to wash the clothes and linens that morning.

Now that she was a little more mobile, Mary felt more productive getting some of the chores done. She'd hated being so confined to the recliner chair. But she also knew that she couldn't have done the laundry without Bethany's help hanging up the towels and sheets earlier. It was one thing to put some pressure on her leg, but too much would make it ache.

Now, as they stood side by side, it was Bethany's company even more than her help that Mary appreciated.

"So then the one *Englische* woman asked whether or not we went to church on Christmas," Bethany said. "She looked alarmed when Edna told her that we didn't."

Mary clucked her tongue and shook her head. "They'd understand more if they held services in their own homes and not a worship house. No one wants the burden and stress of preparing the *haus* for service on the day of Christ's birth!" She set the folded towel into the laundry basket. "Why, I can't imagine trying to clean everything proper *and* prepare for the holiday!"

Bethany made a clucking noise with her tongue.

For a moment, they continued folding the clothes in silence. This was the last week for Bethany to help Edna and, in a way, Mary was glad. She'd missed her daughter being around during the day. It would be nice to have her home again. Besides, Mary had noticed a change in Bethany over the past few weeks. A change for the good. She couldn't quite put her finger on it, but she suspected it had something to do with more than just having been exposed to *Englischers*.

Suddenly, she heard something. "Is that a buggy pulling into the driveway?" Mary glanced over her shoulder, straining to look out the window.

"I don't hear anything."

But Mary was certain she'd heard the sound of horse hooves and buggy wheels. "I'm not expecting anyone." She glanced at the clock. It was just after four thirty. Abram wouldn't be home for another hour yet. "Go check, Bethany. I'm sure I heard something."

Obediently, Bethany set down the towel she'd been folding and, in bare feet, crossed the linoleum floor toward the front door. Seconds later, Mary heard her give a happy sigh and then open the door.

"Hello, John," she said.

Mary caught her breath. Had John Esh come calling on her daughter? And on a Tuesday?

"May I come in a spell?"

Bethany didn't answer, but moments later, she led John into the kitchen.

"What a surprise," Mary said, smiling at Edna's son. "I didn't expect any visitors today." She looked at Bethany as if to ask whether or not she had known that John was stopping by.

Bethany, however, wore a blank expression on her face. But her dark eyes simply glowed with delight. No, Mary thought, she hadn't expected John to visit, but she was certainly quite happy about it.

"Is everything all right at home?" Mary asked, wondering if he might have stopped by to share information about Edna. Mayhaps one of her groups had canceled that week?

But John quickly reassured her.

"Oh *ja*, right as rain." He gave a nervous chuckle. "Maem's probably doing the same as you." He gestured toward the table and the laundry basket. "Only without such an efficient helper."

"That rain yesterday was heavy, wasn't it?" Mary placed her hand atop the laundry pile. "Couldn't get laundry done in such weather. Thankfully it wasn't snow."

"*Ja*, it washed away most of the snow," he pointed out.

Mary smiled. "I know Bethany is happy about that. She hates snow."

To Mary's surprise, Bethany interjected, "*Nee*, that's not true."

"What?" Bethany's confession stunned Mary. She stared at her daughter, her mouth hanging open in surprise. "Since when? All those years you hated the snow. You practically refused to leave the *haus* in the winter whenever there was snow on the ground." She looked at John and gave him an exasperated look. "Getting her to school after it snowed was nearly impossible. She wouldn't even walk there, so Abram had to drive her!"

John laughed.

"Well, mayhaps I learned to appreciate its beauty," Bethany said in a soft voice, her eyes flickering toward John. "Just had to look at it differently, I reckon."

"Well!" Mary put her hand on her hip. "That's most interesting! I never thought I'd see the day when my *dochder* changed her mind about snow!" She raised an eyebrow. "Makes me wonder what else she might change her mind about next."

Bethany flushed and averted her eyes.

John cleared his throat. "On that note," he said lightly, "I was wondering if I might borrow Bethany for a short while."

Mary stared at him, wide-eyed. He'd been so secretive the last time he'd stopped by. Why was he suddenly being so open about calling on her daughter?

"Oh?"

"Going to take a ride into town, and would be nice to have some company." He winked at Mary. "Mayhaps I can find something else for her to look at differently." He shifted his gaze to Bethany. "But only if you wear a heavier coat. No shawl."

Bethany tried to hide her smile.

Mary watched as the two of them quietly walked to the door, John pausing to help Bethany put on a coat before he opened the door for her.

As they disappeared through it, Mary realized that Verna and Wilma had been wrong. When it came to love, no one needed encouragement to hurry it along, for it was clear that love was moving at the perfect speed for John and Bethany.

Chapter Forty-Six

John drove the horse along the back roads toward Shipshewana, slowly guiding it past the houses that were lit up with pretty lights.

"It's so beautiful!"

John smiled at her. "Just wait until it gets even darker. There's one house that is so bright that you'd almost think it's daytime!"

"Oh, I'm not so certain I'll like that house."

"I'm just glad I don't have to live next to it!"

She laughed and he reached under the blanket to hold her hand.

The warmth of his fingers entwined with hers gave her tingles. It was a thrilling feeling.

"I hope you don't mind that I stopped by," he said quietly.

"I . . . I don't mind." The truth was that she had been surprised to see him at the door, but it had been a happy surprise. With his work schedule at the auction house, she hadn't expected to see him at all.

"I didn't want to wait until Saturday." He squeezed her hand. "Sure made for a long week last week."

She smiled, even though he couldn't see it. "*Ja*, I felt the same way."

He turned his head to look at her. “Really?”

She nodded.

“I’m glad.” He loosened his grip on her hand, but still held it. “Listen, Bethany. I . . . I have some bad news.”

Immediately, Bethany tensed. What could possibly be wrong? “What is it, John?”

He pursed his lips and took a deep breath. “I know how much you enjoy the school pageant, but I won’t be able to attend on Friday,” he said slowly. His thumb caressed the top of her hand.

“Oh.” She stared straight ahead, uncertain about how to respond. She didn’t even recall having told him how much she enjoyed the annual pageant, so she couldn’t imagine why he would think she expected him to attend. “That’s okay.”

“It’s the last auction before the Christmas break.” He sounded disappointed. “I would’ve liked to go with you.”

It would have been nice if he could’ve attended the pageant with her. She loved listening to the children singing and reciting Scripture. Sometimes they even reenacted the story of Jesus’ birth. And then, afterward, they’d all share cookies and pie, the perfect combination to celebrate Christmas.

“I’m sorry you’ll miss the pageant,” she said, genuinely meaning her words.

“Me, too. I haven’t been to one in several years. But I always remember how much fun they were when I was in school. And even after, I’d go to watch Jonas and Jeremiah.” He smiled at the memory. “It sure made this time of year feel even more special.”

That was exactly how she felt. Sometimes the teachers would decorate their schools with little clippings from a pine tree, tied to the window sash with pieces of red fabric.

And there were always candles burning on the teacher's desk and a table filled with sweets near the back of the room.

"But after this year," John said, "I won't miss any more."

Bethany's eyes widened. "Oh? Why's that?"

He squeezed her hand. "Just a feeling, I reckon."

They rode in silence for a few minutes until John slowed the horse and turned the buggy down a side road.

"Here. The bright house is just up ahead."

Bethany looked at the small community of *Englische* houses, all of them lit up with twinkling lights on the bushes and trees. Some had electric candles in the windows, and one even had a Nativity scene in the front yard.

"I've never really seen such a thing," she said.

"You've never seen the Christmas lights?"

She shook her head. "We don't often go out at night, and even when we do, we just drive, rather than exploring like this."

He squeezed her hand. "Exploring can be fun."

"Do you explore often?"

"Sometimes, but not too often," he admitted. "It's not as much fun when you're alone."

Bethany didn't particularly consider herself *fun*, but if John thought she was, that made her happy.

Looking down the street, Bethany saw something that made her breath catch. He must have heard her, for he chuckled at her reaction.

Ahead of them was a house so lit up and bright that there was a glow over the roof. Besides the lights on the trees and bushes, the house also had lit-up icicles hanging from the gutter, lit-up figures on the roof, and a yard full of animated characters with spotlights on them.

And there was music playing.

"I wouldn't have believed you if you'd tried to describe this to me!" she said.

"It's really something, isn't it?"

"I . . . I don't know whether I like it or think it's terrible!"

He laughed. "It's fun to look at, though."

"But I definitely wouldn't want to live near this house."

He tightened his hold upon her hand. "Me, neither."

She couldn't imagine that anyone would actually enjoy coming home to such a display. Surely their neighbors didn't like all the brightness. There was something to be said for living a plain life, a life in which less was most definitely more.

"What's it like?" John asked. "Living so close to *Englischers*."

His question caught her off guard. She'd never really thought about the fact that she lived close to *Englischers*, mostly because she didn't interact with them very often. "Our neighbors keep to themselves."

"Do you like that?"

"What do you mean?"

He withdrew his hand from hers and shifted his body so that he faced her. "I just can't imagine living so close to other people and not knowing them."

"Oh, that."

It was true that, unlike most Amish people, who lived together in communities, Bethany's church district was spread out among the *Englische* who lived just off the main street of Shipshewana. To visit with Amish friends, they had to bicycle or take the horse and buggy.

"I've never known any other way," Bethany admitted. "But I do know I would much prefer *not* to live so close to town."

Something changed in his expression. His eyes widened, just a little, and she saw his mouth twitch.

"I always wanted a big garden," she continued. "To grow

more vegetables and to have canning bees. Well, at least I like the *idea* of canning bees."

He smiled.

"And I'd like to not hear the cars all the time. They speed down the road so fast, and some of those drivers just aren't nice."

"Like the woman who stole your photo?"

It took her a moment to remember the day that she'd crossed the intersection and the tourist had taken her photo. That was the day her bicycle broke. She'd almost forgotten that it had been John who rescued her.

"*Ja*, exactly. It's very invasive."

He nodded. "It is."

"What about you?" She leaned her back against the closed door of the buggy. "You live on a farm and you work in town. Seems you have one foot in both worlds."

"'One foot in both worlds,'" he repeated. "That's an interesting way of putting it. The truth is that I don't mind working at the auction *haus,* but I'd much prefer farming." He took a deep breath and turned his gaze back to the house with the lights. "But sometimes we have to do things we don't want to do, *ja*? Like the neighbors who have to endure the bright lights for a few weeks each year. We tolerate what we must in order to help our families."

There was a sorrowful note in his voice. Bethany wished she had something wise to say. "Mayhaps you could talk to your *daed*," she offered as a solution.

"*Ja*, mayhaps." He gave her a small smile. "Well, it doesn't much matter for now. I do have to work tomorrow." He picked up the reins and urged the horse into a walk. "But I wanted to show you this."

"I'm glad you did."

"And I wanted to see you because I won't see you this

week. Since you won't be working for my *maem* anymore after Friday, I thought I could stop by on Saturday."

She felt as if a hollow pit formed in her stomach. She'd forgotten that, after this week, she wouldn't see John Esh on his days off or on Saturdays. After all, Friday was the last meal that Edna had scheduled for the groups from the Destination Amish tours. If John wanted to continue courting her, he'd have to let her know when he was coming to fetch her well in advance.

"I'm supposed to help my *maem* make food for our holiday party. The one we're having at your *haus*." She didn't want to go so long without seeing him, however. "But I'm sure I could visit with you later in the day."

"*Gut.*" He paused. "Because I've something I want to discuss with you."

She felt dizzy. What would he possibly want to discuss with her? Was it possible that he intended to formally ask her to court him? "Wh-what is it?"

He gave her a sideways glance. "Just something. But I can't say anything about it until then. I need to talk to someone first."

"Oh."

Suddenly Bethany knew that if the previous week had felt long, the upcoming one would feel even longer.

Chapter Forty-Seven

After supper on Wednesday evening, Edna was surprised when John joined her and Elmer in the sitting area.

Both Jonas and Jeremiah were out with their friends—Edna never knew where they went, nor did she care to ask. If they weren't out with friends, they sometimes went hunting later in the evening. With pheasant season having just ended, they often hunted deer.

With the exception of the previous weekend, John usually retired early so that he could get up to help his father with the morning milking before he went into Shipshewana for work.

Tonight, however, he appeared to have something on his mind.

Edna rocked back and forth in her chair, working on the scarf she was crocheting. It would be a Christmas present for one of the boys, a small and practical gift that was made with love. Elmer was reading through last week's *Budget* newspaper when John sat down on the sofa.

"Everything all right?"

John nodded. "*Ja*, Daed, everything's all right."

Edna tried to concentrate on the scarf, but she couldn't. Setting down the yarn, she studied John. He'd been such a hard read of late. Usually so thoughtful and kind, he had become a bit quieter and more introspective. Some days, however, he seemed happy in a quiet sort of way. And then, of course, he'd been disappearing quite a bit in the afternoons and early evenings over the weekends.

"Daed," John began slowly. He leaned forward, resting his elbows on his knees and rubbing his hands together in a nervous manner. "I wanted to talk to you about something."

The sound of the newspaper crumpling was Elmer's only response.

Edna looked at her husband and saw that he had put down the paper, his eyes focused on John.

"Well, I was thinking about some things"—he swallowed—"like work and all."

"Work?"

John nodded. "*Ja*, work."

"Everything okay with your job?"

"Oh *ja*, it is. The job is fine, but it's just not for me, Daed."

Elmer frowned. "What do you mean it's not for you?"

Edna rested her hands on the yarn in her lap. She knew exactly what was coming, and to be honest, she was surprised this discussion hadn't occurred sooner.

"I want to farm, Daed. I don't want to work at the auction *haus*. There's no future in that," John said in a somber tone.

At this comment, Elmer sighed. "Some days I'm not so sure that there's a future in dairy farming, either."

"Well, I want to work on the farm, Daed. I've been working at the auction *haus* for six years now."

Edna's eyes flickered to Elmer. After almost thirty years together, she knew him well enough to sense his discomfort with the conversation.

"John, it's not that simple," Elmer replied. "It's about the cost of living, and frankly, we just don't earn enough to support you farming. Plus, we need your income to help get us through the winter."

For a moment, John stared at the floor, still rubbing his hands. He nodded his head a bit as if indicating that he understood what his father had said. He truly seemed to be contemplating Elmer's words, but Edna had a suspicion that John had already anticipated that reaction.

"Mayhaps," John said at last, "it's time for Jonas or Jeremiah to work elsewhere. They've never been enthusiastic farmers anyway. One of them could surely take my job at the auction *haus*."

A fabulous solution, Edna thought. She tried to tamp down her excitement. She knew what this meant. John was thinking about the future. And that future would undoubtedly include a bride. If John worked at the farm, surely he would bring his bride to live with them. Edna could hardly believe her ears. She'd have the best of both worlds: John *and* Bethany.

But she couldn't share any of this. Not yet. The decision would have to be Elmer's.

"Well now," Elmer said, tugging at his graying beard, "seems to me that you've given me something to think about, John." His eyes shifted to look at Edna. "Wouldn't you say so, Maem?"

Swallowing, Edna nodded.

"Why don't we all pray about this for a day or two?"

Edna felt as if her heart skipped a beat. She knew her husband well enough to know that he already had the answer. But he was never one to make a quick decision. He needed time to mull it over and pray until he felt that everyone involved had had enough time to consider all the different angles.

Oh! How she wished that Elmer had simply just agreed. From the expression on John's face, he felt the same way.

The fact that they had to wait would make the next few days painfully long.

"*Danke*, Daed," John said, the disappointment heavy in his voice. He looked drained and tired. "I'll pray on it for sure."

Edna suspected that John had already done that. For days or even weeks, she thought. But she knew that he was far too respectful to push the matter. If his father needed more time to feel comfortable with his decision, John was not the type of son who would demand an immediate answer.

Edna felt her heart breaking for her son as he walked back to the stairs, his shoulders heavy with the burden of having to wait. Surely Elmer would agree to John's request, she thought. It was reasonable enough, especially given his passion for farming, when, as John had pointed out, neither Jonas nor Jeremiah was too keen on being a full-time farmer. Yes, it was time for John to move on to the next phase of his life, and clearly, that included finally doing what he wanted—farming, and most likely with a young wife at his side.

Chapter Forty-Eight

By the time Bethany arrived home on Thursday evening, Mary was already busy making the cookies that she'd promised to bring to the school pageant the following afternoon.

"Land's sake," Mary declared when Bethany shut the kitchen door behind herself. "This day has just flown by!"

Bethany shook the snow from her shawl and hung it on the peg near the door. "It's starting to snow something fierce out there!"

"Fresh snow sure is beautiful," Mary said, scooping a dollop of the peanut butter dough onto the baking sheet. "And you're just in time to help me with these cookies." She smiled at her daughter. "That's a beautiful thing, too, *ja*?"

Sliding onto the bench at the table, Bethany sat down and reached over to pinch the dough. She popped it into her mouth and shut her eyes. "Peanut butter cookies. My favorite!"

"I'm making extra for you, don't worry. And we've sugar cookies that need icing." Mary pointed to the bowl on the counter. "I've already made it."

"I can help with that," Bethany said.

While she got up and fetched the bowl of icing, Mary took the opportunity to observe her daughter. She appeared relaxed and at peace, something that Mary realized was more common these days. She'd definitely come out of her shell since she'd begun helping Edna.

"You've really enjoyed working at Edna's, haven't you?"

"*Ja*, I have." Bethany leaned her elbow on the table and rested her cheek against her hand. "I've learned a lot from Edna."

"Oh?"

Bethany nodded.

"Like what?"

"Well, like how to time cooking for such large crowds and how to organize the kitchen for better efficiency."

Mary made a face. "Are you saying that my kitchen isn't efficient?"

Bethany laughed. "*Nee*, Maem. But it's different when you only cook for three people and Edna is cooking for thirty!"

"I see." But Mary had known Bethany was teasing. "Mayhaps you'll miss riding with John anymore."

At the mention of John, Bethany pursed her lips and her shoulders tensed. Mary wasn't certain how to read her daughter's reaction.

"But you'll see him again on Christmas Eve at the holiday party, *ja*?" Mary scooped some more dough onto a spoon. "That'll be nice, won't it?"

For a drawn-out moment, Bethany didn't respond. She rolled some cookie dough between her palms and then placed it on the baking sheet. "*Ja*, Maem, that *will* be nice."

Now Mary understood. She could remember her own days of courting Abram. They would see each other on Sundays during fellowship. It had been a long thirteen days between each time they'd be together, and she'd often felt apprehensive while they were apart. Would he meet someone else? Would he lose interest? They hadn't courted for long before they married, something that was common back in her youth. Today, however, the young people tended to court more frequently and for longer, probably because they saw each other more often.

"It'll get easier, Bethany," Mary heard herself saying.

She looked up. "What will?"

Before Mary could answer, someone knocked at the door.

"I'll get it."

As soon as the door opened, Mary knew who stood on the other side: John.

"I hope you don't mind that I stopped by," he said in a whispered voice, probably intending to avoid being overheard. "I was on my way home from work and just thought I'd visit for a few minutes."

"I don't mind." Bethany glanced toward the table. "We're making cookies for the school pageant tomorrow."

"Ah." He paused. "I'm interrupting, then."

Mary held her breath.

"*Nee*, not at all," Bethany replied quickly. "*Kum* help us."

Mary breathed a sigh of relief.

When Bethany led John into the kitchen, Mary couldn't help but notice the way her daughter's face glowed. Her eyes brightened and a hint of a smile touched her lips. There was a happiness about Bethany that Mary hadn't seen before.

"John Esh!" Mary greeted him with a cheerful smile. "Have you come to help us bake cookies?"

He pursed his lips and assessed the table. It was covered with bowls and flour and baking sheets. "Well, I have been known to help my *maem* with her cookies." Leaning over, he lowered his voice as if to tell them a big secret. "Why do you think people love them so much? It's my secret touch." He winked at Bethany.

Mary laughed. "I know that is not true."

"So, what can I do to help?"

Bethany fetched another knife and handed it to him. "You can help spread the icing on the cookies."

"Icing. Got it." He walked over to the sink and washed his hands. Bethany stood by his side and handed him a dish towel when he finished. When he set it on the counter, his eyes met hers and he smiled. "Show me how?"

"I thought you were the master cookie baker at your *maem*'s?" she teased.

"Oh. Well." He made a face. "Maybe I exaggerated a little bit."

"Well, it's rather simple." She walked over to the table and picked up one of the sugar cookies. Dipping her knife into the bowl of icing, she slid it across the top of the cookie. "See? Easy."

He picked up a cookie and began to ice it. "So I understand you'll be preparing for the Christmas Eve supper at my *maem*'s on Saturday?"

Mary gave him a curious look. She hadn't told Edna that. How had John heard? "*Ja*, that's our plan."

"Mayhaps I could stop by later. I have an errand in town, and if you'd like, I could pick up your food to bring back home so you don't have to worry about it on Tuesday?"

For a second, Mary almost refused his offer. Among her, Abram, and Bethany, they could certainly manage transporting their contributions to the supper. But then she realized that John wasn't really asking about that. He was asking something else.

"Oh, well, I suppose that would be greatly appreciated." She focused on rolling her peanut butter dough into small balls. "But I would insist that you'd stay for supper, then."

John finished icing his second cookie. "Supper, eh? Well, that would be greatly appreciated." He leaned over and nudged Bethany's arm with his shoulder. "Your *maem*'s smart. She knows that if I took the food home on an empty stomach, I'd probably eat it."

Bethany gave a small laugh.

"Whoops! Hold on a minute," John said. "Come here, Bethany."

Confused, Bethany frowned. "What?"

Mary watched as he placed his hands upon Bethany's shoulders and turned her toward him. His blue eyes studied her daughter's face.

"What is it?" Bethany asked, her cheeks turning pink.

"You've done it again."

She blinked. "Done what?"

He reached up and touched the tip of her nose. "Icing." He turned his finger around so she could see it. "You seem to have a knack for always getting things on your face!"

Her blush deepened.

"Good thing I'm always around to wipe it off!" He laughed and popped his finger into his mouth to eat the icing.

"Good thing, indeed," she managed to say.

Mary smiled to herself. She liked watching the interplay between her daughter and this kind man. And she suspected that she'd be seeing much more of it in the days and weeks and possibly even years ahead.

Chapter Forty-Nine

On Friday, Bethany woke up and could hardly believe that today was the last day she'd be working for Edna Esh. The past few weeks had flown by for Bethany, and now that they were almost over, she knew that she would miss helping her mother's friend.

But the one thing she wouldn't miss was having to ride home with Jonas in the afternoons.

"Your last day working," her mother said when Bethany went downstairs for breakfast.

"*Ja*, it is."

"Are you sad about it?"

Bethany *was* sad, but she suspected not for the same reasons her mother thought. "I am, but Edna mentioned something about helping her again in the spring. A more permanent situation."

Her mother raised an eyebrow. "Oh *ja*? That would be nice."

Bethany nodded. She didn't mention that it was John who had brought up the subject of creating a more permanent situation. She wasn't certain what he had meant by that, but she definitely liked the idea of being around the Esh farm again, even if she had to deal with Jonas from time to time.

"Well, be certain to say hello to Edna, Verna, and Wilma today," Mary said, a forlorn tone to her voice. "Oh, how I wish I could go along with you. I so miss our cookie club days."

Bethany paused and looked at her mother.

"What?"

She shrugged. "Nothing, really. I just always thought you didn't like calling it a 'Cookie Club.' That's the first time I've heard you mention it so casually."

Her mother wore a blank expression, and then she gave a little laugh. "I did, didn't I? I reckon the name's stuck on me after all!"

As luck would have it, Jonas showed up to fetch her later that morning. Wrapping her shawl around her shoulders, Bethany hurried outside and got into the buggy.

"*Gut martiye*," he said.

"*Danke*, Jonas. You, too."

"Did I tell you the story about when I went hunting with Jeremiah near Blue Springs?" Jonas asked as he drove her to his mother's house. "The six-point buck that I bagged?"

Bethany stared out the window, shutting her eyes. He'd told her the story at least twice already, and frankly, she hadn't liked it either of those times. Bragging about killing a beautiful animal didn't sit well with her. But she'd learned that it was sometimes better to let him talk. Time passed faster that way, and the more he talked, the less she had to.

"Mayhaps," she said. "But tell it again."

She barely listened to him as she stared out the window. Later that afternoon, she'd return home and then attend the children's pageant at school. With no work tomorrow, Bethany could truly begin to enjoy the Christmas season.

And she needed the time to figure out what to make for John for Christmas. She knew that she wanted to give him something special, but she just didn't know what. Even though she now had a little extra spending money, buying something from a store felt far too impersonal. And yet, she didn't have time to make him something so grand as a blanket or quilt.

She hadn't yet come up with any one idea that jumped out as the perfect gift for him. He'd already given her so many! He'd taken her to the lake in the snowy moonlight. He'd driven her to see the lights on the *Englischers'* houses. And he'd helped her to stop feeling shy and quiet in front of strangers . . . or at least in front of him.

What gift could she give him that summed up everything he'd done for her?

Fortunately, Jonas didn't realize that she wasn't paying any attention, and by the time he'd finished his story, he was pulling into his parents' driveway.

Inside the house, Bethany hung up her shawl and hurried over to get started by washing the dishes in the sink. Over the past few weeks, she'd developed a little routine with Edna. As soon as Bethany arrived, she cleaned up any pots and pans that Edna had already used. After she dried them and put them away, she'd set the tables. Then, together, they'd finish cooking whatever needed to be warmed up before the guests came.

"Oh, Bethany! There you are!" Edna hustled into the kitchen, a big box in her hands. "I normally have everything ready for when Verna and Wilma arrive so that it's really just a matter of mixing the ingredients. Could you help me measure out the flour?"

Together, they measured the dry ingredients so that everything was already on the table. Bethany suspected that Edna didn't really need Verna and Wilma's help to make cookies for the worship services on Sunday. In fact, knowing Edna, she could've made cookies blindfolded, or even in her sleep.

"You sure do enjoy having your friends over." It was an observation more than a question.

Edna smiled and nodded. "I do. Although I have missed your *maem*."

"*Ja*, she said the same thing this morning."

"Well, she'll be healed up soon enough, *ja*?"

"First week after the New Year, I believe, is when the cast comes off." Bethany couldn't imagine having to wear that big, clunky thing on her leg for six weeks. She made a mental note to always check stepladders before she stepped on them. "Although it hasn't really stopped her much."

Edna agreed. "That's right. Look at how she managed to get us all to make knot quilts the other weekend. She's a good-hearted woman, your *maem*."

Bethany knew that to be true. And she certainly hoped that, one day, she might be viewed as the same sort of person: kind, compassionate, good-hearted, and giving. Perhaps she might even have her own children one day to pass those traits on to.

"Well, everything's set here." Edna surveyed the kitchen table and appeared satisfied. "Let's set those tables, and then, if you don't mind, you might run out to the chicken coop for me? Feed those hens and collect their eggs."

Bethany knew she'd miss working for Edna with her hustle and bustle and focus on getting things done. As she'd told her mother the other day, she had learned so much from Edna over the past few weeks. She'd never met anyone who could get more done in a single day. And, despite all she'd learned, Bethany knew that Edna surely had more to share.

Perhaps she would be able to return in the spring . . . just as John had mentioned to her the other week.

Chapter Fifty

Edna could hardly believe that it was Friday at last.

"Well, Edna, you survived the busy season," Elmer said to her as he sipped his coffee. "I wasn't so certain you'd make it—"

"Elmer!"

"—but you sure did. Came through with flying colors, thanks to that Bethany Ropp, I reckon."

She gave him one of her looks. "You thought I wouldn't be able to handle it?"

Elmer laughed and moved over to the stove so that he could pour himself a mug of coffee. "Well, I knew *you'd* survive, but I wasn't certain if *we* would."

She tossed a dishcloth at him.

He grabbed it and, still laughing, set it on the counter. "So how does it feel?"

The truth was that she felt fabulous. After paying for food *and* Bethany's help, she'd earned over five hundred dollars a week. That money would go a long way toward helping the family over the next few months. But she didn't say this, for fear of hurting Elmer's feelings. He was, after all, the provider for the family.

"I feel tired, that's what I feel!"

"Mayhaps you shouldn't attend the school pageant this afternoon, then."

Her eyes widened. She'd no sooner miss the holiday pageant than she'd miss a worship service! "Why, Elmer! You know that the *kinner* would be sorely disappointed if I didn't bring them cookies." She made a face at him. "And I wouldn't feel like it was the holidays if I missed it."

He chuckled. "I know, I know. I'm just teasing you some."

A noise caught his attention from outside the window. "Well, sounds like your cookie club has arrived." He glanced at the clock. "And that's my cue to get back to work."

He disappeared out the door just in time to bump into the women. Edna could hear their voices exchanging greetings, and then the door opened and Wilma practically burst into the room.

"We've a surprise for you!" Wilma exclaimed as she walked into Edna's kitchen. She dropped her large black bag just inside the door and wandered around the room, her eyes wide and her mouth open as she stared at the red ribbons strung from one corner to another. "Land's sake! How many Christmas cards did you receive?"

Edna watched as Wilma took in the sight of the holiday cards she had strung from the ribbons. Besides the white candles she set on the kitchen window frame, the holiday cards were the only indication that December was a special month in the Esh household.

"That's what happens when two large families join together," she said to Wilma. She didn't display the cards to make anyone feel bad, but she didn't see any sense in just stacking them in a basket. Besides, all of those cards made the room appear festive and that put her in such a good mood each year.

Verna stood in the doorway, shaking off her shawl. She, too, seemed dumbfounded by the multiple ribbons and

Christmas cards. "Every year I say that I'm going to do this," she said as she hung up her shawl, "and every year I forget!"

Laughing, Edna gestured toward the table. "Then go home today and do it!"

"It *does* look joyously charming, doesn't it?"

Wilma snorted at Verna. "Collects a lot of dust, I bet." As if to prove her point, she sneezed.

"Oh, Wilma!" Verna swatted at her friend's arm. "Don't be such a holiday grump!"

"So, what's my surprise?" Edna asked, hoping to change the subject before they got into a disagreement.

"Elmer is fetching it now."

"Oh?" She walked over to the doorway, and upon seeing Mary, Edna cried out. "What a *wunderbarr gut* surprise!"

Elmer helped Mary into the house, even though Mary protested that she could manage on her own and didn't need to lean upon him.

As she climbed the steps to the porch, she greeted Edna with a quick embrace. "Oh, how I've missed coming here," she whispered. "In fact, I've missed going places, period!"

Wilma grinned. "We thought we'd steal Mary away from the *haus* for a few hours. She didn't even know we were coming for her."

Mary looked nervous. "I'm so glad you did, but I'm afraid Abram won't like it one bit."

Edna dismissed Mary's comment with a wave of her hand. "Nonsense. A broken ankle doesn't mean you can't go places. But please sit down. I don't want you overdoing it."

"And if I'd known that they were coming, we could've brought Bethany with us, instead of sending your son to fetch her." Mary looked around. "Where is she, anyway?"

"Fetching the chicken eggs, I imagine." Edna took advantage of the girl's absence to praise her to Mary. "I'll surely miss having her around. She's quiet enough but still good company. And such a hard worker."

"Well, your loss is my gain." Mary limped over to the table and pulled out a chair to sit. "I've missed having her home."

Verna glanced at Edna. "Mayhaps someone else will miss Bethany being here," she said, a mischievous gleam in her eye. "Or have we made any progress with our little project?"

Edna clucked her tongue. "You're incorrigible."

Wilma, however, immediately jumped into the conversation. "Well? Are you going to answer her question? I'm dying to know, too."

Seeing that she wasn't going to get out of responding, Edna took a deep breath. "I suspect that there might be a special friendship developing, but I can't be certain."

Verna clapped her hands. "Oh, joyous news!"

"Let's not get ahead of ourselves," Edna cautioned.

"I agree," Mary said. "Although I will say that he's been over to the *haus* a few times."

The room fell silent, all eyes on Mary.

Stunned at her friend's announcement, Edna's mouth opened. So, her suspicions about John's courting Bethany were correct. "Mary! You need to provide more details."

Immediately, Mary paled. "Oh, I don't think I should tell tales out of turn."

Undeterred, Edna persisted. "When was he there last?"

She looked uncomfortable. "I . . . I guess that would be last night."

Wilma raised an eyebrow. "You guess or you know?"

"I mean that, *ja*, he was there. He . . ." She paused and glanced toward the door as if to make certain that Bethany wasn't about to walk in. "He helped us make cookies for the school pageant today."

"Why didn't you tell us?" Verna playfully hit Mary's arm.

Mary bit her lip. "And—"

"There's more?" Wilma's eyes widened.

"—he's coming to supper on Saturday."

Edna pressed her hand to her chest. "Land's sake! I had no idea."

"Oh, we'll have a wedding before you know it," Verna said cheerfully.

Hearing Bethany's footsteps on the porch, Edna held her finger to her lips. Quickly, she changed the subject just as the young woman entered the house. "I thought that, today, we'd make little Christmas tree–shaped sugar cookies." She held up the cookie cutter and smiled at the other three women as Bethany walked into the room. "Now, doesn't that sound like fun?"

Chapter Fifty-One

Mary watched as Bethany helped Edna serve the *Englische* guests in the house. When Wilma and Verna had started getting ready to leave at eleven, Mary had asked if she might stay a bit longer, and Edna had readily agreed.

During their time together, the women had made their plans for the holiday gathering on Tuesday. Mary could hardly wait to begin cooking on Saturday. It would be such a joyous occasion to have the four families together once again. She was even looking forward to seeing Myrna, although she knew that Verna would certainly talk about nothing but the upcoming baby that was due in the early spring.

"What time does the pageant in your district start?"

Sitting at the table, Mary helped dry some of the dishes. It was the least she could do, even if she wished she could help more. "Three o'clock."

"Ours, too. We'll have plenty of time to get there." Edna peeked over her shoulder at the women still gathered around the tables. "And I might even have enough food left over for Elmer and the boys tonight."

Mary lowered her voice. "Keep some back so you'll have it ready. Then you won't have to worry none."

Bethany walked into the room, carrying two empty

baskets. "More rolls needed." She walked past her mother and headed to the counter, where there was a big container of fresh rolls.

"Oh, Bethany," Edna said in a casual voice, "everyone enjoyed your ham loaf the other night."

Mary looked at her daughter and noticed that her cheeks flushed pink. "You made ham loaf?"

She nodded. "I made some yesterday for Edna's guests on Wednesday."

"The leftovers were right *gut*," Edna said. "In fact, John had three helpings."

Bethany's cheeks grew even more flushed.

"Did he now?" Mary tried to hide her smile. "A *gut* appetite is always a sign of a *gut* worker."

"Or a *gut* cook," Edna tossed back at her.

"Mayhaps both."

Carrying the refilled bread baskets, Bethany hurried back into the far section of the room, where the guests' tables were set up.

Edna came over to the kitchen table and sat down opposite Mary. "I suppose you don't have anything more you want to share with me?"

Mary blinked. Did Edna really think that she'd disclose more information about Bethany and John? "Not unless you have something to share with me."

Frowning, Edna sighed. "I know nothing, Mary. Except that something is going on."

"Well, as I said, I have seen John stop by the house a couple times recently," she admitted.

"And he was very eager to pick her up and drop her off when he wasn't working."

Mary stole a peek to make certain Bethany was still occupied. "Do you think that . . . ?"

"I do think that . . ."

Neither one of them wanted to say the actual words. Mary sighed. "Then I guess we'll just have to keep thinking 'that' until one of them confirms what 'that' truly is."

Edna stood back up. "So infuriating, isn't it? I don't think we gave our parents so much to think about, do you?"

At that comment, Mary gave a little laugh. Surely her friend spoke in jest. Back when she was growing up, things were different. There wasn't so much influence from the outside world, and the rules were even stricter. Mary had no doubt that their parents had wondered and fretted over their children during those courtship years. It was hard to not butt into a courting couple's business, that was for sure and certain.

"Oh, I'm very confident that our parents did their own amount of speculation during our running-around years. We were probably just as—if not more—secretive."

"Well, then, I feel terrible for putting my *maem* through this."

Bethany walked back toward them. When she saw them at the table, she stopped short. "What are you two laughing about?"

"Parenthood," Mary said. "The joys of raising children."

Bethany made a face and continued toward the sink.

"I'm excited about Tuesday, aren't you, Mary?" Edna asked her.

"Having the families get together in the evening is a wonderful idea."

Edna glanced at Bethany. "It was your *dochder*'s idea."

Bethany looked as if she might refute the claim, but it was easy to see that Edna was teasing her.

"But seriously, Edna, are you sure you want to have it here?" Mary asked. She felt terrible that Edna would have to do all that work by herself on Saturday when she should be enjoying her first day without people coming for the noon meal. And then Tuesday, everyone would come to her house and she'd be left with *that* mess. "After all the entertaining you've done for so many people. Mayhaps Wilma or Verna could host the supper."

"I'd have it no other way, Mary Ropp."

"Well, I won't argue then." She wasn't about to quarrel with her friend. "It will be roomier here, that's for sure. And mayhaps you can ask Wilma's *dochders* to come help clean up on Monday."

Edna stared at her, a look of bewilderment on her face. And then, realizing that it was Mary teasing her this time, she broke into soft laughter.

"Mary! I almost thought you were serious." She shook her head. "*Nee*, I have my helper, that's for sure and certain. If she'll come back in the spring, that is."

Mary turned to look at Bethany, uncertain whether or not she had heard Edna. But when Bethany shut off the water and turned away from the sink, she gave Edna a shy smile.

"I'd like nothing better than to help you, Edna."

Edna gave a sigh of relief. "*Gut!* Because after having had you by my side, I don't think I could do it without you."

It was a bittersweet moment for Mary. Her daughter was coming into her own at last, and for that, Mary was thankful. But it also meant that, come spring, Bethany would be gone again. She had missed having her around all day, and now, with a more permanent work relationship being discussed, Mary realized that this was only the beginning, especially if their suspicions about John's interest in Bethany came to fruition.

Chapter Fifty-Two

Oh, how she loved the school pageants!

Bethany sat at one of the small desks and, with her hands folded on her lap, watched as the children sang their Christmas hymns. Their faces were so angelic and pure, the light practically shining from their eyes. Standing in front of the schoolhouse, dressed in their Sunday dresses and suits, they exuded cheer and joy as they performed for their parents, grandparents, and neighbors.

The teacher had decorated the school with simple greens from a nearby pine tree, tied with a white ribbon and positioned at the bottom of each window. And several candles flickered from the edge of her desk. At the back of the room was the long table, covered with sweets and treats for the children after their pageant was over.

The building was packed with people who had come to watch the annual pageant. It was always full, the men usually standing in the back while the women sat at desks and benches that had been brought in to accommodate the audience. It was a building filled with love.

This, Bethany thought, *is what Christmas is all about.*

She had thought a lot about the buggy ride she'd taken with John to see the lit-up houses. Clearly people who lived outside of her community celebrated Christmas in much different ways from the Amish. She knew that just from the way people talked and from things she had personally observed over the years. Always at Christmastime, tourism picked up in Shipshewana, the traffic heavier on the streets. Whenever she had to go to the store, it was more crowded—the stores filled with people buying Christmas presents.

But that wasn't the way of the Amish.

Christmas was about being together to celebrate the birth of Jesus. It was a time to sing and to share, to eat and to laugh. Gifts were kept small and always practical. And lights were limited to a few battery-operated ones or plain white candles.

To Bethany, Christmas was about showing love to God and Jesus. Nothing else mattered. She felt that the flashing lights and over decorated houses took away from God's gift. Bethany couldn't imagine enjoying the holiday if she had to celebrate it any other way.

She felt her mother's hand on her arm. Tearing her eyes away from the front of the room, Bethany saw her mother leaning toward her. "I thought you said John wasn't going to make it," she whispered and then nodded toward the back door.

Startled, Bethany quickly turned to follow her mother's gaze. Sure enough, there stood John, his hands behind his back as he rocked a little bit on his feet in perfect time with the song being sung by the children.

She couldn't have stopped herself from smiling if she tried.

Somehow seeing him there made everything right. If she hadn't realized it before, now she knew that Christmas wouldn't have been complete without John Esh standing in the back of the room, watching the children honor Jesus through their singing.

Turning back around to face the front of the room, Bethany tried to focus on the children. But her mind remained on the back of the building where John stood. She sat there for a few minutes but then gave up trying.

"I'll be right back," she whispered to her mother.

Quietly, she slipped out from the desk chair and made her way to the back of the schoolhouse.

"Bethany." His whispered greeting could barely be heard over the children's song.

"You came."

He smiled and leaned down to respond in her ear. "I wanted to enjoy Christmas with you." His eyes traveled to the front of the room. "All of Christmas."

For the rest of the pageant, she stood by his side, enjoying the hymns. As usual, the children saved the best one for last: "Silent Night." Outside, with the sun already beginning to set, the room grew darker as the children sang in German.

Stille nacht! Heil'ge nacht!
Alles schläft; einsam wacht
Nur das traute hoch heilige Paar.
Holder Knab' im lockigen Haar,
Schlafe in himmlischer Ruh!

By the time they got to the last verse, Bethany felt as if her heart would burst as tears welled in her eyes. Such a beautiful song, and hearing the innocent voices sing it as one only enhanced its impact on her.

After the song ended, Bethany and John went over to where Mary still sat. John helped her get up and assisted her toward the area of the school where everyone was gathering.

"What a nice surprise," she said to John. "I thought you had to work today."

He nodded, his eyes traveling from Mary to Bethany. "I

asked to leave early so that I could be here." His gaze stayed on Bethany. "I didn't want to miss this. It's been quite a few years since I've been inside a school *haus*." He looked around, taking in the blackboard and Bible verses hanging on the walls. "I haven't really missed it."

Mary laughed. "It's smaller than you remember, I bet."

"Indeed, it is."

"And did you enjoy the pageant?" Bethany asked.

"I most certainly did." He smiled at her. "It was nice to hear the songs and see those children honor God in such a loving and innocent way. You were right, you know."

Surprised, Bethany tilted her head. "About what?"

"The pageant does put you in the mood for Christmas." He leaned down and whispered, "Just like snowy nights at the pond and brightly lit *Englische* neighborhoods."

She couldn't help but smile. "*Ja*, John, those things do put you in the mood for Christmas, too."

"Looks like we're both showing each other new things." He gave her an impish grin. "I like it."

"Me, too," she whispered, uncertain whether or not he heard her.

Chapter Fifty-Three

On Saturday morning, just as everyone was about to leave the breakfast table, Elmer surprised Edna by clearing his throat and asking that everyone stay for a few extra minutes.

"What's this about, Elmer?" she asked in a hushed voice.

"Just clear the table and then bring over the coffeepot, if you don't mind. It's time for a family meeting."

Without asking another question, Edna got up and gathered the breakfast plates. For now, she set them on the counter by the sink. She'd wash them later. Her curiosity was certainly piqued by Elmer's most unusual request.

After refilling the coffee cups, she set the pot onto the table, making certain that it rested on a pot holder to protect the table from a burn mark. Then she sat down and stared, wide-eyed, at her husband.

Elmer straightened his shoulders and tilted his chin, adopting a serious look. He reached up and stroked his beard. That was when Edna knew something important was on his mind.

"It's almost Christmas," he started in a slow, deliberate manner. "And I often do a lot of reflection at this time of year. God sent His son to us, an innocent and pure baby, to take on the sins of the world."

Out of the corner of her eye, Edna noticed Jeremiah and Jonas fidget.

"Christmas represents new beginnings and change. So many things changed for the people of Israel because of God's gift. So many things changed for people everywhere in the world, and they continue to change. All because of God's gift." He paused and reached for his coffee mug. Slowly, he took a sip. It was clear that he wasn't about to rush this discussion.

"Change." Elmer set down the mug again. "Change can be good or change can be bad. As an Amish man, I've learned that worldliness can lead to change, and frankly, I associated change with bad things. Electricity, automobiles, cellular phones. They all represented change and were to be shunned."

He met Edna's questioning stare.

"Recently, we've had a lot of change on our farm. Decreased revenue from our milk production led to increased work responsibilities for your *maem*. Not necessarily good change there."

Jonas frowned. "But increased work for Maem helped with the decreased profits."

Elmer nodded. "That's true. We can always look at things from two different perspectives. And that's what I'm going to ask you to do when I tell you about some new changes we're going to have around here."

The silence in the room felt heavy. Edna caught John giving her an inquiring look, as if to ask her if she knew what this was about. She gave a tiny shrug, indicating that she had no idea where her husband was going with this conversation.

"Change *can* be good, especially when it benefits the whole." He scanned the faces of his three sons. "And by whole, I mean our family, those seated around the table today." He leveled his gaze at John. "And those who might join our family in the future."

John coughed and averted his eyes.

"So, beginning in the New Year, I am asking John to return to the farm."

Immediately Jonas and Jeremiah bristled.

Elmer held up his hand. "One of you boys will apply to take over John's position at the auction *haus*. The other one will look for employment, possibly in construction."

Edna's mouth practically fell open. Elmer was going to send *both* of the boys to find work away from the farm?

"You can't do all this farmwork with just you and John!" Jonas cried out. "It's already impossible with the three of us!"

But Elmer disagreed. "*Nee*, Jonas. It will be fine with just me and John to tend to it."

Jonas gave an incredulous laugh.

"It's true," Elmer continued. "Let's face it. Neither you nor Jeremiah is as enthusiastic about farming as John is. And his work ethic . . . well, let's just say that he knows how to pull his weight two or three times over."

Edna hoped that Jonas didn't press his father, for she could imagine how hard Elmer was trying to select words that would not overly upset Jonas and Jeremiah. She snuck a look at John and saw that he appeared as surprised as she felt. Frankly, she hadn't thought too much about John's conversation with Elmer earlier in the week. She'd been too busy planning the previous week of serving meals to tourists and preparing for the school pageant later that afternoon. From the expression on John's face, he, too, hadn't expected an answer from his father so quickly, and possibly hadn't expected it to be in his favor.

"But why both of us?" Jeremiah asked.

Elmer gave him a simple explanation. "I don't want your *maem* working so hard come springtime. She took on far too much work this fall."

His words surprised her. She'd never complained about working so hard. It was, after all, her family, and she liked being able to help. "Oh, Elmer. I didn't mind."

But Elmer held up his hand, cutting her off before she could say anything else. "*Nee*, Edna. You need time for yourself, too. You make cookies for Amish Aid, for church, for sick people. You crochet blankets for charity. You make quilts to cover the homeless. And you serve all those meals. While I'm grateful that you had help these past few weeks, I don't want you taking on so many meals. One . . . maybe two a week. But no more. It's too much work for you, even if you have help."

When she heard Elmer list all of the things she had been doing, Edna realized that he was right. It *was* too much for just one person. She needed more downtime so that she could focus on the most important of jobs: taking care of her family as well as herself. And the fact that Elmer felt that way made her heart fill with even more love for him.

What a wonderful Christmas gift her husband had just given to her.

Chapter Fifty-Four

Mary stood at the stove, stirring the cranberry sauce so that it didn't stick to the bottom of the pan and burn. A sugary sweet smell filled the kitchen. She kept thinking back to what Verna had said at Edna's the previous day. A wedding. Was it possible that John and Bethany would get married?

She knew that they hadn't been courting each other very long, but Mary also knew that it didn't really matter. She'd spent far less time with Abram during their brief courtship. When God wanted two people to be together, He found ways to make it happen. At least that was what she believed.

Bethany walked to the stove and peered over her mother's shoulder. "How's that coming along?"

"*Gut.* Almost ready to put into the mold."

"I'll fetch it."

As Bethany went over to the counter, Mary watched her. If what Verna said was true, Bethany might not be living at home for very long. It was moments like these when Mary wished she could've had more children. She wasn't ready to be without her daughter's company, although she knew that she'd been blessed for the past nineteen years.

Bethany placed the metal mold on the counter. "What's that look for?"

"What look?"

"You look sad."

Mary gave her head a little shake. She hadn't realized that Bethany had been watching her. "It's just . . . the holidays. Makes me think about a lot of things, I suppose. Memories of the past. Thoughts for the future."

Bethany placed her hand on her mother's arm. "Those should both be happy, Maem. No reason to look so forlorn."

She tried to smile. "You're right."

Bethany took the wooden spoon from her mother and stirred the cranberries one more time. "I think it's ready to pour." She reached for the pot holders and carefully removed the pot, tipping it so that the liquid filled the wreath-shaped mold. "There!" Standing back, she assessed her work. "That'll be right pretty on a plain plate, don't you think?"

A knock on the door interrupted their conversation. This time, Mary didn't have to wonder who it was. Surely it was John.

She watched as Bethany hurried over to the door to let him in, a quickness to her daughter's step that brought a wistful smile to Mary's lips. Young love was always a special time in a person's life. Over the years, Mary had always enjoyed attending weddings and witnessing the coming together of two young—and sometimes not so young—people for a lifelong union. The thought that, just maybe, her daughter would soon be standing before the congregation to exchange her vows before the bishop, claiming John Esh as her husband, a lifelong commitment before God, made her feel warm inside.

John entered the kitchen and paused, sniffing at the air. "It sure does smell like Christmas in here!"

His cheerful greeting brightened the room. "You think so?"

He nodded. "Oh *ja*. I definitely smell cranberries."

Mary gestured toward the mold on the counter. "We just finished making the Christmas mold."

John glanced at it. "If it's as good as it smells, I'll be certain to have two helpings of it."

"Just wait until you taste my *maem*'s corn casserole," Bethany said. "It's always a favorite on the Christmas table."

The compliment made Mary flush. While she always enjoyed cooking, she wasn't used to hearing such flattery. "Oh, now." She waved her hand at Bethany, modestly dismissing her words. "No more so than Edna's, I'm sure." Turning her attention to John, she motioned for him to take a seat at the table. "We won't be finished for you to bring food home with you, I'm afraid. But please sit. Bethany can fetch you some coffee while I finish up supper."

He made himself comfortable, removing his coat and hanging it from a peg on the wall near the door. "Feels like snow out there again. Sure am glad that we got all that wood cut up. Will be cold working outside this upcoming week."

"Looks like it'll be a snowy winter this year, that's for sure." Mary took a mug out and handed it to Bethany. "And your *maem*? Is she ready for Christmas Eve? Such a lot of work for her after she's been so busy these past few months."

Once Bethany had given John the coffee, she stood by his chair as if wondering what to do. Mary tilted her head toward the table, urging her daughter to join John.

"Oh *ja*, she's busy as all get-out today." He sipped the coffee. "But she always was a hard worker." He set down the mug and examined Bethany with great regard. "Mayhaps that's why you got on so well with her. You bustle about, too. Active like a little bee!"

Mary watched her daughter blush.

It was heartwarming to listen as John playfully teased Bethany.

A few minutes later, John stood up. "Well, I hate to do this, but I'm going to have to renege on supper tonight."

Mary heard Bethany catch her breath.

"Oh?" She sounded disappointed.

"*Ja*, I'm terribly sorry."

Mary felt just as saddened by his announcement. She'd been looking forward to getting to know John better. "Is everything all right?"

"Oh *ja*, right as rain. Or snow, in this case." He gave a little laugh. "Something came up and I've an unexpected errand in town. I need to get there before the stores close and then get back to the farm." He leveled his gaze at Bethany. "But, if you've a moment, mayhaps you'd walk outside with me to the buggy?"

As they walked to the door, John paused to collect his coat. Mary saw him observing Bethany reach for her shawl.

"*Ach!* Not that shawl!" He made a *tsk, tsk* noise as he shook his head. "It's too cold. You'll get sick."

"Germs make people sick, not the cold air," she said as she pulled the shawl over her shoulders. "Plus, I like my shawl."

He made a face at her. "You'll catch the flu and will miss all the holiday festivities." He wagged his finger at her. "You'll miss your *maem*'s corn casserole!"

She smiled at him as he opened the door, and she slipped under his arm.

Mary stood near the counter, watching from the window as John took Bethany's arm and helped her down the stairs. Just as John had predicted, a few flurries were falling from the sky, a soft blanket beginning to grace the tips of the bare trees and ground. As they crossed the yard, they left footprints behind.

Sighing, Mary turned away and gazed across the room. There was a feeling of emptiness there, one that she suspected she'd have to get used to soon enough. It was a bittersweet realization that it might be a foreshadowing of what life would be like in the future if John and Bethany *did* marry.

Chapter Fifty-Five

Her heart pounded as she walked beside him. He didn't stop at the horse and buggy but guided her along the driveway. They moved together, their feet in tandem as they made their way to the edge of the property.

"Something happened today," John said quietly.

She lifted her face, the tiny snowflakes brushing against her cheeks, so that she could see him better. He stared straight ahead, wearing a serious expression. She hoped that whatever he had to tell her wasn't bad news. And then she remembered that he'd told her earlier in the week that he had to discuss something with her. But whatever had happened today couldn't have been related to that.

"What is it?"

He stopped walking and shoved his hands into his coat pockets. He appeared to be avoiding looking at her, and that caused Bethany a moment of concern.

"I did what you suggested, Bethany."

Her mouth dried and she had trouble swallowing. What had she told him to do?

"And . . . I never would've had the courage to do it if you hadn't pushed me."

Her eyes widened. She didn't remember pushing him to do anything at all.

"Now I have the chance to do everything I've wanted to do in life." His blue eyes sought hers. "All thanks to you."

She narrowed her eyes, trying to make sense of what he was telling her. "I'm sure I don't understand."

He reached out and hesitated just a moment before he took her hand in his. "The farm. Daed says I'm to return to the farm full-time after the New Year."

Bethany caught her breath. She knew how John had wanted that to happen, and she remembered encouraging him to talk to his father. She hadn't realized that he had actually followed her suggestion. "Oh, John! That's *wunderbarr gut* news!" How happy she was for him!

He nodded his head. "And both Jonas and Jeremiah will be working off the farm."

At this news, Bethany frowned. "I don't understand."

John gave a nervous laugh. "Daed's going to leave the farm to me, Bethany. That's what it means. Neither of those two ever wanted to be a farmer. But because I was older, I had to look for a job off the farm."

"But both of them? Won't that mean more work for you? You'll be doing the work of two men."

He made a face. "Have you seen them work?"

An image of John's two brothers came to mind. "You have a point."

He laughed again and tightened his grip on her hand. "There's more, though, Bethany. Remember I said I wanted to talk with you about something?"

She nodded.

"Well, I wanted to talk to my *daed* first and knew I'd have to wait to hear his decision. You see, even though I'll now have the farm, there's still something missing."

"Oh?"

"I can't run the farm like this."

Stunned, Bethany stared at him. What did he mean by *that*? It was what he had told her he wanted. "But I thought you wanted to run the farm. What could possibly be missing?"

He took a deep breath. "I do want to run the farm, but I can't. Not alone."

She didn't understand. Wasn't his father still going to help him?

"Mayhaps I'm not saying it right, Bethany." He shuffled his feet as he stood before her. "I *want* to run that farm, but I *can't*. Not unless I have you by my side."

Standing before him, his hand holding hers, Bethany felt light-headed. Oh! How she had hoped and prayed that *this* might be what John wanted to talk to her about. But now that he had said the words, she almost didn't believe she had heard him properly. Had he truly just said that he wanted to marry her? Or did he mean something else?

"I . . . I think I know what you're saying."

He laughed. "I'm not saying anything, Bethany Ropp. I'm *asking*. I'm asking you to marry me and move onto the farm."

She felt dizzy and was thankful that he was holding her hand. "Oh."

"You said you wanted to live away from town," he hurried on. "And I want to give that to you. I want to help you grow a big garden so you can have those canning bees in the late summer—"

"I'd have no one to invite!"

"I'd come, Bethany. And so would your *maem*!"

Her heart pounded, and she had to will herself to breathe. "Where would we live?"

"We'll stay in the main house until I can build us a *dawdihaus* that we can move into come spring." He bent his knees so that he could stare at her eye-level. "And you could help my *maem* with her business. Mayhaps, as she grows older, you could even take it over."

She gasped. "Take it over?"

He nodded. "She won't want to do that forever. And you bake the most wonderful pies."

"How do you know?"

His eyes sparkled. "Maem saved some for us. You'd have people coming from all over the state just to sample your apple pie, that's for sure and certain."

"But . . ." Her mind whirled with a dozen questions. How could she run a business? Would she have to move away from her mother? When would they tell their families? And yet, as she looked into John's eyes, she knew there was only one question that truly mattered, and that was whether or not she wanted to spend the rest of her life with the man standing before her.

John must've read her mind. "So, what do you say, Bethany? Will you marry me after the New Year? Shall I talk to the bishops tomorrow after worship?"

She nodded, slowly at first and then with more emphasis. "John Esh, I will marry you." She felt as if she might cry, there was so much joy overflowing inside of her chest. Everything had happened so fast, but she knew it was the way God intended it. "Happily."

A smile broke onto his face and he wrapped his arms around her, pulling her close to his chest as he embraced her. She heard him sigh, a satisfied sound. "You've just given me the best Christmas gift ever." He leaned down, placed his hands on either side of her face, and then pressed a gentle kiss against her forehead. Staring into her eyes, he whispered, "I love you, Bethany."

She could hardly believe that she'd just heard those words slip through his lips, and yet, upon hearing them, she knew how right they felt.

"And I love you, John."

Chapter Fifty-Six

"Well, Edna," Susan Schwartz said, underscoring the "well" as they waited for the rest of the congregation to arrive at the Millers' house for Sunday worship, "what's this I hear? Whispers about a Christmas wedding?"

As she stood with the other women in a semicircle, all of them dressed in black, waiting to greet newcomers, Edna felt a need to collect her thoughts. Susan's words had indeed caught her off guard. Was it possible that other people in the church district knew about John and Bethany? She couldn't imagine how such a rumor would have started. As far as Edna was concerned, their discretion had been complete.

"Oh, Susan," Edna replied at last, "I wouldn't pay attention to such gossip."

"Truly?" The older woman sounded disappointed. "We had only one wedding this past season. I had rather enjoyed the idea of a late December wedding."

Late December? Edna blanched at the idea. That seemed far too soon. She'd only just gotten used to the idea of John courting Bethany! "I don't know why you listen to such things. There have been no announcements, and considering there's only a week or so left in the month, I wouldn't put much stock in silly tittle-tattle."

"Oh, I'm sure it's more than tittle-tattle." Susan leaned over and lowered her voice. "Seems a certain young man"—she raised an eyebrow—"was seen in Shipshewana just yesterday evening."

Edna pursed her lips and made a stern face. She remembered John leaving the house yesterday afternoon, but she had thought that he was having supper with the Ropps. And he'd returned early enough. How could he have managed to find time to go into town?

"And he was shopping!"

Edna clucked her tongue and rolled her eyes. "My word, Susan! There's nothing suggestive about shopping, I'm sure."

"Oh?" Susan wore a smug expression, clearly enjoying the fact that she had a secret she intended to share. "What if I tell you that he was at Lehmans' Variety Store and he purchased a motion clock!"

Edna's mouth opened. "A . . . clock?"

With a satisfied smirk, Susan nodded. "You know. The big ones that play melodies on the hour."

"Oh my," Edna whispered. Her eyes scanned the room as if seeking John, but the men were still outside, for there was still time before the worship service started. "Are you absolutely sure?"

"I'm as sure as I'm standing here talking to you. My cousin Dorothy heard it from her neighbor Karen, who was there shopping in the store when John walked in, and she heard him talk to the salesclerk about the clocks."

Edna wanted to comment that it sure seemed Karen had wasted no time in telling Dorothy, who, as quickly, had found a way to share the news with Susan. "Mayhaps she mistook John for someone else?"

"*Nee*, it was none other than your son, John Esh. She recognized him from the auction *haus*. He does work there, right?"

None of this made any sense. "A clock? Are you sure?"

"I'm quite sure that's what they told me."

But Edna couldn't quite believe it. Surely Karen thought she'd seen John Esh, but it was really someone else. After all, a young man usually bought the clock for his girl *after* she'd accepted his proposal. It was a common engagement present from a man to his future wife. If that were indeed the case, it would mean that John had already proposed to Bethany; but when would *that* have happened? And why on earth wouldn't he have told them?

She tried to remember how John had behaved that morning. He had seemed a bit more quiet than usual, but given the excitement of the previous day, when Elmer had held their family meeting about changes in the upcoming year, it was no wonder. Jonas and Jeremiah were both still sulking about it, although Edna suspected that was partially for show.

No. Nothing at all had seemed terribly different that morning.

"Now, now, I wonder whom your son would be buying a clock for," Susan went on, putting her finger to her cheek.

Edna knew that Susan surely suspected someone, but she wasn't about to make her own suggestions. Anything she said would surely filter back to the grapevine. "I'm sure I couldn't say."

"Couldn't?" Susan laughed. "Good choice of words, I'm sure."

Edna gave her a look of reproach.

"I'm sure your good friend Mary Ropp might be able to say." The older woman reached over and patted Edna's arm. "Don't worry. His secret is safe with me. Just make certain I get an invitation, *ja*?"

Two women entered the house and Susan straightened to greet them, leaving a perplexed Edna wondering about what she'd just learned. If John had already proposed to Bethany, he had given no indication of it. Clearly, he hadn't wanted to let anyone know yet. She'd just have to wait for John to announce the news. In the meantime, she hoped that Susan Schwartz would be able to keep that secret to herself for just a little while longer. Surely she didn't want to ruin John's surprise.

Chapter Fifty-Seven

After Sunday worship, while the tables were cleared from the first seating of fellowship, Mary noticed that Bethany seemed anxious. She kept looking at the clock and then at the door, as if expecting someone to show up.

"What's going on with her?" Verna asked as she carried some platters back to the kitchen.

"I'm not quite sure."

"I've never seen her so antsy." Verna set the plates on the counter and turned around, standing beside Mary. "I wonder if it has anything to do with our little project."

Mary didn't need to ask what "project" Verna was referring to.

"Speaking of John," Verna went on in an even lower voice, "how was supper last evening?"

Mary took a deep breath, visibly embarrassed that she had to admit the truth. "He didn't stay for supper."

Verna widened her eyes, clearly incredulous at the news she'd just heard. "What?"

"You heard me."

"Did he just not show up?"

Mary shook her head. "*Nee*, he came, visited for a few minutes, and then left. Said something had come up and he had to go to town. It's a shame. I really hoped to get to know him better. Even Abram was disappointed."

Verna squinted at her as if not believing what she'd just been told. "He visited and then left? Right away?"

"Well, he *did* talk with Bethany outside, and when she came back in, she didn't talk much, either. In fact, she was quiet all evening." Mary felt a tug at her heart. Bethany was not one to be overly talkative, but she had been even more pensive than usual after John had left. And after supper, she'd quickly retired to her bedroom. "What if he broke it off with her?"

Verna waved her hand impatiently. "Nonsense!"

"I'm serious, Verna." Mary scanned the room to make certain Bethany wasn't nearby. "She seemed so distracted when she returned to the *haus*. And she had been so happy and cheerful when he first arrived."

"You're imagining things, I'm sure."

But Mary insisted. "*Nee*, Verna. I wasn't imagining it."

"Then mayhaps she was just disappointed that he couldn't stay."

That was a possibility that Mary hadn't considered. Perhaps she *had* jumped to the wrong conclusion. Her maternal instinct had kicked in, and she feared anything that might hurt her daughter. That had always been her way. Abram's, too.

"You're overthinking it, I'm sure," Verna continued. "If they are in love, she'd be sorely disheartened to hear that he couldn't stay. Wouldn't you have felt the same way about Abram?"

Verna was right. Mary would've been terribly distraught if she'd been anticipating enjoying a meal with Abram and he'd had to cancel at the last minute. "I suspect you're right."

"Of course I'm right!" Verna gave her a stern look. "Why,

I remember how *ferhoodled* you were when Abram came calling on you. You walked around with your head in the clouds half the time. You thought you hid it so well, but I knew."

A small gasp escaped Mary's lips. "You did not!"

"I most certainly did! Neither one of you was terribly discreet about slipping away from singings or fellowship so that he could take you home in his buggy. All that hymn humming!"

Just the thought of those nights, way back when, made Mary smile. She remembered exactly what Verna was speaking about. After the first two times Abram had sent a friend over to inquire if she might ride home with him in his buggy, they'd devised a secret code for when Abram would want to leave. He'd collect his hat and coat and head to the door, passing near her while humming his favorite hymn.

"You remember that?"

Verna rolled her eyes. "My word! How could I forget? That Abram was always humming and looking for you at the singings. And as soon as you heard him, you'd get up to leave right away." Even Verna laughed at the memory. "All in the name of discretion, and yet everyone saw right through it!"

Mary couldn't help but laugh, too. "And here we thought we were being so sneaky."

Verna nodded. "So trust me, Mary Ropp. You mark my words. We'll be celebrating their marriage soon enough, and then, hopefully, a *grossboppli* by next Christmas."

Just the thought of being a grandmother was enough to make Mary lose her concentration. Her daughter getting married was one thing. Having a baby was quite another.

"A *boppli*? Oh help!"

"Well, of course a *grossboppli*!" Verna gestured toward

Myrna, who sat nearby at a table, her belly protruding from her black dress. "That's the order of things, isn't it? Courtship. Marriage. *Kinner!*"

"I can't think of such things today!"

Verna shook her head and made a face. "This time next year, I promise you that you'll be holding a sweet *boppli* in your arms."

The thought *did* warm Mary's heart.

"And just think," Verna exclaimed. "Mayhaps Myrna's *boppli* and Bethany's will be friends as well as second cousins. The next generation of members in the Cookie Club!"

Even though she laughed with Verna, Mary felt as if the wind had been knocked out of her. Moving over to the sink, she took over the task of washing platters and serving trays. She needed to keep herself busy so that her mind would stop whirling.

Of course, she knew that Verna was right, but it hadn't been something Mary had considered. Why, she couldn't even begin to imagine her daughter having a baby. Mary knew that her own struggles with pregnancy, followed by so much heartache when she'd miscarried, had tainted her view of her daughter having babies. Everything would be in God's hands, she told herself, but she still knew that it was a mother's prerogative to worry.

Chapter Fifty-Eight

Somehow Bethany knew it was John long before the horse and buggy slowed to a stop beside her on the road. Amid the snowy flakes that fell from the sky, she stood on the side of the road, waiting for him to slide open the door on the right side of the buggy.

"*Kum* quickly," he called out. "It's too cold outside."

Smiling, she clutched her shawl by her throat, shivering as she climbed into the buggy. He had a blanket ready for her, covering her lap so that she could warm up.

"*Ach*, you must be freezing!"

She shook her head. "*Nee*, it's not so cold out there. Just my toes got chilly." She glanced down at her black shoes. These were the pair she always wore on Sundays to worship. The thin soles did nothing to keep out the chill of walking on snowy roads.

"And you're wearing that shawl again!" He gave her a look of exaggerated irritation. "I can't have my new fiancée catching a cold just before Christmas."

"I won't. I promise." She smiled as she settled into the seat. "What are you doing over here?"

He clucked his tongue and jiggled the reins. The horse took its cue and started walking again, the buggy wheels rolling over the pavement with a creaking noise. "Why, I've come to talk to your bishop."

She flushed. She'd forgotten that he had told her of his intention to speak to both of their bishops today.

"Plus, I wanted to see you," he added, giving her a wink.

"I'm glad you did."

"Now, tell me why you were walking home?"

She didn't want to admit that she'd been feeling anxious. Her mind continued to whirl as she mulled over the fact that she'd soon be married to John and moving away from her parents. It was exciting and frightening at the same time. During the second seating, when she should have been enjoying the noon meal with other members of the community, she'd gone to her mother and, claiming a headache, told her she wanted to go home early.

"I . . . I just couldn't sit still, I suppose."

"Really?" He wore a concerned expression. "Is everything okay?"

She nodded. "*Ja*, everything's right *gut*." She hesitated before she reached out to touch his hand. Holding the reins in one hand, he entwined his fingers with hers, and she smiled. "Especially now that you're here."

A look of relief washed over him. "That's how I felt today, too, especially after I spoke with my bishop."

She caught her breath. Oh, how glad she was that it was the man who needed to inform the bishops. She wouldn't have been able to do such a thing!

"And now, I'm on the way to have a word with *your* bishop."

She knew what that meant. In two weeks, when their districts gathered for worship, the bishops would announce their upcoming wedding to the two congregations. But Bethany and John wouldn't be there. It would be a day spent together, alone, discussing their wedding plans. He'd probably come over to her house and she'd make him some breakfast so that they could have some quiet time while the rest of the community learned about their engagement.

As soon as her parents returned to the house, it would be time to finalize wedding plans. Most likely they'd get married at the Esh farm, as her parents' house was too small for a wedding celebration. There would be no wedding halls or churches to accommodate such an event. That was not the way of the Amish. In accordance with their traditions, members of the *g'may* alternated hosting religious services and special events at one another's farms. But there would be invitations to write, many of them because everyone in the community would have to be invited, and a new dress to make. She'd plan the wedding meal with her mother and Edna, helping to prepare the food in the days preceding the event.

It would be a very busy time, for sure and certain.

And then she'd have to get ready to move to the Esh farm.

So many things to plan as she prepared for the next phase of her life as John's new *fraa*, she pondered.

"January fourteenth," he said. "That will be our wedding date."

Bethany took a quick but deep breath. "Oh," she whispered.

He glanced at her. "Something wrong?"

"It's just so far away."

John laughed. "Only three weeks or so. We've a lot to do in between now and then. It will be here before you know it."

For Bethany, it couldn't come soon enough.

"Will you be sorry to move away from your parents?" he asked.

"*Ja*, I will," she admitted. *That* thought had troubled her more than anything else. "I can't imagine my *maem* being alone in the *haus* all the time."

For a moment, he didn't respond, respecting her comment with silence. Finally, he cleared his throat. "I was thinking about that, Bethany. Mayhaps, during this winter, we could stay with your parents."

Immediately, she brightened. "Really?"

John pulled the reins, slowing down the horse for a stop sign. He looked both ways before continuing down the road. "It'll give me more time to build our *haus* and give you more time to be with your *maem*, especially during the cold winter months."

"You'd have to drive there every day."

He smiled at her, his blue eyes searching her face. "It's a very small sacrifice that I'm happy to make if it means making you look as happy as you do right now." He leaned over and gently kissed her forehead. "Now, why don't I drop you off at your *haus*, then?"

"Or . . ." She leaned against his arm and peered up at him. "Mayhaps we could go for a ride? It's pretty outside today, with the snow and all, and I like just being here with you."

He pursed his lips as if considering her request. Then, slowly, he nodded. "You know, Bethany, I think that's a right *gut* idea. I'd like nothing more than to take a nice, leisurely ride with my girl seated by my side. I can talk to the bishop later this afternoon, I reckon."

She tucked her hand into the crook of his arm and moved closer to him. She felt warm and safe seated next to him in the buggy. It was a place she would sit for many years to come, and that realization made her happy.

Chapter Fifty-Nine

"Straighten out that tablecloth, Jeremiah! And Jonas, I need more pine branches. Please cut some from the tree outside."

Edna bustled about the kitchen. Everyone would be arriving in an hour, and things were not perfect yet. The food was cooking and the room smelled like the place to be, but she hadn't finished setting the tables. And, frankly, Jeremiah and Jonas were not the best of helpers.

"Where's John? I don't see *him* helping!" Jonas grumbled.

"Never you mind about your *bruder*," she snapped back. But she knew that John was outside, talking with Elmer. She suspected she knew what they were discussing, for she saw them walking around the back of the house, where John pointed to a section of the yard. She wanted to give her oldest son the time and privacy he needed to have that discussion with his father. Keeping Jonas and Jeremiah occupied, however, was proving most difficult.

"I can't get this stupid cloth straight," Jeremiah cried out in frustration. "I pull it this way to cover the end; then the other side is too short."

"Then pull it back."

"Come help me, Jonas."

But Jonas was heading to the door. "Can't. I have to go

cut pine branches," he shot back and then disappeared out the front door.

Edna rolled her eyes and walked over to the table. The white cloth was bunched in the middle. Sighing, she shook her head at him. "Honestly, Jeremiah. This isn't that hard. Look." Gently, she moved the tablecloth and positioned it perfectly in the center of the table so that the edge hung evenly on both sides. "See?"

He gave her a sheepish grin.

"Now, let's set this so that everything's ready when my friends arrive."

He groaned.

Ignoring him, Edna suspected that she'd better enjoy John's wedding, for it would be a long time before her other two boys got married. What Amish woman would want to handle either of them?

"Hey, what's this?" Jeremiah pointed to a box situated on the floor by the counter. It was wrapped in plain brown paper with a beige ribbon around it.

Edna looked at it. She hadn't noticed it earlier. "Why, that looks like a present!"

"That's a big present. Wonder who it's for?"

Edna didn't have to wonder. She suspected it was a gift for Bethany from John. But the box didn't look like it was big enough for a clock.

Jeremiah picked it up and shook it.

"Set that down," Edna scolded.

"It's not heavy."

"Jeremiah!"

"Okay, okay." He put it back on the floor.

She moved over to the two long tables and helped him place the plates, glasses, and utensils at the table. The white plates with rose floral rims looked pretty against the white tablecloth. The set of china had been her mother's, a collection she had inherited from *her* mother. She was fortunate that, as the family had grown, her grandmother and her mother had continued buying more plates for the set. With over thirty plates, there was enough for all the place settings rather than having to use everyday plates, too. The precious heirlooms were only used for very special occasions, such as holidays and birthdays. Hopefully she'd be able to use the set again soon—for a wedding.

The door opened and Jonas walked in with two branches from the pine tree in his arm. "This enough, Maem?"

She took them from Jonas and carried them to the sink. As she snipped off the smaller branches, she wondered about that present. What could John possibly have bought for Bethany, and why would he have left the gift out in the open like that? Her curiosity was definitely piqued.

After collecting her clippings, Edna began arranging them in a white porcelain water pitcher and set it onto the table.

She stood back and assessed the table. Everything was looking just picture-perfect. With the hope that an announcement might be made, Edna wanted the kitchen to be warm and inviting, a place for the four families to gather around the table and share an evening of fellowship.

Happy with the table, she moved back to the kitchen and, returning her attention to the food on the stove, peered into the pot of boiling water and reached for a fork to test the potatoes. What was a Christmas Eve meal without mashed potatoes?

The sound of footsteps on the porch steps preceded the voices of Elmer and John as they walked into the kitchen, both of them slapping their arms against their sides.

"Definitely going to snow later," John said. "Bitter cold out there."

"*Ja*, but this smells like the right place to be!" Elmer hung up his coat and placed his hat on the counter.

"Elmer!" Edna put her hands on her hips. "Put that away. I'm trying to keep everything tidy."

He made an apologetic face and picked up the hat.

She waited until he returned and tried to catch his eye. She knew better than to outright ask what John had been discussing with Elmer, but she was eager to know. Although he avoided looking at her, there was a hint of a smile on his weathered face.

"Well," she said at last, "everything all right outside, then?"

Elmer's lips twitched and he gave a simple nod. "*Ja*, right as rain."

Edna frowned. Clearly her husband wasn't going to give her any hints. Oh, he'd hear from her later! But in the meantime, she still had work to do in preparation for her friends' arrival for their Christmas Eve supper.

Chapter Sixty

"Look at you! No cast!"

Mary smiled broadly as she walked into Edna's house. Her leg still felt stiff, but she was so happy that the cast was gone.

"I thought it was coming off after the New Year," Edna said.

"Me, too. Abram surprised me by taking me to the doctor yesterday."

"Well, let's avoid that stepladder today," Edna teased.

"And tomorrow and the next day," Abram quipped as he walked past his wife.

Mary was glad to see that everyone was already there. When she went to join Verna and Wilma in the kitchen, she felt a sense of comfort. Oh, how she'd missed being with her friends. And now that her cast was off, it would be much easier for her to climb in and out of the buggy, to ride along with Wilma and Verna when they went to Edna's to bake cookies.

"Myrna's come down with terrible morning sickness," Verna said as they stood together near the sink.

Mary found Verna's daughter, seated in a rocking chair with Ezekiel's daughter on her lap. Myrna looked a bit peaked and pale as she held the little girl.

"Has she tried sage tea?"

Wilma made a face at Mary's suggestion. "That never worked for me!"

"Oh now, Wilma! If memory serves me well," Edna laughed, "you had heartburn, not morning sickness!"

"Did not!"

Verna joined in. "She's right. You ate too much pie all the time." She looked at Mary. "Don't you remember?"

"Actually, I do." Mary put her finger to her head as if thinking. "Cherry pie was your favorite, if I recall."

Wilma scowled. "It *was* morning sickness," she mumbled.

All three of the other women looked at her and, simultaneously, said, "Cherry pie!" and then began laughing. Even Wilma joined them.

"Okay, maybe I did indulge just a little too much in that," she admitted. "But sage tea sure didn't help me."

Verna cleared her throat and nudged Mary. "Look," she whispered and gestured to where John stood near Bethany in the back of the room.

Wilma looked over her shoulder to see what they were gawking at. "Oh my! Do I sense an announcement?"

"Hush now, Wilma," Edna hissed.

Wilma, however, called out, "What's going on over there?"

Bethany flushed, but John grinned. "I've a present for Bethany and she says she doesn't want to open it in front of everyone."

"A present?" Wilma raised an eyebrow and turned back to look at Edna and Mary. "Well, I'd love to see this present. Wouldn't you, Mary? Edna?"

Mary felt light-headed. Seeing the two of them together, standing off to the side and talking with their heads together, certainly made it clear to her that everything was more than right between John and Bethany. Surely this would be the moment when their intentions were announced. Mary held her breath.

John reached down and picked up the package. He held it in his hands as if it were the most precious thing in the world. Handing it to her, he whispered, "Go on. Open it."

Mary saw that Bethany's hands shook as she removed the ribbon and slid her finger along the seam of the brown paper. John helped to hold the package as she carefully lifted the top. Mary craned her neck, trying to see what was inside, but all she could see was white paper.

Bethany tried to hide her smile.

"What is it?" Mary whispered to Wilma.

"I can't see."

"Well? What is it?" Edna called out, her eyes wide and bright.

John started to reach into the box. "I hope you don't mind, Mary, but I bought your *dochder* a new coat." He withdrew the black coat and laid it across Bethany's shoulders. "To replace that shawl on cold winter days and nights."

"Wish us luck trying to get her to wear it," Abram said.

John stood behind Bethany, his hand lingering on her shoulder. "Mayhaps I'm the one who will need luck, Abram. You see, there's more," he said, his expression sobering as he looked at his mother. "We're getting married." He paused. "On January fourteenth."

Mary felt her heart skip a beat. January fourteenth was just three weeks away!

Abram's eyes widened. "Married? But she's too—"

Mary nudged him with her elbow. "Hush now, Abram," she whispered.

Edna, however, brightened, and she clapped her hands together. "Oh, blessed news!"

Wilma nudged Verna. "I told you so."

"You told me nothing."

"Did so."

John nodded, his hand still resting on Bethany's shoulder. "Daed and I already picked out the spot in the back where we'll build an addition to the *haus*," John said, mostly to Bethany but so everyone could hear. "Weather permitting, we'll begin working on it after the wedding and it should be finished before long."

"A *dawdihaus*?" Mary gasped. She hadn't thought about the possibility of John building something for them. Bethany wouldn't be living with Edna exactly after all! She'd have her own house.

"And, if Mary and Abram will have us, we'd like to live at their place until it's ready. Say springtime?"

Mary could hardly believe her ears. Nothing would have pleased her more. She suspected that John and Bethany could've lived at Edna's *haus*—it was certainly big enough. Shifting her gaze from John to Bethany, Mary saw that her daughter was smiling at her. Clearly John had suggested this arrangement to benefit both her and Bethany.

"I reckon we could arrange that," Abram said. "Would be right nice to have another man around the *haus*."

"*Ja*, but just until I can build something small for us to get started, and then, later, we'll move into the big *haus*."

Edna wagged her finger at them. "Don't think that means you'll be getting rid of us," she teased. "I don't mind moving to the smaller *haus*, but I plan on being around to help with lots of *bopplin*!"

Bethany's cheeks turned bright red, and Mary felt her own drain of color.

"First things first," John said, clearly sensing his fiancée's discomfort.

Jonas and Jeremiah walked inside, with Rachel and Ella Mae following.

"What ho! What's going on here?" Jonas took one look at his brother standing beside Bethany and he broke into a grin. "Well now! Didn't see that coming!"

"And here we thought he was courting that old *maedel* Bessie!" Jeremiah said.

Mary couldn't help but laugh with the rest of her friends. It was definitely turning into a very merry Christmas indeed!

Epilogue

Bethany knelt in the dirt, her bare toes tucked into the soil, as she weeded her garden. She loved spending her afternoons there, plucking the little green intruders that popped up overnight and tending to her tomato plants. A rabbit had eaten all of the lettuce she'd planted, and while John had put wire fencing around it, Bethany hadn't yet had time to replant it.

Two months ago, they'd moved to the *dawdihaus* at the end of April, coinciding with the return of the tourist season. And while Bethany helped Edna with the baking, her mother had offered her help with serving and cleaning. Edna had been thrilled for the help and company, while Bethany was just happy to see her mother on a regular basis during the week.

"Looking mighty *gut*," John called out as he crossed the yard toward the garden.

She sat back on her heels and covered her eyes. The sun was setting behind him as he approached. "We'll have plenty of tomatoes for sauces and salads, that's for sure!"

"Mayhaps Jonas can make you a roadside stand for selling your vegetables," John said as he opened the gate and walked over to her. "He's really gotten good with making things ever since he started that job with the builder."

Bethany brightened at the suggestion. "What a *wunderbarr* idea!" She wouldn't even mind having to talk to strangers, not if it was about the food she grew. "Do you think he would?"

"I reckon it's worth asking. And Jeremiah could help him on Saturday when he's off from the auction *haus*." Reaching out his hand, he helped her to her feet. His hand brushed against her belly, and he let it linger. "How's the *boppli* doing?"

"Kicking away," she laughed.

He held his hand there as if trying to feel the baby move. Bethany knew the moment he felt something, for his face lit up.

"Such a miracle," he whispered.

She covered his hand with her own, staring up at him. She'd never known that such joy was possible. Living in the small two-bedroom *dawdihaus* on the farm brought her endless peace.

"Let's go inside," she said. "I made some fresh meadow tea and baked you some sugar cookies."

He lifted her hand and brushed his lips against her fingers. Together they walked out of the garden, pausing to shut the gate behind them. As they headed into the house, the clock that hung in their entrance room played a gentle melody and the sun set behind the roof of the barn, another day ended on the Esh farm.

Recipes from the Amish Cookie Club

Bethany's Gingerbread Cookies

1 cup unsalted butter
1 cup dark molasses
1 cup brown sugar
½ cup water
1 large egg
1 tablespoon vanilla extract
6 cups unbleached all-purpose flour
1 teaspoon cinnamon
1 teaspoon ginger
1 teaspoon nutmeg
1 teaspoon cloves
1 teaspoon baking soda

Cream the butter, molasses, and brown sugar in a large bowl until smooth.

Mix in water, egg, and vanilla.

Combine the flour, spices, and baking soda in a separate bowl.

Combine the dry mix with the butter and sugar mix.

Put in refrigerator to cool for 2–3 hours.

Preheat oven to 350° F and line several baking sheets with parchment paper.

When ready to bake: drop the dough (about one healthy tablespoon each) onto the cookie sheets and flatten using the bottom of a large glass or coffee mug. Alternatively, roll out into 1/3-inch dough and cut shapes.

Bake for 10–12 minutes or until golden brown.

Makes approximately 4 dozen cookies.

AMISH STARRY NIGHT CHRISTMAS COOKIES

½ cup walnuts
½ cup almonds
2⅔ cups unsalted butter
2½ cups brown sugar
3 large eggs
2 tablespoons honey
1 tablespoon vanilla extract
½ teaspoon sea salt
4 cups unbleached all-purpose flour
6 cups rolled oats
1 cup raisins
1 cup white chocolate chips

Preheat oven to 350° F and line several baking sheets with parchment paper.

Coarsely chop the walnuts and almonds and set aside.

Cream the butter and sugar in a large bowl until smooth.

Mix the eggs, honey, vanilla, and salt together until smooth.

Combine with the butter and sugar. Beat until creamy.

Slowly work in the flour and oats.

Add the raisins, white chocolate chips, and nuts into the dough and mix well.

Shape dough into large balls (approximately 1½ inches in circumference) and put on the cookie sheets and flatten using the bottom of a large glass or coffee mug.

Bake for 12–15 minutes or until golden brown.

Makes approximately 3 dozen cookies.

Amish Molasses Nut Cookies

1 cup almonds
1 cup unsalted butter
2 cups white sugar
2 large eggs
1 cup dark molasses
1 teaspoon vanilla extract
6 cups unbleached all-purpose flour
1 teaspoon sea salt
1 teaspoon cinnamon
2 teaspoons ginger
1 teaspoon baking soda
1 cup buttermilk

Preheat oven to 350° F and line several baking sheets with parchment paper.

Coarsely chop the almonds.

Cream the butter and sugar in a large bowl until smooth.

Mix in the eggs, molasses, and vanilla.

Combine the flour, salt, cinnamon, ginger, and baking soda in a separate bowl.

Combine the dry mix with the butter and sugar mix.

Slowly add the buttermilk.

Beat until creamy.

Add the nuts into the dough and mix well.

Drop the dough (approximately one healthy tablespoon) onto the cookie sheets and flatten using the bottom of a large glass or coffee mug.

Bake for 12–15 minutes or until brown.

Makes approximately 4 dozen cookies.

Read on for an excerpt from Sarah Price's
next heartwarming Amish romance,

AN AMISH COOKIE CLUB COURTSHIP,

coming soon!

Edna braced herself for what she knew was inevitable: another desperate plea from her friend Wilma.

It was Wednesday morning, and just as she did every week, Edna had invited her three best friends over to bake a batch of cookies for Yoders' Store in Shipshewana. Ever since the previous year, they'd been baking cookies for the store to sell, a way to raise money for Amish Aid in their respective church districts. But, even more importantly, it was another chance for the four Amish women to spend time together and socialize.

They also still managed to find time to meet every other Friday to make cookies for their congregations to enjoy during the fellowship hour following their biweekly worship service. Over the years, the four women had developed quite the reputation for baking cookies—a favorite among young and old alike. They had even become known as the Amish Cookie Club, a nickname that didn't sit so well with Edna but had stuck just the same.

Edna supposed it didn't matter *what* people called them. The most important thing was that the four childhood friends made time to get together and support each other, something that was easier to do now that all of their children were grown and, in some cases, married.

With the cookies baking in Edna's large commercial oven, the sweet scent of cinnamon wafting through the kitchen, the four women sat in the back room, keeping their hands busy crocheting (or, in Verna and Wilma's case, knitting) while they visited. This part of the day was even sweeter than the cookies they baked.

Four months had passed since Edna's son John had married her friend Mary's Bethany. Four long, peaceful months filled with a new sense of energy in her house. Despite living in the small *dawdihaus*, John and Bethany often spent their evenings visiting her parents who now lived alone. While Edna missed having her son at her kitchen table every morning and evening, she found herself thoroughly enjoying the company of his young wife during the day. They often spent their mornings together, baking and cooking or sitting by the wood-burning stove in the back room, crocheting blankets. Indeed, this past winter had proven to be the most joyful one that Edna could remember in many years . . . for Bethany had brought a new sense of calm to the farm and refreshing female companionship to Edna's life.

Unfortunately, all of that was about to change.

MayFest was rapidly approaching—just a few weeks away. And that meant the unofficial start to the summer tourist season in Shipshewana. With the return of the tourists, Edna's business serving meals to the *Englische* would start up once again. And, of course, that also meant it was time for Wilma to try pawning off her twin daughters as helpers for Edna.

"Rachel and Ella Mae are both eager to help you," Wilma said as she sat in the rocking chair, knitting a lap blanket. She rocked back and forth, a sweet, angelic look on her cherubic face. "Why, just the other day, Ella Mae asked when they could start!"

Edna caught Verna's eye and noticed that her friend choked back a laugh.

"What?" Wilma asked.

"I bet she did just that."

Wilma scowled in Verna's direction. "I'm telling you, she did!"

"I'm sure."

"Bah!" Waving her hand at Verna, Wilma redirected her attention to Edna. "And I know how busy you are. Surely you need help."

It was Mary, however, who quickly interjected. "But Bethany is part of the family now," she reminded Wilma, peering at her friend over the rim of her round eyeglasses. "And *she* will be helping Edna."

"Oh, fiddle-faddle!" Wilma scoffed. "It doesn't take a doctor to see she's pregnant, and with her being so fragile—"

Mary frowned. "She's not fragile!"

Verna raised her eyebrows. "She's pregnant?"

"—she'll be too tired to help out Edna."

Edna sighed and shook her head. "Clearly the cat's out of the bag now."

"Why didn't anyone tell me?" a bewildered Verna asked, looking from Mary to Edna. "I'm always the last to know anything anymore!"

"We were going to tell you soon," Mary said in an attempt to soothe Verna.

"Hmph!"

"Besides—" Wilma pursed her lips, adopting an air of innocent superiority. "I'd be surprised if John let her work much longer anyway, seeing how protective he is of her."

Edna clucked her tongue and was about to refute Wilma's claim, but Mary, who sat beside her, placed a hand on Edna's knee. "He *is* just a little bit overprotective," she whispered gently.

Edna gasped. Coming from Mary, Bethany's own mother—the queen of overprotection!—that was certainly rich!

"I heard that!" Wilma lit up, pointing in Mary's direction. "Even her own *maem* agrees!"

Inwardly, Edna groaned. She couldn't—simply couldn't!—have Wilma's daughters helping her with the *Englische* customers. Why! They'd merely bicker and argue with each other the entire time, for sure and certain!

"Besides, it's not fair," Wilma added, puffing out her chest and putting on a face. "All three of you have married off your *kinner* and now have grandbabies on the way, but not me!"

Verna rolled her eyes. "You have plenty of grandbabies from your older *dochders*!"

"And *sohn*, too!" Mary chimed in.

"Bah!"

But Edna couldn't get past what Wilma had just said. Something wasn't making sense. And then it dawned on her. "Wait a minute, Wilma." She leaned forward in her chair and stared pointedly at her friend. "Who, exactly, are you intending your *dochders* to marry if they are helping me serving *Englische* tourists? Their *Englische* sons?"

A silence fell over the room.

After a brief hesitation, Wilma raised one eyebrow, arching it in a perfectly inverted V. "Well, you *do* have two *sohns*, you know."

With wide eyes, Edna stared at Wilma. If Mary had a feather in her hand and brushed it against Edna's arm, she'd have surely fallen over! She had to repeat Wilma's words—not just once but twice!—to realize that she had, indeed, heard her friend correctly. And then, she noticed that neither Verna nor Mary said one word.

Slowly, Edna turned her head and stared at Mary. "Did you know about this?"

Mary licked her upper lip and averted her eyes.

Edna shifted her gaze to Verna. "You?"

"I . . . uh . . . well . . ." she stammered, but then she, too, looked away.

"Land's sake!" Edna exclaimed at last. "I see exactly what's been going on!" She dropped her crocheting onto her lap. "The three of you have been scheming behind my back!"

"I wouldn't exactly call it 'scheming,'" Mary mumbled.

"Hush now!" Edna pressed her lips together. "Scheming is exactly what it is. No amount of confectioner's sugar will sweeten this bitter cookie!"

Verna looked as if she might laugh.

"I'm simply shocked," Edna said at last. Both Mary and Verna knew how difficult Wilma's two daughters could be. Why on earth would either of them think, for even one minute, that Jeremiah or Jonas would be a good match for Rachel or Ella Mae? In fact, Edna couldn't imagine *anyone* being a good match for those two quarrelsome girls! "If you wanted your *dochders* here to learn how to suppress their opinions or work as part of a team, well, *that* I could understand, but to try to marry them off to *my* boys?"

Wilma blinked her eyes. "What's wrong with that?"

"Wilma!" Edna gave her a sharp look. "It hasn't slipped your notice that Rachel and Ella Mae do nothing but argue, has it?"

"Well, I—"

"And that's not necessarily a personality trait that will interest any young man?"

"I suppose that—"

"And I can assure you that, despite your *dochders'* pretty faces and desire to work, neither of my *sohns* would find anything appealing about a young woman who does nothing more than compete with her own *schwester*!"

Wilma pouted. "I think you're being a bit harsh—"

"*Nee*, I'm not!" Edna shook her head. "And both Verna and Mary are aware of it, which makes this little scheme even more surprising to me."

Wilma took a deep breath and exhaled slowly. She bent her head, and an awkward silence filled the room.

For a moment, Edna felt terrible. Perhaps she had been too hard on her friend, although, truth be told, Wilma had been pestering her for well over a year about this matter. Still, she should have held her tongue and found a kinder, gentler way to dismiss Wilma's dozenth attempt.

Suddenly, the hint of a smile crossed Wilma's lips, and she lifted her gaze, her eyes catching Edna's. "Still, you never know, Edna. God does work in mysterious ways."

"Oh help," Edna muttered, tossing her hands into the air.

"And you *did* say you'd help them to learn how to suppress their opinions and work as part of a team—"

Edna's mouth fell open. *Had* she said that? She couldn't remember exactly what she had said in the heat of the argument.

From the corner of her eye, Edna saw Mary cover her mouth and Verna titter, both of them clearly amused. The truth of the matter was that, while she had scaled back to just three days a week—the previous season had been far too much work for her—Edna most likely *would* still need help. Three days of cooking, baking, serving, and cleaning was an awful lot of work for just one woman.

As for Bethany, she had not fared too well recently, morning sickness having stricken her in the past two weeks. And Edna knew that John *was* overprotective of his wife.

Now that he was working on the farm, he often stopped inside to check on her, making certain that she wasn't pushing herself too hard.

His attention was sweet, but Edna could see that John would not permit Bethany to work for long, especially if she continued feeling poorly.

Wilma raised her eyebrows. "So when, exactly, should Rachel and Ella Mae start?"

Defeated, Edna exhaled and let her shoulders slump. "Next Wednesday."

Wilma cheered while the other two women laughed. Edna, however, only felt the heavy burden of defeat. Suddenly she wasn't looking forward to the following week after all.